Murder Unleashed

By Dorothy Bennett

Concerning a vanished priest . . .
a dead farmer . . .
and the curious murder of the "White
Flower" of San Francisco's night life!

Originally published in 1935

Murder Unleashed

Published by Resurrected Press

This classic book was handcrafted by Resurrected Press. Resurrected Press is dedicated to bringing high quality classic books back to the readers who enjoy them. These are not scanned versions of the originals, but, rather, quality checked and edited books meant to be enjoyed!

Please visit ResurrectedPress.com to view our entire catalogue!

LIKE us on Facebook to get updates on new publications! http://Facebook.com/ResurrectedPress

ISBN 13: 978-1-937022-99-0

Printed in the United States of America

Resurrected Press Books in A. E. Fielding's *The Chief Inspector Pointer Mystery* Series

RESURRECTED PRESS CLASSIC MYSTERY CATALOGUE

Journeys into Mystery
Travel and Mystery in a More Elegant Time

The Edwardian Detectives
Literary Sleuths of the Edwardian Era

Gems of Mystery
Lost Jewels from a More Elegant Age

Anne Austin
One Drop of Blood
The Black Pigeon
Murder at Bridge

E. C. Bentley
Trent's Last Case: The Woman in Black

Ernest Bramah
Max Carrados Resurrected:
The Detective Stories of Max Carrados

Agatha Christie
The Secret Adversary
The Mysterious Affair at Styles

Octavus Roy Cohen
Midnight

Freeman Wills Croft
The Ponson Case
The Pit Prop Syndicate

J. S. Fletcher

The Herapath Property
The Rayner-Slade Amalgamation
The Chestermarke Instinct
The Paradise Mystery
Dead Men's Money
The Middle of Things
Ravensdene Court
Scarhaven Keep
The Orange-Yellow Diamond
The Middle Temple Murder
The Tallyrand Maxim
The Borough Treasurer
In the Mayor's Parlour
The Saftey Pin

R. Austin Freeman

The Mystery of 31 New Inn from the Dr. Thorndyke Series
John Thorndyke's Cases from the Dr. Thorndyke Series
The Red Thumb Mark from The Dr. Thorndyke Series
The Eye of Osiris from The Dr. Thorndyke Series
A Silent Witness from the Dr. John Thorndyke Series
The Cat's Eye from the Dr. John Thorndyke Series
Helen Vardon's Confession: A Dr. John Thorndyke Story
As a Thief in the Night: A Dr. John Thorndyke Story
Mr. Pottermack's Oversight: A Dr. John Thorndyke Story
Dr. Thorndyke Intervenes: A Dr. John Thorndyke Story
The Singing Bone: The Adventures of Dr. Thorndyke
The Stoneware Monkey: A Dr. John Thorndyke Story
The Great Portrait Mystery, and Other Stories: A Collection of Dr. John Thorndyke and Other Stories
The Penrose Mystery: A Dr. John Thorndyke Story

The Uttermost Farthing: A Savant's Vendetta

Arthur Griffiths
The Passenger From Calais
The Rome Express

Fergus Hume
The Mystery of a Hansom Cab
The Green Mummy
The Silent House
The Secret Passage

Edgar Jepson
The Loudwater Mystery

A. E. W. Mason
At the Villa Rose

A. A. Milne
The Red House Mystery

Baroness Emma Orczy
The Old Man in the Corner

Edgar Allan Poe
The Detective Stories of Edgar Allan Poe

Arthur J. Rees
The Hampstead Mystery
The Shrieking Pit
The Hand In The Dark
The Moon Rock
The Mystery of the Downs

Mary Roberts Rinehart
Sight Unseen and The Confession

Dorothy L. Sayers

Whose Body?

Sir William Magnay
The Hunt Ball Mystery

Mabel and Paul Thorne
The Sheridan Road Mystery

Louis Tracy
The Strange Case of Mortimer Fenley
The Albert Gate Mystery
The Bartlett Mystery
The Postmaster's Daughter
The House of Peril
The Sandling Case: What Would You Have Done?

Charles Edmonds Walk
The Paternoster Ruby

John R. Watson
The Mystery of the Downs
The Hampstead Mystery

Edgar Wallace
The Daffodil Mystery
The Crimson Circle

Carolyn Wells
Vicky Van
The Man Who Fell Through the Earth
In the Onyx Lobby
Raspberry Jam
The Clue
The Room with the Tassels
The Vanishing of Betty Varian
The Mystery Girl
The White Alley
The Curved Blades

Anybody but Anne
The Bride of a Moment
Faulkner's Folly
The Diamond Pin
The Gold Bag
The Mystery of the Sycamore
The Come Back

Raoul Whitfield
Death in a Bowl

And much more!
Visit ResurrectedPress.com
for our complete catalogue

FOREWORD

The 1935 mystery novel *Murder Unleashed* is interesting for a number of reasons. First it is interesting for what it is not as much as what it is. It doesn't follow the then prevailing pattern of the English mystery with a clever crime presented as a puzzle and an even cleverer detective to unravel it. Nor does it fit the mold of those light hearted American mysteries full of witty dialog and snappy one-liners and a hint of romance that were so popular in the films of the period.

Stylistically, it owes most to the hard-boiled school of detective fiction pioneered by Dashiell Hammett and Carroll John Daly. The settings and the crimes are gritty and realistic, not glamorous, the motivations of many of the characters petty and shallow. And as with many of those stories, the hero finds himself caught up in events he doesn't understand against a backdrop of the corruption that money and power bring. Yet the hero is not a hardened private detective, not a Sam Spade or Phillip Marlowe, or even a jaded newspaper man, but instead is a singer on a late night radio program, a former college boy and football player who has had his life turned upside down by an incident in his past.

The setting of the novel is San Francisco and central California in the early 1930's, in many ways the same San Francisco as that of Hammett's *The Maltese Falcon* and the same California as his Continental Op stories. But it is also the California of Steinbeck, not the Steinbeck of *The Grapes of Wrath*, but the Steinbeck of *Tortilla Flats* and *Cannery Row*, for the roots of this mystery lie in the small towns of the agricultural country south of San Francisco.

The crime, itself is brutal enough, a young woman lured to a hotel room only to be stabbed with a kitchen knife and left for a stranger to discover. Yet the novel is not so much about the solution of the crime, but about the hero coming to terms with himself and the incident in his past that had caused him to cut himself off from his past life. It is this emphasis on the psychological aspect that separates Murder Unleashed from the hard-boiled school. Detectives such as Sam Spade have already made their choices in life, while Dennis Devore still has his in front of him.

The author, Dorothy Bennett, is something of a mystery, herself. Her only two works are *Murder Unleashed* and *How Strange a Thing*, a mystery in the form of a poem that came out in the same year, 1935. After that, despite the promise of Murder Unleashed for all intents she disappears. Though some have attributed the novel to the screenwriter and playwright of the same name, evidence would seem to argue against this. That person was born in Indiana and was working in New York and Los Angeles at the time *Murder Unleashed* must have been written. She would not have had the comfortable familiarity with the culture and places of San Francisco and its vicinity that the author must have had. Instead, she seems to have been someone who had grown up in the area and attended the University of California, Berkeley campus, possibly writing both works while a student.. There is a note on a copy of *How Strange a Thing* that she donated to the U. C. Berkeley library that would seem to indicate this.

Whatever the facts of her life may be, for a first (and possibly only) novel, Murder Unleashed is a remarkable work, well written, well plotted, and well thought out. Resurrected Press is pleased to offer this new edition of a long forgotten work.

About the Author

Little information is available about Dorothy Bennett. It would appear that she grew up in Berkeley, California and probably went to the university there. Her mother was Mary Richardson Bennett, to whom she dedicated a murder mystery in the form of a poem entitled *How Strange a Thing* which was published in 1935, the same year as *Murder Unleashed*. Evidence indicates that she is not the same person as the playwright and screenwriter Dorothy Bennett, who wrote the screenplay for *The Brasher Doubloon,* the movie based on Raymond Chandler's *The High Window.*

Greg Fowlkes
Editor-In-Chief
Resurrected Press
www.ResurrectedPress.

TABLE OF CONTENTS

I. BEGINNING OF WISDOM

IT BEGAN that foggy November night in San Francisco when Dennis Devore stuck his key in his hotel-room door, shoved it open onto blackness, and lit the light.

He stood on the threshold of the little snug, neat room. It might have been anyone's room, or no one's, so neat, so impersonal it was, with its bed neatly made, sheet turned down, reading light over the headboard, graceful walnut furniture, windows looking out onto the dark and the scattering lights below the hill, where Market Street and the downtown theater district still crawled along like great gold snakes through the night. Only a pocket-size radio standing on the table, a few packages of cigarettes thrown around on cloisonne ashtrays, and a pile of untidy books spilling over on the bureau made it his.

He preferred it that way. Light travel, long journey. He always felt nowadays as if he had to be free to get up and go in a second, if he wanted to. He carried his personal life in his dark and ruffled head.

So now he looked with satisfaction around at his snug and tidy den where he'd holed up for the winter. And as he looked, he saw something dark and untidy—like a solid sort of shadow—on the floor beyond the central table. He stepped around to see better, and then he stood staring down at the floor, eyes widening—widening . . .

He put his hand out automatically and clutched the edge of the table. His eyes still stared downward. They were wide with horror, as a moonless night is wide open to darkness.

There was a woman on the floor—a woman he'd never seen in his life before. She had red hair, loosened, coming down to her shoulders—a very white face—dark blue eyes that looked at him—and she was dead.

He knew that. He couldn't mistake it. She was dead, and those dark sapphire eyes stared at him incuriously. Her skin had the whiteness of milk, and her hair was like flame playing over her head. She was beautiful, and she was dead.

He didn't quite know what he did in the next few minutes. When he caught himself up again, he was still looking down at her, and his hand had clamped the table edge as if it had grown onto it. He couldn't have moved, then. But he'd gone through a very dark way in that short time.

But now he had hold of himself again. What had to be done would be done. He gave himself orders to move, to break that intolerable vise of stillness and horror that held him. And very slowly he went on over to the telephone on the wall, took up the receiver, and said, "Get me the Hall of Justice, will you?"

He listened a second, then, "Police department, please. Hello—will you . . . you'd better send someone over. There's a woman dead here."

It sounded for another second like a hoarse deep crackle of machine-gun barrage at the other end of the line. Dennis shrugged his shoulders wearily. He gave the name of the hotel.

"How do I know?" he said. "I found her."

He hung up. Then he passed one hand over his head, in a puzzled gesture. He couldn't think. He only knew that he had to keep that still figure within the edge of his sight. It couldn't hurt him, of course, but—he couldn't quite turn his back on it. He discovered that he was shivering, uncontrollable deep shivers like waves that tried to wrench his sanity from its moorings.

He had to hold onto himself. He did.

There was something he'd forgotten to do. Notify the hotel people. That was it. They'd have the police busting down doors in a minute if he didn't.

He went to the phone again. Suddenly, desperately, he needed communication with some outside help, the sound of a human voice. He felt like a diver abandoned on the ocean floor.

He raised the reassuring voice of the desk clerk downstairs.

"Listen," he said, "send the manager up here right away, will you?"

"He's just gone up in the elevator," the clerk said. "Told me he was going up to your room. The telephone girl gave him some message. Anything wrong?"

Dennis said, "Thanks. I'll let you know later."

The still figure on the floor was always within range of his vision. He mustn't lose sight of it. He'd go crazy with a primitive, superstitious fear if he did. The powers of darkness . . .

You had to face them boldly. Then they couldn't get you.

He knew that. He'd faced them.

There was a knock on the door. Life thundering out its command to open and face things. A quiet, sharp knock that meant to be obeyed.

Just as Dennis said, "Come," hoarsely, the door opened anyway and the hotel manager came in. He stopped inside the room and looked at Dennis, before he let his glance go around. His face was rigid, pitiless, hard with distaste that anything had happened in his hotel. His eyes were keen as lights shining in darkness.

"What's happened Ah!" he interrupted himself, as those keen hard eyes came to the woman.

"Someone—killed." Dennis found his voice dry. He forced it out of his throat and found that it dried up on him like one of the little California rivers sinking into a sandy bed in summertime.

"Killed?" The manager took him up sharply. "You said over the phone just now . . . dead."

"Look," Dennis croaked.

His hand pointed. There wasn't any need to say anything else. They both saw it—a little dark river drying on the taupe plush carpet. A little river of blood, whose source had been the back of that silent, black-clad figure. It had crawled a few inches and then sunk into the carpet. Or else—she had been killed at its farther end and had moved, before she died, in a convulsive gesture of escape. Not a pleasant little stream.

Dennis thought wildly for a brief moment of escape, of cottonwoods waving along a wide, sunny river, of water so shallow you could wade across, seeing the sun on the sandy bottom—of the wind in his face, the same wind that waved the trees.

That was far away—months and sunny afternoons away. It was a foggy November night, and he was in a close little hotel room, and that beautiful, white-skinned figure in the filmy black evening gown was lying at their feet. The grave blue eyes questioned them, swept them aside as unimportant. She looked as if she mustn't be disturbed—as if she were listening to, were looking at, something really important. Her whole attention elsewhere, beyond them.

And slowly, beyond the horror and the superstitious dread of death, Dennis began to feel stirring in his heart an ache of resentment that something so beautiful should die—should die before its time. The waste of beauty—the pity, the pity!

What had she done? Did it matter? She didn't deserve to die. No one so beautiful did. Not, his heart said fiercely, even if she'd done things terrible or treacherous. She'd given the world something in return, anyway. She'd been—her own excuse for being.

"Who is she?" asked the hotel manager, still staring at her.

Dennis's dark head came up on that with a jerk.

"How do I know?" he retorted. "I never saw her before in my life!"

"H'm," said the manager.

On that exchange they ended, until the police arrived about a minute later. The room seemed suddenly full of very substantial men in overcoats and felt hats, of deep voices questioning, commanding—of wide shoulders, hard eyes, straight glances.

The passage with the hotel manager had been just a preliminary. This was the main event.

There were two of them—Inspectors Sullivan and Cassidy. Dennis didn't have a chance.

The hardly veiled doubt of the hotel manager was nothing to the unbelief expressed by Inspectors Sullivan and Cassidy. Cassidy was a sharp-voiced man with a driving manner. He asked questions and expected answers. But Sullivan was like a smothering mountain in bulk and in manner. He sort of loomed. His comparative quietness was all the more impressive. Dennis felt smothered by that watchful silence and that ominous reticence.

They asked questions.

"Who is she?" Cassidy demanded, jerking his head first at the woman and then at Dennis.

Dennis said wearily and a bit automatically, "I never saw her before—in my life."

"Huh," said Cassidy, dropping this for the minute.

They crossed over to her, after warning the two men watching them not to move or touch anything in the room. They dropped to their knees and touched the corpse gently. Dennis and the hotel manager, who looked like a sharp black-and-white glossy raven in his dinner clothes, looked on silently.

Cassidy's head went up like an alarm signal. His hard blue eyes sought them.

"She's still warm!" he rasped. His sandy face flushed a bit with excitement. "She's still warm, I tell you. And the blood hasn't dried yet. This was done recently."

Sullivan nodded. The massive head went up and down once.

Cassidy jumped to his feet, turned on the other two.

"Who did it?" he demanded. "Who did it?"

He was like a fierce little hunting terrier now, sharp in excitement, merciless. He turned to both of them in turn.

"I don't know," Dennis said. That brought the gaze of those pitiless blue eyes on him then. He braced himself to meet them, and Sullivan's appraising deeper ones in the background.

"Who are you, anyway?" Cassidy snapped.

"I phoned you," Dennis said dully. "I—I'm in this room. When I came home tonight—just now—I found — that. I found her there."

"Yeah?" Sullivan came into it now. "What's your name?"

"Devore," he told them. "Dennis Devore."

It sounded like a silly sort of name now. He wished he'd picked a better one while he'd been at it. At the time, it had sounded good enough for what he wanted to do.

"What time'd you come here?" Cassidy asked.

"I don't know exactly," Dennis said. "I was on at the studio—broadcasting studio, you know—at eleven forty-five, for fifteen minutes "

"Broadcasting studio?" Cassidy picked him up.

"I'm a radio tenor," Dennis said. "I sing over it every night, at the same time."

"Eleven forty-five to twelve, eh?" Sullivan said, expressionless. "That brings you to twelve o'clock. Go on."

"I guess I left the studio just after twelve," Dennis thought back. "The next number was on when I left. It was a one-o'clock program tonight. It took me, say, fifteen minutes to walk home—I climbed the hill—and came right in here."

"Clerk might remember," Cassidy said briefly.

"It was about twelve fifteen, I guess." Dennis set his guess at that. "Then I came in " He set his teeth on that.

"Lights on?" Cassidy said, glancing around the room.

"No, out," Dennis went on, grateful for the shove over that hard place. "It was all dark in here. I had to open the door with my key and then turn on the lights at the door."

"The door was locked, eh?" Sullivan boomed in.

"Locked," Dennis nodded. "But anyone could have opened it—with a passkey. *He* did, just now." He jerked his head at the hotel manager, that unfriendly black-and-white raven in smart glossiness.

"Did, eh? What for?" Cassidy asked.

The gentleman he indicated shrugged.

"The telephone girl passed on Mr. Devore's message to the police to me," he said. "The policy of the hotel —well, there are some things we like to handle ourselves. Unfortunate publicity, you know "

"Some things you like to handle for yourselves!" Cassidy took him up, snarling. "To *keep* to yourselves, you mean! But not murder!"

The manager shrugged again and lapsed into silence.

"Go on. What about this passkey business?" Cassidy was on Dennis's trail again, yapping at his heels, as it were. "Why was it necessary?"

"It wasn't," Dennis retorted. "He knocked on the door, and before I could open it he'd shoved right in on his key."

"Before you could open it?" Sullivan said. "What were you doing that took up your time, anyway?"

At that Dennis looked at him with the first faint shine of a smile in his dark eyes, like a rather rueful sunrise coming in on a cold and wintry day. A smile at his own expense.

"Just—looking," he said softly and huskily.

"I was afraid that Mr. Devore might have stepped out, after—er—doing his duty by the police," the hotel manager struck in smoothly and nastily.

An unfriendly bird, Dennis decided dispassionately.

"Stepped out a second? Did you?" That was Cassidy.

"No, I tell you! I was in the room when he came in. I told you—I was—just looking."

Dennis had too much to do to hold his own with these two men to think about the hotel manager just now.

"Touch anything?" Sullivan asked now.

"Only the phone—and the table, I guess. And the door, of course."

"Fingerprints?" the hotel manager said.

"We'll see," grunted Sullivan, turning from them. "Coroner's men'll be here in a minute. Get the doctor's opinion. Not much doubt, though. Someone stuck a knife in her—and it's still there. Accounts for not much blood shed."

He turned softly, prowling lightly for all his bulk, to the windows, staring down at the sills a minute, at the latches still on the catch, at the dark fire escape beyond going down into the night. He didn't touch anything there, though.

Cassidy turned briskly to the hotel manager.

"Have to get list of people on this floor," he said to him. "Who're in these rooms along this hall, anyway? Did they see anyone or hear anything? What were they doing when she was killed here?"

The manager shrugged again, as one who gives up riddles.

"If it comes to that," he said, slowly, "I should be glad to have an explanation of some things myself. Why, for instance, should anyone select Mr. Devore's room in which to do such a terrible deed—a murder?"

The implication wasn't pleasant. No one pretended that it was. You couldn't gloss such a thing over. They all stared at Dennis for a second like, he decided swiftly and irrelevantly, hungry tigers picking out their special steaks.

There was now a confused noise beginning in the usually noiseless, plush-padded corridor outside.

"Doctor—coroner's men—likewise police reporters," diagnosed Cassidy quickly. "Let's get going."

Sullivan moved into action, slow, massive, somehow like the fabled irresistible force joined to the immovable body.

"We'll have to take your fingerprints," he said to Dennis, "if that's agreeable."

"Why not?" Dennis said. "Of course."

Cassidy was letting in something that resembled a pack of hunting hounds, eyes bright with excitement of the chase, giving tongue impartially to any trail that looked good. A blue-coat was helping him sort out visitors at the door. Cassidy had underestimated the population waiting outside. There were elevator boys in trim blue uniform, plainclothes clerk, and a few negligee guests from the same floor joining in the chorus.

The officially approved ones came in. Sullivan nodded to one unobtrusive little man with a case.

"Prints," he said briefly. The little man nodded and set out things on the walnut center table. There was something black and smudgy, like the sort of thing you press an election rubber cross against to ink it. Dennis reached out one hand. The little man seized it suddenly, firmly pressed down his fingers one by one in a quick rolling motion over the black stuff, transferring each print to paper before he took another finger. Then he dropped that hand, took the other one, and went through the same procedure. Dennis was left with two black-fingered hands. He was a bit ashamed and angry with himself because his hand shook a little. There'd been something so impersonal and ruthless in the procedure of taking his fingerprints that there was a sort of degradation about it—about him, he felt.

It was sort of frightening. Was this the way they treated prisoners—real prisoners? It was like being a wild animal in a cage. No regard for your personal will or spirit.

Someone came up to Sullivan, leaving the group gathered at the woman's body in a buzzing circle. A little man, with eyes like birds', bright and inquisitive and not unfriendly, in a thin brown face. A black overcoat almost too big for him draped him grandly. A black felt hat tilted jauntily over the lean little face.

"Kennedy—from the *Star*," he introduced himself in a hoarse chirp. "Took me off a losing poker game Can we smoke, chief?" he interrupted himself and lit a cigarette without waiting for Sullivan's approval or disapproval. That huge detective glared at him, but the undaunted intruder was conveniently blind and deaf to certain rumbles from the big throat.

"Murder, eh?" he went on.

"And what else would it be, with a knife sticking in her back?" broke in Cassidy with a certain bitter sarcasm.

"Trace the knife?" Kennedy thrust at him.

"Sure—if you want to trace every breadknife the chain stores have ever sold here," Cassidy thrust back. "You saw it—you can buy one like it for fifty cents. We could indict anyone in San Francisco who ever cut a loaf of bread, nearly, for having one in their possession."

"Yeah—and you could find out where it was last sharpened," the police reporter cut in. "I've got one of those things myself—I'm baching it—and I'm here to tell you they couldn't cut putty unless they'd been darn near a grindstone, a good grindstone, for an hour or two."

Sullivan turned to Dennis.

"You can go in the bathroom and wash your hands of that ink," he said.

Dennis went through the crowd. He caught Kennedy's half-whisper to Sullivan as he went. He tried not to see what was on the floor or what they were doing.

"Who's that guy?"

Sullivan rumbled an answer. Dennis knew what it was.

When he came back, Sullivan was waiting to meet him.

"We're going over to the Hall of Justice to report," he said. "You'll have to come with us, Devore, and explain why someone used your room for a murder party. I'm curious myself."

Dennis caught Kennedy's bright eye as Sullivan tried to hustle a way for the two of them out of the crowded room, without answering any of the questions that blocked his way.

"Listen," said that bright, keen little man intently, not unfriendly, "you're in a bad way, kid. Anyone you want me to call up?"

Then Dennis remembered someone.

"There's a man I know," he said, "a bird named Peter Byrne. If you'd call him up—I'd be glad. Thanks."

"Don't thank me. It's a swell story," Kennedy retorted. "A bird named Peter Byrne, eh? Right! What is he—a friend?"

"He's a lawyer," Dennis said hurriedly, as Sullivan grasped his arm and made a way for them impatiently.

Kennedy whistled, keeping pace with them.

"They find a beautiful dame dead in your room, and they haul you off to the coop," he remarked appreciatively. "You sure are in a tight place, kid. My boy, you don't want a lawyer—you need a can opener, to get you out of this."

"Will you shut up?" growled Sullivan and swept Dennis with him past the half-opened mouths and wide-open eyes of elevator boys, half-dressed guests, and other onlookers, down to the elevator, and so out to the street.

II. A BIRD NAMED PETER

Peter Byrne, awakened by a wild ringing sometime well after midnight, wondered why there were such things as telephones in this very imperfect world. He was a wide-awake young man when he was awake, and he went in for sleeping just as whole-heartedly.

After a few seconds he decided to answer the call.

He collided first with the bureau, whose location he knew as well as he knew that of the nose on his face, and then with the telephone chair. After that he was ready for anything, sleep shaken out of him.

"Huh?" he said to the crisp voice over the line. "What's that? Dennis Devore?"

"He's a tenor over the radio—one of these midnight canaries," chirped the shrewd, not-to-be-denied voice. "Come clean, Byrne—he says you're his lawyer—a lawyer, anyway. And he's in a jam, all right."

Peter forgot the midnight cold waves coming through his pajamas, attacking his bare feet. He clamored for details.

The voice then identified itself more explicitly. "I'm Kennedy, doing police for the *Star*," it said. "Devore asked me to call you. He's on the carpet at the Hall of Justice now."

"Not," thought Peter grimly and a bit wistfully, "such a bad place to be, at that."

He couldn't think of any Dennis Devore he knew who was a tenor over the radio. However, he was willing to learn more, as long as he didn't have to turn on the radio and listen to this Devore canary at this time of night.

"What's he in for?" he asked.

"Not what you think," the shrewd voice sort of grinned at him over the phone. "There ought to be a law, I admit—but we haven't got around to it yet. We will, we will. Just give us time—"

"Say," said an indignant and now thoroughly roused Peter Byrne, "what is this, anyway? A debate? Go—"

"Whoa!" said Kennedy calmly. "I'm coming to it. There's no law against tenors, as I said—but there certainly is against murder. Your friend Dennis is up for entertaining a lady corpse unbeknownst to him in his room tonight. He claims it was there when he got home from the studio. The police just said 'Yeah?' and hauled him off to the Hall of Justice—about 1:30 a. m. Pacific Standard Time. Are you standing by? The gong will indicate the police patrol, this time."

"Wh-what?" said Peter, inadequately.

"And so, friends of radioland, we come to the end of another swell pogrom—I mean program—and the beginning of the next. It's probably going on at the Hall of Justice now, where they're socking the truth out of your client."

About to say, stunned, "He's not my client!" Peter Byrne paused, on the very words.

The picture this shrewd chirper indicated wasn't a pretty one. Murder? Maybe so. A woman killed in this Dennis Devore's room. And no one to stand up for Dennis, whoever he was—and what a rotten name he wore! thought a fastidious Peter—except a casual pick-up acquaintance of a police reporter. And this Devore had given him Peter Byrne's name. Sort of last resort, maybe, because Peter couldn't place him at that. Not even with all the details he'd just listened to, that surely should excite any faint memory of this Dennis whatsoever. It was, when you came to think of it, sort of like an S O S coming out of the night to him.

And, as though accurately guessing the state of Peter Byrne's mind about that time, Kennedy's cool bird chirp changed to something colder and harsher, more like a challenge.

"Well?" it said, slowly, deliberately, a bit contemptuously, into the continued silence.

"Well what?" Byrne growled back at him.

"Are you in this or aren't you?" the police reporter wanted to know, still in that deliberate, rather deadly voice. "That is the layout. Either pick up your cards and play 'em or pass. I've told you all I know, Byrne. Just that Devore handed me out your name. I told him I'd get the situation before you. Are you in or not?"

A muffled roar answered him. To anyone who had ever spent an afternoon at the zoo it would be reminiscent of an aroused bear, shaking a shaggy head from side to side, coming out to battle. Peter was getting mad. His friends simply didn't go around bumping people off and then getting insolent, cold-voiced police reporters to call him up at an ungodly hour at night to bait him like this.

"Okay," said Kennedy, perversely mistranslating this roar. "I'll slip word to the boys his lawyer is coming around. You probably won't be able to get your client out of hock before morning, though. Might use a habeas-corpus grip on 'em to make them give him up if they're holding him too hard."

Peter had quieted down to deadliness himself. "I'll get him out," he promised simply and grimly. "I want to talk to him myself."

He hung up with a bang.

The light went on in the hall then and revealed Peter sitting there in blue-and-white pajamas, shaggy brown head at one end of his attire, large brown bare feet at the other. He blinked a startled pair of deep blue eyes from under strongly accented eyebrow ledges. He was impressive, built on the battering-ram principle.

His sister Blake was coming down the stairway. She wore a striped flannel dressing gown of blue and orange and brown, and a pair of blue bedroom slippers with orange pompons. She had a bright head of boy's golden brown hair weirdly ruffled up now, and a sleepy red mouth. Even when she was walking half asleep she carried her head with a sort of pride that straightened her slim body into a rushing grace.

"Blake," Peter said, puzzled, "do you know a guy named Dennis—Dennis Devore?"

"Heavens, no," Blake said. "Who is he, and why?"

She dropped into the big chair by the hall table and managed to wind herself up in its seat like a cat.

"I *thought* I'd brought you up better'n that," Peter grunted in great satisfaction. "I bet he's someone I knew at Stanford. There's always a lot of fellows you never remembered seeing in your life before, calling you up and saying they were at Stanford with you, when they want something."

"What does *he* want?" Blake asked, to be agreeable, seeing that her adored Peter was ready for a bit of midnight conversation.

Peter gave her the conversation, briefly.

"Guy's in jail. On a murder charge. Lady friend of his killed. He says he never saw her before, stranger to him. He gave a reporter my name to call up. Oh, yes—and he's a radio tenor—sings over the radio."

"Pete!" said Blake. She sat up. Her eyes were shining. Her bright boy's head lifted swiftly. "Go in and get him!"

"With what?" said Peter. "My bare hands?"

"He gave your name," Blake said softly.

Her brother grunted again.

"What are you doing down here in those clothes?" he demanded. He rose slowly, impressive in his scantier ones. "You'd better go to bed again."

"Where are you going?" his sister asked, preparing to go.

"I'm going to dress," he said briefly. "They don't allow pajamas down at the Hall of Justice when you're calling there just for a short visit—not a week-end stay."

"You lamb!" said Blake very softly and surely, pausing on the turn of the stairway to smile down at him before she disappeared.

That was about three o'clock in the morning. Peter was patient, he was forceful, he pulled wires. But it was around eight o'clock in the morning when the police decided to release his involuntary client from further questioning—for the moment.

They met in a small gray anteroom. Peter surveyed the wilted figure with frank interest. Dennis gazed up at Peter's more respectable and imposing heights.

"Hullo!" Peter said. "You Devore?"

Dennis nodded. "You're Byrne, aren't you?" He hesitated a second. He gave the impression, to Peter, as if he'd just held out his hand and then decided to snatch it back swiftly. A gesture of the mind rather than of the body.

He grinned faintly, instead.

"'Dr. Livingstone, I presume,'" he murmured.

Peter couldn't help grinning back before he thought about the seemliness of it.

"How'd you know me—of me?" he asked. He dropped onto the strongest-looking chair and motioned his client toward another. They settled down more at ease. Peter produced smokes, with a guilty glance of defiance toward the door. The dark head opposite him bent down swiftly over a match held out, inhaled luxuriously, exhaled a long wreath before it straightened up again.

"Missed those," he said simply. "You? Oh, I'd seen you at the studio—you came in with a party one night, remember?—and last night, when I couldn't raise any other name to save my life, you for some unknown reason stuck out in my mind. Favorably," he added hurriedly and respectfully, looking at Peter's two hundred pounds. "Perhaps it was because I'd remembered what a devil of a good guard you were and I knew I'd need a good fighter with me in this mess."

Peter grinned again. Then he made his face sober.

"Well, what happened in there?" he nodded toward the closed door.

"Plenty," said Dennis.

His eyes were dull and impenetrable all of a sudden.

"You didn't get fresh with them, did you?" Peter asked.

The wilted figure faced him indignantly.

"Fresh!" he echoed. "Do I look as if I was fresh?"

"You look as if you needed a shower and a shave," Peter commented frankly on his appearance. "And breakfast."

"Breakfast?" said Dennis wistfully. "What's that?"

"An old American custom," Peter explained. "We have it at our house every morning."

"I'd sort of lost track of it," Dennis apologized.

He got to his feet rather quickly, as if something had just got into his mind.

"Well," he said, "thanks very much—for all you've done. Sorry to have bothered you, but—thanks."

"What for?" Peter asked.

"Thanks for the lift," Dennis said. "I—I suppose this is where I get off. Good-bye." He did hold out his hand this time.

He couldn't very well make a graceful exit with two hundred pounds of solid Peter at the other end of his hand. He wanted to make a swell exit, too. He thought he had just about that much left in him.

"I said we had breakfast at our house—every morning," Peter repeated. "An old American custom."

"Oh!" Dennis said. "As I said, I'd sort of lost track of it."

III. TRICKS

After Peter had taken care of the necessary formalities they left the Hall of Justice and returned to Peter's house, where Dennis was now being introduced to that good old American custom, breakfast, at the Byrnes'.

"Tell us about it," Blake said, leaning brown elbows on the white cloth.

So Dennis told them about it.

At the end Blake's eyes were wide and almost as dark as Dennis's own, and Peter's eyes had narrowed like an armed force behind strong walls, ready, watchful, wary.

Dennis watched Peter like a man at the end of a long dangerous journey, beneath the walls of a strong and safe refuge, wondering if those walls would take him in.

Peter came out of his fortress then, having surveyed the countryside.

"What a beautiful jam!" he said with professional joy.

Dennis grinned, a bit crookedly this time.

"That's what Kennedy said," he reported. "'My boy, you don't need a lawyer—you need a can opener!'"

"Well, Devore—where did you get that name, anyway?" Peter paused to inquire en route.

"Pulled it out of a hat," said Dennis.

"Never do," grunted Peter.

"Oh, well—most people never get past the Dennis part." Their guest was still engrossed in pancakes and coffee, but willing to do his part in polite conversation at that.

"Well, Dennis," Peter gave in, "what happened down at the Hall, after that?"

"It was a great deal like being X-rayed," he replied. "Any little secret I'd ever had couldn't have stood a chance with those birds."

"But they do think you are holding something out on them?"

"Well, I must be cleverer than I give myself credit for being, then," Dennis said cheerfully. "They even shared my baby days with me."

"Well,"—Peter was being ponderous, but walking softly—"they did find the body in your hotel room, you know. And people don't—"

"Don't they?" Dennis asked grimly and surveyed the abashed faces about him. "I'm here to tell you they did!"

Something old and cold and wise had entered that bright and gay little sun room in that minute. They felt it.

Things did happen that way. People were murdered. Innocent men were accused. Innocent men had been hung.

"We've got to get Dennis out," Blake announced firmly. "First, who was she? We must find out everything—everything the police find out, and more. The whole truth. Then, was she killed outside somewhere and then brought into the room, or was she killed in your room?" Blake went on keenly.

"The police think so," said Dennis. "In the room. They hardly suspect me of lugging her along under my arm from the broadcasting studio."

"Yes, but we have this advantage," Blake pointed out. "We aren't narrow, like they are. We are free to suspect anyone, and we aren't trying to pin it onto Dennis, especially."

"Thank you," said Dennis, with that faint grin flashing out. "Only I plop for the room, too. Because why? First place, it's too darn risky doing it outside and bringing her in. Second, I saw her. And I don't think she'd moved—much."

Peter asked the same question the hotel manager asked. But he asked it in a very different sort of way.

"But why," he wanted to know, "your room?"

Dennis looked at him steadily with dark eyes staring through him and far away beyond him.

"'An enemy hath done this,'" he said, under his breath. "That's one answer. To put me in bad, maybe. Whoever had a grudge against her may have known me.

"There's a link there," Peter pointed out cautiously.

Dennis nodded, as though the interruption had been hardly registered on his mind.

"And then—why *not* my room?" he went on. "No one who's actually committed a murder can afford to have a body around. Put it on someone else. Say it was someone staying in the hotel—must have been—and they knew I was singing every night except Sunday from eleven forty-five to twelve at the studio. Room would be absolutely free then. Smallest risk of any in the hotel, probably. They arrange then for a murder party between those fifteen minutes. Easy, if it's been planned out. Wrong room. Lady enters it—it's in darkness, you know. Killed before she realizes it's a trap. Murderer goes out. Back to own room. Waits for alarm."

"Clever!" said Blake, shuddering a bit.

Dennis cocked an appreciative eyebrow at her.

"Oh, yes—if you like cleverness," he agreed. "Personally, I think it's a very overrated quality. I prefer depth."

"Quit sparring," ordered Peter. "This brings up a new line. Do you realize that it needn't have been anyone you know, any enemy of yours? It might be an absolute stranger!"

"Ye-es," said Blake. "But—let's combine both theories. Keep the best qualities of each. She was killed by someone who knew and hated Dennis, too, and she was killed in Dennis's room because he was away singing over the radio at the time. That clear?"

"Perfectly," said Peter. "Only—who did it?"

Dennis withdrew his gaze from the tablecloth that he'd been staring at.

"Look here," he began, "you're taking an awful lot on faith. Me, I mean. Isn't there—isn't there anything you'd like to ask—about me?"

"Well, but—I've seen you before," said Peter. "Were you at Stanford?"

He waited suspiciously for those familiar words of a claim on him to come.

Dennis laughed.

"No, I went to your dearest enemy and rival," he retorted. "At Cal we look upon Stanford as a training place for a good practice team for us."

"Got it!" said Peter suddenly in great satisfaction. "Last time I saw you, you were pushing your hand in my face. It was two years ago, at the Big Game. I was playing in the line, and you were a back trying to come through with the ball. You straight-armed me, and when I got up you'd wriggled past the second defense and were about thirty-three yards to the good. I remember that play, all right."

"I never did like guards," said Dennis airily. "They are apt to get in your way when you're in a hurry. You did, even when you weren't supposed to."

"Only I don't remember anyone on that team named Devore." Peter's relentless memory was still tracking.

"There wasn't any," Dennis said softly.

"Oh?" said Peter as softly.

"No. But it would be easy, of course, to look up the names of the team and find out who played in the backfield," Dennis said.

"Got no time," said Peter. "I'm a busy man. Don't play kid games any more and get my face shoved in."

"Well—" said Dennis softly but more huskily.

They heard a faint ring at the front door. Blake opened one of the casement windows and leaned out in the morning sunshine, peering down, trying to see who stood below.

"It's your police-reporter friend Kennedy, Peter," she reported. "He's on our doorstep."

She called down, and a minute later Kennedy came in and nodded to them.

"How's tricks?" he asked. "Mind if I smoke?"

"Do," said Blake. "Tricks are rather slow, at first," she told him. "You see, we don't know what's trumps. Would you say—clubs?"

"I'd say spades," Kennedy said. "For day after tomorrow, anyway. Coroner's inquest. If the verdict is death by someone unknown, you've still got a chance on the outside, kid. But if it's death by the hands of one Dennis Devore, the police'll take charge of your case for you and your client."

"A labor-saving device," said Dennis, "the police force."

He tried to smile.

"Go in with us," said Blake suddenly to Kennedy.

That hard-bitten gentleman eyed her suspiciously. "Oh, yeah? How?"

"We want to keep Dennis out of jail and get the right person who did the murder."

"I'll accept the invitation," Kennedy decided, after a second, grinning. "And it's not for your *beaux yeux* either, guy," he informed Dennis. "It's simply because I believe that a radio tenor is a subject for murder, a murderee, not a murderer."

"First, who was she?" Blake cut in ahead of Peter, to his indignation. "We've got to know!"

Kennedy's lean brown face hardened. He leaned forward.

"Listen," he said, "I'll tell you who she was. She was Bianca Fior! That mean anything to you? She played in big-league company, and she could hold her own beside a battery of beauties like Helen of Troy or Cleopatra as a siren."

"Bianca Fior," Dennis only said slowly. "That means white flower, doesn't it? I told you I felt that way when I saw her. As if I'd stumbled by mistake into some kind of bloody fairy tale."

"This isn't being in a fairy story," Blake said softly and sharply.

"It's better than being in a nightmare," Dennis answered.

IV. DE MORTUIS

"Bianca was a home-grown goddess," Kennedy said. "Statue of Liberty of North Beach. There's a lot of mystery about her beginnings, and a lot about her end. You see her like that big dame in New York Harbor, big, beautiful—God, she sure was!—and with a past and present like a sort of foggy mist around her. Who was keeping her? The police'd like to know. They might run up against something dangerous. Some big politician, maybe. An ex-rum-runner's gal, maybe. They're moving cautious. Too many prominent men in her background. Too much politics, maybe. They'd be a lot easier in their minds if Bianca hadn't been bumped off."

Blake nodded wisely.

"She was beautiful—and bad," she emphasized. "And we're going to find out about her. Peter, you'll take headquarters, won't you? And tackle Dennis's inspector?"

"Okay by me," said Peter. "What's his name? Sullivan? I'll find out about the inquest, too. I've got to get to the office first, and I'll go on from there."

"That reminds me, brother," Kennedy said to Dennis, "you've got to come clean with me. We need pictures—lots of 'em. Papers are hollering for them. And that's a funny thing. I looked around your room a bit after you'd gone last night, and I couldn't see a single picture, or letter, or anything of yours there. Just some cigarettes and books. No wonder the lady mistook that room for hers, or for an empty one. No one'd know you'd ever lived there. Nothing personal around."

"I don't like a lot of truck," Dennis said.

"I'll say you don't," Kennedy said dryly. "Your room would make the Sahara desert look all cluttered up with Victorian keepsakes. But don't let me trouble you."

"You don't," Dennis retorted, grinning. "Was that all you had on your mind?"

Kennedy, under cover of lighting another of his eternal fags, gave him a long, cool appraising look from bright cold eyes.

"All," he said briefly, puffing out blue smoke. "Just to find the lady's stabber, and to cover police at the Hall, and to get some pictures of one Dennis Devore, radio singer, released by the police after an all-night questioning."

The bright little green-and-gold sun room had begun to be filled with blue tobacco smoke since Kennedy had come. He'd turned it into an office.

"Is that necessary?" Blake asked.

Kennedy nodded. "Play in with me, and I'll play in with you," he said. "That's fair, and I've got to hold down my job. Do I get them?"

"Yes," Dennis said. "You'll have to take them yourself, though. I mean—the broadcasting studio hasn't any of me."

"So I discovered," Kennedy said. "We'll take 'em on our way to our good deeds today. Stop by at the office with me, and it's done. Where'll we four meet next?"

"What are you going to do, Blake?" Peter asked.

She raised innocent eyes to his. "I'm a lady novelist looking for local color," she said simply. "I'm going to interview the hotel staff, on Dennis's corridor. To find out about those other guests who *didn't* find a body in their respectable rooms."

Peter got up then, preparing to go.

"We part here," he said, "then. Dennis, what are you going to do? We've ruled you out of the Hall of Justice and the hotel part of it."

"I'll have to go to the studio and settle up accounts," Dennis said. "I'll bet you a nickel, even, they'll cancel my contract."

"Or else raise your salary," Kennedy grunted. "You'll be a great drawing card now, kid."

"Oh, yeah?" asked Dennis coldly. "Because I might be a murderer? If they offer to do that, I'll fire myself!"

He'd gone white around his nostrils. His eyes blazed darkly, and he breathed a bit quickly. Kennedy watched him, that inquisitive bird's head of his on one side.

"I'd sure like to play poker with you," he said.

Dennis cocked an arrogant eyebrow at him.

"Do you think I look like a professional card player?" he asked, rather coldly still.

Kennedy grinned.

"No, you wouldn't be as dangerous if you did. You're scared, and yet you're cool and dangerous," —he emphasized his points with his lighted cigarette stabbed into the smoky air, leaning forward—" and you're picking your way through this with the brains of a quarter-back. The way you're using all of us– you remind me of a great back I once saw picking his way through a broken field at full speed."

Dennis looked at Kennedy and finally smiled it off.

"I've often wondered what happens to great football players," he said, airy again. "Beyond becoming wrestlers or candidates for the Old People's Home."

His eye lit on Peter in passing for an infinitesimal instant, without expression. Peter blushed.

Kennedy said, "This one I'm telling you about got in a jam, after he graduated. He ran down a man on a dark night on the highway down near Salinas way, and he didn't stop. Didn't even turn up till next morning to leave his name. Man died. He was some Italian wholesale dealer up here, I think. Pretty important. And this guy'd been speeding, evidently. They tried him for manslaughter, and he got off pretty well—on probation for a year, I think. Then he disappeared."

Blake said, in a soft rush, "Oh-h-h!" and stopped.

"He didn't stop, or come back until next morning?" Peter inquired, expressionless. His big brown face was like a rock.

"There was a girl in the car with him," Kennedy said. "Her name never came out. I think this football bird I'm telling you about got her home okay."

"Really?" said Dennis.

Kennedy stared at him. There was a short, intense second of silence, almost unbearable to Blake and Peter. Dennis went on smoking.

"I *said* I'd like to play poker with you," Kennedy remarked. His voice was that of the most lively admiration.

He hoisted himself to his feet.

"Well, come on," he said. "You're coming with me to the office, you said, for pictures."

Dennis got up, too, in a swift motion that reminded Peter of Blake's way of moving.

"After today," he said, "there probably won't be any Dennis Devore, radio tenor. I—I hope you'll think kindly of him."

That irrepressible grin of his just faintly touched dark eyes and sober mouth.

"He wasn't a bad guy," he gave him his requiem. "*De mortuis*, you know."

He turned to go, after Kennedy.

"Dennis," Blake said suddenly, "where are you going?"

"I don't quite know." Dennis wrinkled his brow mildly. "I can't live at the hotel—I suppose I'll get a room somewhere."

"I told you I was baching it," Kennedy broke in grudgingly. "I've got two rooms over on the north side of the city. Lots of room there for two. Thought I told you."

"You didn't," Dennis said. "But thanks. I'll accept." His voice was brief and bitter.

"You needn't thank me," Kennedy growled as ungraciously. "I like to have my exclusive story under my eyes all the time."

Clearly it wasn't one of those hospitable impulsive invitations. It looked regrettably like an invitation by *force majeure*. Dennis had an ominous semblance to a prisoner being led off to a dark dungeon that he hadn't inspected and chosen himself.

"Be here for breakfast tomorrow," Blake said hastily and impulsively, as this aspect of it struck her.

Dennis nodded and smiled at her reassuringly and followed Kennedy down the stairs.

Peter said, a bit heavily, in the silence, "I feel as if I were riding a surf board. Things seem to happen fast, when that Dennis guy is around. But—I don't know. It may be dangerous, but it's exhilarating." He grinned sheepishly.

"Yes," Blake said. "I feel that way, too. Rather— short of breath."

"What are we in for, anyway?" Peter said, sobering.

"I don't know," Blake said. "But we sort of had to do it, Peter. There didn't seem to be anything else to do."

"Not at the time, no," Peter agreed. "We just held onto our surf board and let it ride. But now—you heard what Kennedy said. About that ex-football hero who ran a man down and let him die in the road? If I thought Dennis was the one he meant who did it, it would be something else again. What do you think, Blake?"

He was suddenly impressive again, with a stern weight of integrity in him that bulked sheer as his big self.

"I think," Blake said slowly, "the only thing the matter with Dennis is that he's too chivalrous."

"What?" said Peter.

"Look how he acted about that Bianca woman, and she's the one that's got him into all this trouble," said Blake sturdily. "I shouldn't wonder—if he hadn't been too chivalrous at some other time in his career."

"Well," Peter said, "you'll cure him of that if anyone can, I'm sure."

"*De mortuis*," said Blake softly, "*nil nisi bonum—* indeed! I wonder just what he was thinking of—besides Bianca."

Peter began to laugh.

"I've just thought," he explained to her questioning eyes. "I've got two old codgers coming in to make a change in their wills today. I'll have to put 'em off. They're in no danger. They've lived to their placid eighties already— they can wait. Nothing's ever happened to them much. It's Dennis who needs to worry about reaching the ripe age of thirty alive!"

V. CHURCH OF SAINTS PETER AND PAUL

Another conversation was going on between Dennis and Kennedy, on the front smoker of a Kearny Street car going down into Market Street.

"What's the idea," Dennis asked stiffly, "of the third-degree stuff?"

"Meaning what?" Kennedy said, raising an eyebrow and impassively puffing away.

"Well, I'm coming to stay with you, and it's not for your *beaux yeux* either, guy," said Dennis bitterly. "You practically blackmailed me into coming," he reminded his host.

"Better than being blackballed at your hotel," Kennedy grinned. "Listen, Devore—you want to keep out of jail right now. That's your aim in life—or it ought to be. Undercover stuff. And I'm not keen on having a good story wandering around under other people's noses—and eyes. I want to keep it to myself—for a while, anyway. You stay under cover at my place, where no cop'll think to look for you, and we'll both be covered."

"Why don't you spill your story right now?" Dennis asked. "Afraid? Or looking for fingerprints? There aren't any—I can tell you that. Nothing for the cops to compare, either."

"Or anything else," said Kennedy. "I noticed that. You sure made a clean break. I don't doubt someone swiped the records and the prints and all that. They would."

He looked sidewise at his rather sullen companion.

"Her folks had quite a lot of influence down there, didn't they?" he asked, grinning.

"Will you shut up?" said Dennis in a restrained but ferocious voice. "And go to—"

"The office," interrupted Kennedy brightly. "Here we are."

They climbed off at Market Street, where the traffic swirled around Lotta's slim fountain. They crossed the street and went up into an elevator, then left that and changed to another, rickety one.

"About that story," Kennedy finally said. "I might aim to keep it, and then produce it for what our British cousins would label 'Sensation in Court.' And then again I might not. It all depends."

"On what?" asked Dennis.

Kennedy grinned at him again.

"On people," he said. "I've seen a lot of 'em. Especially at the Hall of Justice. And they nearly all wilt, innocent or guilty, when they get in there. Something in it gets them. You didn't, and yet you had a lot to be scared about—things like this coming out, for instance. But you didn't lose your nerve. I don't think you've ever lost your nerve. And yet this bird back in Salinas did, according to the story. But it never did seem reasonable to me that a great back, used to thinking quickly, would have lost his nerve so completely, the way that bird did. He'd have thought things out quicker. People are funny. But I know them. That's one thing being on police does for you, anyway. You get so you can't be fooled about people much."

"Oh," said Dennis, thinking this out.

They got out and banged on a rickety wooden door that reminded Dennis of a model speakeasy. A center hole in it opened. A face appeared. Kennedy nodded at Dennis, and the face withdrew. The door opened.

"Scotch," murmured Dennis hopefully.

"No, Danish," Kennedy said following him in. "He doesn't like to be disturbed, that's all. Danes are funny that way."

"I know," Dennis nodded. "I had a Great Dane once. He didn't like to be disturbed, either—especially when he had a bone to pick." He fingered a scar on his right wrist reminiscently.

He sat on a hard chair and looked around a very bare room. It had great windows to the north and west, and an unpainted kitchen table and a couple of hard kitchen chairs in it. Otherwise it looked as if the carpenters and plasterers had just gone away and nobody else had moved in yet. Their host appeared in silence, a round rosy face, and a wet and chemically-smelling black rubber apron. He set up black apparatus, a little way in front of Dennis.

Dennis stared at it calmly and curiously. Only his eyes went black and impenetrably dull again, and the white lines came around the base of his nostrils.

He thought in a vivid flash of Sullivan standing by while a little unobtrusive man seized his hands, and, finger by finger, rolled them in inked stuff. There was a sort of degradation in having these things happening to one, instead of making things happen as you pleased. Like being an animal, and having to stand for whatever people did to you!

The flashlight went off then in a great sound, lots of smoke and a bright light. The little man nodded to them and disappeared into his warren. Kennedy got up.

"We won't wait for the prints," he said. "Thanks. I guess they'll turn out okay."

"They'd better," Dennis said. He got up, a bit stiffly.

"Smoke?" Kennedy said and fished out a packet of cigarettes. Dennis took one out carefully and lit it from Kennedy's light. His hands didn't shake. He could control his poised body more coolly than he could his hot and impatient mind.

"We'll go all the way down in this crazy thing," the police reporter said when they were in the rickety elevator again, descending slowly and cautiously. "No use letting people know where you are, if anyone's watching the front entrance."

They got out in a basement of gray concrete and walked through a sort of gray tunnel, landing outside in the dirty sunshine of an alleyway. Kennedy looked away carefully and quickly.

"Okay," he said softly. "No one'll pick you up here, anyway."

He signaled to a lurking plain dark taxi just on the corner where the alley joined a main street.

"Our special brand," he murmured to Dennis. "Warranted not to talk out of turn."

They got in the taxi without another word. Kennedy leaned forward and spoke to the driver.

"We can stop by at your studio, kid," he explained, sinking back again. "You can fix things up there, and then we'll go on to my place. I wouldn't go back to the hotel if I were you."

Dennis involuntarily shuddered and then held himself rigid again, commanding his betraying body. He saw a lighted hotel room, the graceful walnut furniture, the bed with the sheet turned back—and, beyond the table, that dark and untidy sort of shadow . . .

"I haven't the least desire to go back there, I assure you," he said through stiff, dry lips.

Kennedy looked at him again, that sidewise, quick, stab of a look from bright birds' eyes.

"Don't let it get you, kid," he said more gently.

Dennis looked at him coldly with his dark head haughty again.

"Nothing's ever 'got' me," he said coldly. "Not even getting my picture taken like a San Quentin boarder!"

Kennedy shrugged. They stopped before the entrance to the studio building.

"I'll wait here," the police reporter said. "You won't be long, I guess."

"Not if I can help it," Dennis grunted, getting out.

He wasn't. It was about five minutes later when he came down the stairs to the street again, the hatless dark head moving swiftly and surely through less sure traffic of people.

"I told you," he said only, getting in. "There goes Dennis Devore, poor fellow! Canned."

"By request?" Kerinedy asked.

"Does it matter?" Dennis retorted. "Sure it was by request—my own request. I asked for my time."

"And you got the air," Kennedy punned pitilessly. "Well, there's one less radio canary singing. That's all to the good."

Dennis laughed. He was oddly released and happy.

"You never heard me!" he said. "That remark proves it."

"And I hope I never will!" Kennedy said grimly.

They were in the sunny north section of the city now. Brown-faced, beautiful children with dark hair and great soft dark eyes like deer played about the narrow streets. The taxi went up, and stopped in that position, still going up. They climbed out precariously.

"My joint," said Kennedy. It was a new, clean-looking apartment house—two stories, four apartments, Dennis estimated swiftly. Better than he'd thought it would be. And there'd be a swell view of the Gate, glittering in noon sunshine.

There was. There was something else, too, that he hadn't reckoned on. A grand piano in the small living room. His eyes widened, seeing this. A swell grand piano! He knew the sort of tone it would have—dark and lovely, like itself.

"*Cantabile*," he muttered reverently, like a sort of Italian oath.

Kennedy's place was a surprise. He'd thought of something bohemian, which meant dusty and rather bare, like the camping place of a hardened old campaigner. Or else cluttered up so you couldn't move. This was—different. A grand piano. And the shelves of the room covered with books of phonograph records, music scores.

Kennedy was in the small bedroom. Dennis stepped over and looked at some of the books of records. His eyes stayed wide and dark with astonishment. He whistled softly. Into those astonished eyes came the faint flickering of mischief beginning again.

Kennedy came back again, slipping an overcoat on quickly.

"I'm due at the Hall now," he explained in a hurry. "I'll be back around six, I guess. You'll stay holed up right here till I get back. Get me? There's some stuff in the icebox when you get hungry."

"Aye, aye," said Dennis a bit absently. His eyes were veiled, but eager.

He surveyed the records gleefully when his host had gone.

"Blackmail, eh?" he said thoughtfully. "So I'm to stay in all day? We'll see."

He then proceeded to get drunk. He had a cocktail of Gershwin's, consisting of the Concerto, and the Rhapsody in Blue, then a full-bodied draft of Wagner's Ring taken straight, and blissful ecstasies from Beethoven. He began tapering off with Mozart. When Kennedy came back around six o'clock, he was sitting bright-eyed and white-faced at the piano playing and singing, lustily.

His host muttered softly. Dennis turned around, letting one finger pick up and trail the tune in the meanwhile.

"I saw Sullivan," Kennedy announced, discarding coats. " He got after me for letting you go this morning. He's just about made up his mind to take you in again. The inquest is coming, and he needs a goat to sacrifice. Threatened me with lese majeste and a few assorted crimes, but I told him there wasn't any warrant out for you yet and he'd better wait till the inquest is over. You're not to go out till then, either. You stay right here, holed up."

Dennis nodded, trailing a cigarette from the corner of his mouth and turning loose on the piano.

Above the syncopated din his voice rose, melting, tender. He was in the throes of sentiment.

Kennedy writhed, bearing up nobly. Finally:

"Do you *have* to do that?" he yelped.

Dennis looked at him.

"I have to do *something*," he said gently. "I'm bored."

Kennedy sat down in the armchair and groaned aloud.

"He's bored," he said bitterly and blankly. "Sullivan's after him, and that big stiff usually grabs what he's after; there's a murder inquest up, and he's bored. Did anyone ever tell you there was wirehaired fox terrier in you?"

"No," said Dennis truthfully.

"Well, there is," Kennedy grunted. "If you wait till I can get my things on again will you promise not to sing? There's a roof-garden ex-bootlegger across the street, on top of that apartment house. No one'll be likely to look for us there."

Dennis grinned and gave up the desecrated piano reluctantly.

"It's blackmail," Kennedy said as they went on down the stairs cautiously. "And you know it. You looked at my music stuff there."

"Blackmail?" said Dennis. He raised an elegant eyebrow. "Where have I heard that word before?"

The roof garden was cool. It had a view of part of the city to the south and sloping down to the north, where the dark Gate ran swiftly in the darkening evening. There were nondescript potted green things around, palms or rubber plants or what Dennis called hotel foliage.

Kennedy talked to the proprietor, a dark-faced but pleasant person with a picturesque version of a dinner suit. Dinner began to come—chicken, taglierini, red wine. They had a table at the edge of the roof, where the wall came up to their shoulders as they sat there.

"What's that big building—the gray one?" Dennis asked.

"Church," Kennedy said. "All the Italians go to it. It's St. Peter and St. Paul's."

Their host bent over them in an aroma of garlic, dark mustachios highly perfumed, and greasy vestments.

"All," he said, gutturally mysterious about it. "Yes. But not one—no more. She will be there for Mass, and she will never hear it. No more. Ah, *bella—fior d'Italia!*"

All of a sudden he wasn't a greasy, intrusive speak-easy host trying to be mysterious. He was a poet, a lover, a representative of a lover's race, mourning a lost beauty.

"Who d'you mean?" asked Dennis, with quickening breath.

"I mean her—the one they killed." He turned to Dennis as to a confidant. "You heard? They called her Bianca—Bianca Fior."

"You know her—about her?" Kennedy thrust in, keen as a bright thin dagger's blade.

The man shrugged. His dark eyes looked at them from beneath a dark fringe of hair. Honest, mournful eyes.

"No one knew her," he sighed. "Just—the house she lived in, the restaurants she danced in. No one knew her, signor, as she really was. Only I—a little. Two nights ago, just before sundown, I saw her. She was coming from the church, and she was weeping. I saw that. She had been to speak to her friend, the priest. Old Father Malletti. She came there sometimes."

Kennedy looked at Dennis. His eyes were bright as steel.

"Confession?" he barely breathed.

Their host shrugged again and mopped the table absently.

"No, not Confession, I think. She went to the parish house. Not to the church. I think old Father Malletti knew all her sorrows. As a friend, not a priest, perhaps. He would come to the door and stand on the stairs watching her go away. He did so the last time. He raised his hand. She did not dare to go too directly to God, I think—that beautiful one!—but old Father Malletti would dare to go for her. He is—a saint."

He made the swift, almost invisible passage of one brown, unwashed hand across his greasy white shirt-front, and went back to his noisy kitchen region. Dennis and Kennedy stared out at the thickened darkness. In the closing night the tall gray church of the Saints, Peter and Paul, stood impassively fronting them.

Dennis cleared his throat finally.

"Well," he said, "I'm not such a dumb dick after all, am I?"

Kennedy stared at him pityingly.

"Kid," he said, "for dumb luck, no. You ought to be down on your knees."

VI. "HE IS GONE ON A JOURNEY"

Dennis yawned with immense exertion, through the thick soft feathers of sleep smothering him. His head drooped forward.

"Wake up!" said Kennedy hastily. "We're going places."

"Now?" said Dennis wonderingly.

He sighed deeply and shook sleep away from him, and obediently followed Kennedy down the stairs and across the street. He stood swaying a little, wand-in-the-wind fashion, waiting for Kennedy to take the lead into the apartment house.

That bothersome, small, hard-bitten gentleman sized him up wearily.

"Look here," he decided, "can you stay awake long enough for me to ask a question at the corner church?"

Dennis just nodded, or rather let his head drop down once. It was too much trouble to open his mouth and say yes.

He followed Kennedy, still half in his dream, to the still-lighted doorway of the priests' residence of St. Peter and St. Paul's. Kennedy rang the bell. After a minute the door opened. The housekeeper stood there, light falling on her old-fashioned big white apron and on her sturdy, lined face.

"Father Malletti?" asked Kennedy.

"Oh, you're wanting to speak to *him*?" the woman asked shrewdly. "In particular? Well, I'll have to call someone, sir. I don't just know . . ."

Dennis heard the voices, saw the lighted faces, from far away. Like people on a lighted stage.

The housekeeper turned. A tall young priest stood there behind her. A beautiful masculine voice, like a struck bell, thought Dennis, enchanted, spoke out effortlessly.

"You wanted Father Malletti?" said the beautiful voice. It came from the tall young priest. "Ah, he's away. He's not here."

"Where is he?" Kennedy took him up quickly.

"He is gone on a journey," said the young priest, "to the country. He went Saturday night. A former parishioner of his was dying, and they sent a big, dark car for him to come."

"Where is this place?" Kennedy asked.

"It's near Delroy." The beautiful voice seemed to hang in the air, sighing, over each word. Dennis listened to the sound, not the sense. He was too sleepy. But a word caught his ear.

"That's funny," he said, after they'd thanked the priest and had gone down the sidewalk again. "Delroy! That's where— "

He yawned and forgot again.

"Aren't we ever going to sleep?" he said plaintively. "Or will we keep this up all night? The Chinese torture. You're as bad as Sullivan."

"That's where—what?" his active small tormenter said.

"Oh—that's where I've got a small ranch," Dennis answered. "I'll invite you down some time. We've got the best beds—"

"If Father Malletti doesn't get back tomorrow morning," Kennedy said, halting at their door, "I'll take you up on that right away."

Something seemed to strike him then with a curious kind of worry, as though something were—out of tune, and he couldn't locate the note.

"Some people," he said slowly, "are a long time dying, aren't they? A big, dark car coming . . ."

He shook his head. He was blaming himself for the wrong notes. They were in his head, not in the things he'd heard.

There was a wall bed let down in the living room for Dennis. He was in it almost as soon as it was down. A pair of Kennedy's pajamas draped him sketchily. He tucked his head down into the pillow. The light began to grow dim.

"Delroy!" he said very drowsily. "There's a river . . . and cottonwoods . . . cottonwoods . . ."

They were waving in the little wind. He saw the shallow ripples of the broad stream, and the glint of gold under them as the sun struck through to the ledges of smooth sand underwater. A smile curved his mouth. .. .

"Say," Kennedy said, "I'm going to the Hall of Justice to take the night shift. I may be back late, but I'll try not to wake you up. Can I trust you to stay here while I'm gone?"

There wasn't any answer. The bright light fell full on the face of one who was far away.

"I guess so," Kennedy grunted, turning off the light.

VII. THE LONG LEASH

"Fellow-members of the Dennis Defense Society," said Blake impressively, "we are met here to—to—"

"To do honor to a man who," rattled off Dennis glibly, "I should say needs no introduction—a man who has the welfare of this great country at heart—a man who, under a cast-iron exterior, has a heart as soft as a properly boiled egg—a man who—"

"Charter members of this society will please come to order!" said Blake. "Silly nuts—"

"Decline the nomination," said Dennis. "I was only calling attention to your cook. Under that Mongolian exterior rests an artist. His pancakes are a poem. I," he said pensively, "should know."

Blake succumbed. "Louie is an old-timer," she said carelessly, puffed with pride. She helped herself to a cup of clear topaz coffee, sniffing delicately with pleasure as she did so. "He says he used to wash gold in the Sierra creeks, just after the forty-niners were there."

"There's gold in them thar eggs," said Peter, opening one as if he expected to find a nugget in it.

Dennis grinned. He'd been absurdly blithe at an absurd—to his reporter host—hour in the morning. Ever since he'd gotten up around half-past seven, rustled around the small apartment shaving, bathing, and borrowing things from a Kennedy sound asleep, and had finally shaken his indignant host awake to tell him he had a breakfast date, he'd been, if not obnoxious about it, at least fearfully glad-handed. He belonged, said Kennedy bitterly, with one of those early-bird exercises on the radio. The cheerful kind. And now would Dennis let go his shoulder and let him get some sleep? He didn't give a hoot if he was going out to run into the entire homicide squad, out for his blood. Dennis, said Kennedy, growing eloquent, could go to several places whose location Kennedy seemed to know well. Or he could get taken up by the police if he wanted to. Let the police, if so, do the worrying. He didn't owe them anything.

"I'll be back after breakfast, maybe," Dennis said reassuringly, giving that indignant limp shoulder a final shake, this time meant in all friendliness of good-bye.

"Not," said Kennedy, "if I see you first!"

"Your ties are rotten, anyway," Dennis retorted. "I had to wear my own."

That final sally woke Kennedy up completely. He spent some uneasy moments wondering just what Dennis had decided to borrow from him before he decided to call sleep a lost cause and get up and see the worst.

By that time Dennis was knocking at the door of the dark old Byrne house on Russian Hill, being let in by Louie, the Mongolian image graven with nearly inch-deep lines on his mahogany old face.

And the Dennis Defense Society had greeted one another and were assembled for breakfast again by Blake, in the little green-and-gold sun room. The day was beginning with a little mist, a slight fog of San Francisco, so they had a fire in the very small fireplace by the north wall. Blake wore a creamy sort of silk dress, with blue heavy beads around her neck. Peter had blossomed out in a dark blue tie with minute red dots in it, worn with his usual blue suit. This would have signified, in a lesser man, an outbreak of vivid whorls, lightning blazes, and patterned arrows—something, as the salesmen say, pretty dashing, sir. Dennis gave the impression that he was actually wearing something of that sort anyway—red and gold, or blue and orange in heavy bars. He wasn't. His tie was immaterial, though. It was his vivid face, his eyes lit up in excitement, his dark head poised, that gave that impression. His spirit was wearing that sort of tie. All uncontrolled color and dash.

Just about this time Kennedy said to himself, with immense conviction, surveying the somehow crowded room that Dennis had so blithely left behind him, "Talk about serpents! I'd trade a wirehaired terrier in the house for a serpent, a nice quiet serpent in my bosom, any day!"

But Blake, curiously enough, at this time was looking at Dennis across the table, seeing the altogether blithe and somehow untouched spirit in him, and she felt a sort of sadness coming on her. She couldn't explain it. She only knew that suddenly she felt as though she were growing old—and Dennis wasn't. A sort of cold feeling, as though she were lonely. She couldn't understand it. The merest touch of a loneliness of spirit. She thought:

"Doesn't he *feel* anything?"

It was like a curious sort of balance. As Dennis's mind and heart and spirit went up, hers went down.

As though she'd lost him, a little. She didn't want him sad—but she wanted him with her.

Not so young and—untouched by sadness or mortal pang.

Dennis himself didn't know what was the matter—he simply felt that all was right with the world, like a lark charging skyward, as it were. At the very back of his mind, beyond his own hearing, a sound like a bell swung, clapping, "Delroy! Delroy!" at measured intervals. Perhaps its vibrations came to him, making him merry.

"Who reports first?" he asked, looking up. "We must get to business."

"I like that!" said Blake. "When I've been trying to get you two to pay attention!"

Peter strolled into action, like a large rock detaching itself from the landscape.

"Ladies first," he said.

"I was going to." Blake leaped to the invitation before anyone could get in ahead. She planted her elbows on the table and stared at them with very blue eyes. "You can't *guess* what I've found out!"

"My dear child!" Peter protested beyond endurance. "This isn't charades. If we'd guessed, you wouldn't have had to go and find out anyway."

"Well, then," Blake sorted her thoughts, "I spent the afternoon associating with the hotel servants. If the hotel manager knew he'd have had me thrown out. But the servants weren't a bit averse to making some extra money and to telling all they knew to a writer lady. They were thrilled. I started in with the cloakroom attendant—ladies' maid, you know—and gave her a big tip. Then she smuggled the others in for questioning. She wanted to know,"—she turned to Dennis gravely—"if her picture would come out in the paper."

"I'll take it up with Kennedy," Dennis said. "If she's pretty, that bird would commit grand larceny to get her picture."

Peter looked from the rock ledges of his eyes at Dennis, and then decided not to speak of pictures being in the paper this morning. It didn't seem tactful. He remembered that Dennis had been practically sand-bagged into having his taken yesterday.

"Bianca," Blake was saying, "came up in the elevator to the fourth floor—your floor—alone, about eleven fifty-five or a few minutes to twelve, that night. She didn't stop to ask the desk clerk for the number of any room, or anything—she just crossed the lobby to the elevator. She was wearing a black chiffon evening dress, and a bright Spanish shawl over it. And she was alone."

"That means," Dennis said intently, "that she was going to meet someone—a man—upstairs. We must look for a man alone, then, in the corridor I was in. He probably wouldn't have associates."

"Not in this kind of a deal," Peter rumbled. "Remember, we've decided he had it all planned out—going into the wrong room with her, and all that. He knew what was coming. It wasn't a sudden impulse."

"That makes it terrible!" Blake said, in a softly agonized rush of words. Her eyes darkened. That bright figure, going to death—to a planned death . . .

Dennis nodded. Something of her shadow seemed to have fallen on him. Or his spirit had come down to meet hers, from its first wild swoop upwards this morning.

"Who were my pleasant neighbors?" he asked grimly.

"Your immediate neighbors were"—Blake consulted a scribbled piece of paper—"(1) a honeymoon couple, on your right-hand side. She had dolls with long sprawled legs stuck around the room, the chambermaid told me. Just an ordinary good-looking young couple in looks—she could hardly remember anything extraordinary about them. They're on their way to Detroit now, anyway—to Papa's mills or something.

"Then, (2) a shoe salesman was on your left side—a traveling salesman. He had an exhibit of shoes down in one of the smaller ballrooms. He's there now, for the week, taking orders from the shoe men."

"A man alone?" said Peter, keen-eyed.

"He's a hearty-looking fellow," Dennis said. "I've met him in the lobby. Borrowed a light. Talked. About himself and his business. Brown hair, rather full face. I'm sure you can rule him out. He wouldn't have stuck a knife in Bianca—he might have playfully pushed her out of the fourth-story window at the height of a wild party, but he'd have been awfully sorry afterwards. No, this was cold-blooded and cruel. It was all arranged. That's what makes it so horrible. She came up in the elevator to meet someone, in her bright shawl and black dress, and they were laying for her."

"By the way, that shawl—" Peter said.

"It wasn't found?" Dennis asked. "Why, it wasn't in my room. I'd have seen it—"

"No," said Blake. "Nor an evening bag. Any woman would have had a dinky little bag with her, dressed as Bianca was. The chambermaid says they didn't find a thing like that. They looked in the lobby, and the corridors, too. The detectives asked them questions about these things."

"Make a note of it," Peter said briefly to Dennis. "Someone's got them."

That gentleman, bright-eyed, nodded. "Go on," he said softly.

"The entire corner next to the shoe salesman is a suite of several rooms. It's taken by an old lady who's had it for ages. She's a sort of cornerstone of the hotel. She has a maid, too. But if she's turned from respectability, I'd expect an outraged earthquake to topple the hotel walls down in retribution."

"Always suspect old ladies," Dennis said darkly and helpfully. "I do. All the unlikely people, you know."

"The hotel manager?" suggested Blake, wrinkling her nose.

"If you'd seen his face that night!" Dennis sighed in negation. "I'm afraid that's no good. He'd have thought out a better way than doing it in a guest's room. A man doesn't deny his own character, even at the moment of murdering. No, he'd have lured the guest on to a ferryboat ride and then dropped him overboard neatly. Without a trace, you know."

"How about the elevator man who brought Bianca up?" Peter asked. "He was alone with her up there for a second or two—or more."

"He's a nice young lad," Blake said, reminiscently smiling and shaking her head. "Fresh as daybreak—face, smile, manners, everything. He—if you're going to reconstruct this thing from people's characters, Dennis— would have gone for the point of anyone's jaw with a straight right—anyone that he'd a quarrel with. He wouldn't have stabbed anyone in the back. Least of all a woman. Besides, he's got an alibi. Or else he's the author of the quickest murder in history. He went right down again, after he'd left Bianca on your floor, to take some other people up to the seventh. The clerk noticed that. The people who went up will swear to the exact time, too. One of the women in the party glanced at her wrist watch, while they were waiting for the elevator to come."

"No-o," said Dennis, half to himself. He leaned one elbow on the table and draped himself thoughtfully on it. His eyes were half closed in concentration.

"The man who did this," he said, "wasn't like any of the people we've discussed. He was like this: He had hell's own nerve, to do it this way. Do you realize that? It took all of it to do it—waiting for her, not knowing whether she'd be late or not—or if other people would get out at that floor with her. He bet on his luck. He'd choose a room near as he could get it to mine—across the hallway, say. I can see him," said Dennis, in a queer low voice that made them see pictures, too, in the bright daylight, "with his door open just a crack, listening for the elevator—making sure she was alone on that floor—coming out of his room quickly— 'Bianca!' coming to meet her with his arms out. He was a friend, a lover. She didn't have the least idea she was going to meet an enemy. She wasn't on guard. A woman like her would have been, otherwise. She was a wise baby. He even," said Dennis, in that monotonous thread of a voice with scarlet and black in its even tone — "he even took off her shawl and laid it across his arm, very gallantly—helping her off with it, in my room—and then she turned around, to see the room— his room—"

"*Dennis!*" Blake broke it off', in a sharp gasp. "Don't!"

"The seance," said Peter, "is ended."

He shook himself like a great dog when it comes up out of deep water. He eyed Dennis a bit askance.

"I think we know now," he said, "what the man was like, Dennis. Your demonstration was very effective. All I can say is that I hope for your sake he picked on you just because you sing over the radio at stated intervals. I wouldn't care to have anyone like that in my intimate circle of enemies."

"*Was* he?" Blake asked keenly.

"Known—as the police say—to me?" Dennis shook his head. "He wasn't—favorably or unfavorably. I haven't got anyone like that in my past, thank heaven."

"Well, is that all the bag?" Peter asked Blake.

"No," she said. "It isn't. I was going to say, across the hall from Dennis was, (1) a stage couple, those musical-comedy people who're playing at the Columbia in *Honeyblossom* this week."

"Ah, they'd do it with their tongues," breathed Dennis.

Blake looked at him. He sunk back abashed, making dumb-show promises of penitence and silence.

"And (2)," said Blake severely, "the Anstruthers, and we've gone to dinner parties and met them there, Peter, which I *hope* lets them out."

Dennis showed signs of life again. Peter caught his eye in sympathy. Dennis subsided, satisfied. Blake glanced up from her notes, suspiciously, but seeing no sign of communication attempted, went on.

"Then there's— Dennis, what were you going to say just now?" she pounced suddenly.

"I was only going to say," Dennis murmured, "you can bore people to death, too—at dinner parties. That's one way of doing it."

Blake snorted. A ladylike little snort. Peter grinned.

"Then there's," said Blake with immense dignity, "a Mr. Morgan, a very nice man, at the end room across from your side. And he was down in the Etruscan ballroom all evening dancing."

"What a pity," Dennis broke his silence drowsily, like little bubbles of speech ascending from a recumbent floating swimmer in a calm pool, "what a pity," he repeated, "that it wasn't the Attic ballroom. Morgan— Attic."

"*Den*-nis!" said Blake. He opened his eyes to a frozen atmosphere.

He broke the ice and got out of his perilous position. "What," he inquired intently, "does Mr. Morgan do, besides being so nice?"

"And besides dancing all night in the—uh, Etruscan Room?" Peter wanted to know.

"Why," said Blake doubtfully, "I don't think he does anything, much." She frowned down at her notes. "The help all like him. And he's got money. He just hasn't any business. Maybe he buys stocks sometimes, to keep him busy. But I suppose he plays around, mostly. He knows a lot of people. Plays golf a bit. Likes sailoring—has a nice little launch, or motorboat, or some kind of an amateur ship, at the Yacht Club anchorage. Gives parties. Goes to 'em."

"A clubman," said Peter in a tone of complete discovery. "There must be such beings. You always read about them in the papers."

"Noted," said Dennis, nodding. "Or well known."

"Ah," said Peter, "but do we?"

"Of course you do," said Blake briskly. "I told you all there was to tell about him. He was dancing all evening, anyway."

"We'll file Mr. Morgan for reference, anyway," said Dennis soothingly, " though I agree with you that he's probably harmless. How would a clubman dispose of his enemies anyway, Byrne? I'm a bit at sea there, I confess."

"He'd just drop them," Peter considered and gave a verdict. "Not know them at all—socially, you know."

"I don't think Bianca was the sort of person you could drop," Dennis pointed out. "Not if she didn't want you to."

Peter wagged a dubious head. "It's supposed to cut people to the heart," he said. "Being dropped, you know. They stagger out of their clubs—you've seen them, in the movies—"

"If you two have quite finished your humor," said Blake, gently, "we'll have some more business. That's all my report. The other rooms were vacant. Those were all your immediate neighbors, Dennis."

Dennis smiled at her. "Thanks a lot," he said.

"That's all right," said Blake a bit gruffly.

Darn Dennis! You couldn't get really mad at him, Blake thought, balked. He disarmed you. He was doing it now.

"The committee of the whole has read and approved of Miss Byrne's report," he said, "and orders it filed for reference. And the chairman wishes to say that it's a very nice report indeed."

He turned briskly to Peter.

"Byrne?" He cocked an interrogative eyebrow at that immovable but somehow forceful large person.

Peter smiled slowly. His blue eyes were very clear and untroubled in the depths of their rock ledges.

"Do I hear the whip crack?" he asked. "All right, here come the elephants into the arena."

"You were to meet Sullivan," Dennis reminded him affably.

"What's Inspector Sullivan like?" asked Blake with a proper awe of the constabulary.

"He's like Peter, a little." Dennis turned to her. "That's why I wanted to send Peter against him. He— looms. They remind one a great deal of two tall cliffs standing face to face, and I feel a bit crushed and very vulnerably puny between them. Man facing Nature, and all that, you know. Peter, if not actually getting anything out of Sullivan, could at least outface him. I can't."

"The inspector doesn't like you, Dennis?"

"I wouldn't say that," Dennis considered. "Not me personally, that is. He just wouldn't care much for any criminal. Particularly one he thinks may be a murderer. He just isn't made that way."

"But then—why didn't he arrest you straight off?"

Dennis took another of his long looks into a darkened future.

"The long leash has strangled many fool dogs," he said slowly. "I think that's the inspector's idea, in this case. He's giving me all the rope there is—to get tied up in."

"Oh!" said Blake.

"Not entirely," said Peter. "He's after Dennis, sure. But he told me he wouldn't want to help hang an innocent man. He's puzzled because some of the pieces don't fit in.

He said, 'You can tell Devore it was lucky for him the windows weren't open.' Don't you remember—"

"But they *were* closed," said Dennis, bewildered. "I told you—the room was locked, and all the windows were locked, too. Sullivan saw them."

"Sure he did—and he saw the fire escape just outside them. And he said to himself, if you'd just staged a murder there and wanted an out for yourself, wouldn't you have opened the windows and left the way to the fire escape open, and then called the police? And when the police came, you'd have said, 'A thief's been in here—and he's killed this woman!' and you'd have pointed dramatically to the open window, Dennis. And that's what you didn't do. You let the police come into a closed, locked room and told them you'd found it that way, and expected them to believe someone else had done it. You blundered into the murderer's trap. And, luckily for you, Sullivan had sense enough to see it. Then he wondered if you were outsmarting him, at that.

"He took your fingerprints. He searched the room for strange prints, and he didn't find any. He didn't expect to find any. Anyone that smart wouldn't have left prints there. There weren't any prints at all on the knife. But on the window latch, where he found your fingerprints, he did find a set over yours. It was the chambermaid's. She was the last one to shut those windows. So you hadn't outsmarted him and closed the window and put yourself into a trap so obvious that he couldn't help seeing it. It was the murderer who'd put you there. And, luckily for you, Sullivan saw that and you didn't. Otherwise you'd have gone clever and tried to get yourself out of it."

There was a short but very full silence.

"Well," said Dennis, summing it up at last, "I *told* you cleverness was a very overrated quality!"

VIII. DELROY! DELROY!

"Well," said Peter, "we seem to be agreed that everyone we've discussed in this case couldn't be a murderer. That helps a lot."

The phone rang. Blake took the call on the French extension phone by her chair and then handed the instrument over to Dennis.

"For you," she said.

It was Kennedy. That noble soul had risen above his injured feeling about the rape of his socks and shirts, to answer the higher call of his profession.

"Dennis," he said without preamble, "Father Malletti hasn't come back."

Dennis said, "Then that means—Delroy."

"Uh-huh," agreed Kennedy. "I've been to the church, and they're worried. Young Father O'Bannon —that's the one we saw last night—sort of blames himself. But—well, he can't give us any more help on the details. That's all we've got to go on—a big dark car coming, and a dying parishioner somewhere in the country near Delroy. You say you know the place."

"It's my inning," said Dennis instantly. "I'll go, Kennedy, and if I find him I call you up. Okay?"

"There must be some white man's blood in you," Kennedy said gratefully. "Sew it up tight, Dennis, whatever the dope is, and I'll remember this. I can't get away from the Hall just now."

Dennis put the phone down, softly, thoughtfully, and turned to his frankly interested host and hostess.

"There *is* news," he said. "Listen."

And he told them of the Italian ex-bootlegger's roof garden just across the street from the gray bulk of the

Church of Saints Peter and Paul, and of old Father
Malletti standing on the steps and watching Bianca,
weeping, hurrying across the square—and later that
same night, a big, dark car coming and taking him away.
. . .

His voice faltered to silence. His eyes were dark and
somber, unlit by any light within. He saw pictures. He sat
with his hand propping up his chin—he saw the old man
going into darkness—Bianca's friend. . . .

"Father Malletti was a saint!" he protested. He turned
to Peter and Blake. "The Italian said so! No one would
hurt him!"

"Oh, Dennis," said Peter reluctantly and slowly, but
with his terrible strong honesty, "sometimes saints get in
the way—of devils. And your murderer—you told us so
yourself—was a devil."

"I think," said Blake, on a queer high note of
breathlessness, "we'd better get the car out, Peter. Can
you come with us?"

That stout-hearted gentleman shook his massive
head, still more reluctantly.

"I've got a case coming up in court," he said. "But —I'll
get a postponement! You can go on without me, and I'll
follow later. That okay?"

"Swell!" said Dennis. "I'll see you at Hasta la Vista."

"Wherever that is," said Blake, once again cheerful at
the prospect of action, and persuading herself that all
would go well, since Dennis's face was brightening.

He told them, briefly. "I've got a ranch there. By the
Little San Ramon River. Hasta la Vista—it means, 'Until
I see you again,' or something like that. Sort of a good-
bye."

"Ah, a landed gentleman!" said Peter lazily but
keenly.

"Not yet," said Dennis. "A bachelor. Always have
been."

He flashed that somehow grave, faint grin of his at
Blake.

"Come on," Blake said, getting up.

He was light-hearted again. She felt her own spirits going up recklessly. She put on her brown tweed coat with the big badger fur collar sticking up all around her face, and a snug brown turban on her bright hair. Her eyes looked bluer and bigger, and her cheeks were fresh and cool and pink, in the brisk breeze outside the house. The fog was driving inland, in little puffs of white across the city, in the fresh wind, and the sun was out in a blue November day that was almost a copy of spring.

They got out the old red roadster and waved goodbye to Peter, standing there at the casement window with his pipe in his teeth and his mouth drawn back in a smile. Blake waved and smiled at him, but Dennis's white flash of a smile was almost like a knife cutting them away from him. He was glad to be out, and free, and away.

" Dennis," Blake said curiously, watching him drive, "you love this place of yours, don't you?"

"'Where the heart is . . .'" said Dennis, and fell silent.

But she could almost hear the little merry whistle in his heart, not quite coming up to his lips. He drove with the sound of it in his ears.

Through the warm dust of the Santa Clara Valley, set out with small fruit trees on the brown fields in even rows like rooted chessmen; through the little towns, whose names rang like sweet-toned bells in the sleepy noon sunshine, Palo Alto, San Jose, Gilroy, San Juan, Salinas; through the dark and wooded Santa Cruz mountain pass, to the salt marshes of the open seaside county of Monterey, where the wind blew and lonely cattle grazed; and so at last, about three o'clock in the afternoon, to sunshine again, and the Little San Ramon River winding across yellow fields in a flat country, singing to itself, very sleepily, very softly.

Dennis's country.

There was a little whitewashed ranchhouse set up among a few tall guardians of trees on a little knoll; there were empty corrals a little to one side; there were white chickens scratching in the dirt in a run set conveniently near the kitchen door; there was a wide veranda across the front of the house, and a few bright flowers, dahlias and chrysanthemums, lifting their heads in the brief garden around the front steps.

"Darling!" said Blake approvingly, getting out of the car a bit stiffly.

Dennis said nothing. He only looked. He stood and looked at it all as if he were—hungry, Blake decided. Dennis said, "I haven't seen this place for—nearly a year. I wasn't quite sure—it would be here."

The kitchen door opened. Blake caught her breath. An almost perfect copy of Louie, the old, graven image of a Mongolian, was out on the back stoop with a pan of chicken feed in one thin brown claw. His white apron was spotless. His head was brown and nearly bald. His black eyes glittered from wrinkles numerous as those in a thoroughly dried prune.

"It's Wong," said Dennis briefly.

The graven image saw them. The black eyes glittered. The thin brown hand clutched the tin pan. Wong drew himself up.

"Moah *bettah* you come back!" Wong addressed the errant young master in a thin, indignant high cackle that suggested an extremely nervous hen. "Wotsa mallah you! You think Wong he laise this chicken, laise these egg, laise these applicots, bettah fo' nothing! Wotsa mattla you, Dennis, fo' not coming back heah?"

The thin high cackle of a hen disturbed in her maternal duties beat on them relentlessly. Blake grinned. Dennis was getting nicely done to a lobster red.

"Come on, Odysseus," she said. "The speech of welcome seems to be drawing to a close. Wong's getting out of breath."

"Whew!" said Dennis.

The torrent died down to a mere muttered trickle. The black eyes glittered balefully. The wrinkled old face gasped for breath.

"You darned old heathen!" said Dennis.

Odysseus was home from whatever wars he'd been engaged in, Blake thought.

Pretty soon Dennis came out of the kitchen and grinned at his guest rather sheepishly.

"We stay here for chicken dinner," he said. "And Peter, when he comes. In the meanwhile messengers go forth among the heathen, from house to house and ranch to ranch, assembling the multitude and requiring them to come out and say if any strangers have been around Delroy, or if any big black car has been here—if anyone's dying, and wanting to be prayed for—if Father Malletti's been here, and if he's gone. You see, Delroy is more of a district than it is a town. There's only a main street with a few stores on it, and hitching posts and parking space for us rustics and cowboys when we come in to order our sombreros and neckerchiefs. We'll inquire there, of course. But Father Malletti wasn't called there. He was called to some outlying ranchhouse or shack around here."

"We'll find out!" Blake sounded her battle cry.

"Sure we will," Dennis echoed her blithely. "And there goes the one who'll do it for us."

A thin brown figure was scrambling aboard an antiquated Ford roadster. The Ford roadster went bucking down the dirt road, hitting each deep rut as it passed.

"Dennis," said Blake admiringly, taking off the hat from her hot forehead, "you have, a genius for using people."

"Really?" said Dennis politely.

"Go on being like that," said Blake, undaunted. "I feel a distinct coolness in the air. Delightful."

Dennis grinned and got down from his high horse.

"Sometimes I've been sorry I never had a sister," he said reflectively. "It would have been nice at times to tie her to a post and play Indian-at-the-stake with her. I'm sure."

"Didn't you have?" said Blake.

"No, never. Neither sisters nor cousins nor any aunts," said Dennis briefly. "I'm an orphan."

He got up quickly.

"Do you want a drink of water and to rest in the shade here," he asked, "or do you want to come down and see the river?"

His tone was so hopeful that Blake got up, the obedient guest.

"Let's go see the river," she said responsively.

Dennis and Blake walked side by side through the hot gold sunshine, feeling the warmth of the sandy earth up through their shoes as they went, down to the green-shaded water. The Little San Ramon rippled in the sun brightly, like a shield held up, and the cottonwoods stirred gently, and the world was warm and golden and very peaceful. They had come, Blake thought, from the autumn fogs of the morning through spring to summer again, and it was rather unbearably peaceful and lovely, as though this were a lost summer —last summer's golden day, for instance, forgotten by time. She told this to Dennis, and he nodded gravely and stood looking a moment at the shifting river, from where they were halted up from the bank.

"'Tinkers to Evers to Chance,'" he murmured. "I see what you mean, Blake. Reverse play—going back to last summer instead of forward. Maybe you're right, and I'm making up for the summer I missed here. Time's justice doing me right."

He smiled at her.

"I always see what you mean, Blake," he repeated. He caught her hand suddenly and swung it as they went on again to the river.

Then his eyes went far away, absently, again.

"I'm thinking of Father Malletti," he said softly. "I didn't expect to find him in my house, all ready for us, exactly, but—well, Delroy's such a wide county. He might be anywhere around here, and what chance have we of picking up his trail? Just—chance, that's all."

Dennis dropped her hand.

They walked on in silence. They came to the bank of the Little San Ramon, and Blake sat down on the soft sand, while Dennis propped himself along the trunk of a cottonwood tree and stared at the stream going by, dazzling his somber eyes.

After a while, Blake said softly, urgently, "Dennis?"

He didn't turn around. "Yes?" he said.

"There's something else," Blake said. "You're putting me off, Dennis. You've something else in the back of your mind, always. What is it? We're friends, Dennis. Peter and you and I. You can trust us."

He turned around then in a roughly impatient, single movement that yet held appeal.

"What are friends, Blake?" he asked. "I haven't got a thing to give you—you and Peter. Nothing that'll satisfy you. You know—you must have guessed—I'm the hit-and-run hero Kennedy was talking about. The man who ran into someone down near Salinas here a year ago last July, and didn't give himself up till next day, and all that. I was lucky—I got off with probation. Lucky! How'd you like to report every doing of yours twice a week to a hard-boiled probation officer? It makes you feel like a beast in a cage. You want—space. Freedom. Loneliness. Well, after a year I got 'em."

"And what are you going to do with them, Dennis?"

"Oh, I'm not a woman hater," he said more calmly. "You needn't be sorry for me, Blake. I'm not soured on life, or anything like that, and I don't think all women are crooks because one of them took me for all I had. She was in a tough place, and she used me to get out of it—that's all. She was engaged to a fine guy, and she was a flighty little piece who wanted some fun. He was away right then, so we went around together a lot. And one night we were coming home, along about two in the morning, and she was driving—"

Blake gave a sharp gasp.

Dennis eyed her wearily.

"I thought you knew," he said, uninterested. "Something you said—well, anyway, Kennedy guessed — she was driving lickety-split, and all of a sudden she bumped something, and she began to cry out about hitting someone. But she didn't stop—she stepped on the gas. And by the time I could get her stopped, we were on a side road. So I made her come back, and we saw another car stop and pick him up, taking him to a hospital, I guessed. She was just about crazy then, thinking she'd have to tell all this to her fiance—he was a nice guy, but very strict—so I drove her home and then came around to the town to report it. And they took me up, for hitting him. He was dead.

"That's all, I guess," Dennis reviewed past history dispassionately. "I'd probably have done the same thing if I'd been in her case. I don't blame her. No, it's just that I feel like the name of that ship the Canadian captain had—the one the Coast Guards sunk. *I'm Alone.* I prefer to be. I feel safer that way."

"You pig!" said Blake.

Dennis bowed.

"'At your command!'" he said.

"I wish I had a mustache to twirl," he added plaintively. "I always feel not having one at such moments as these."

Blake laughed—she couldn't help it—above an immense gulf of loneliness.

IX. THE HONEST PLOWMAN

They had no news of Father Malletti—no news of him anywhere. Neither of his coming, nor of his staying, nor of his going from there. Not from the dusty, sun-parched, incurious little town, or from any of the neighboring ranches. Peter, who'd come down by train and been gathered into the red roadster at the station at five o'clock that afternoon, thoroughly scouted the idea of there being any news.

"This is the last place they'd take him to," he asserted, driving them off the main paved highway into the dirt road to Dennis's ranch. "If he was 'taken' anywhere at that, instead of being legitimately sent for. They'd never give the real name of a place in such a case.

Dennis disagreed. He shook his head wearily, stubbornly, unconvincedly.

"I've got an idea they did," he said simply. "They made a slip there. Someone was thinking of this part of the country, and the name came out. It's so pat, somehow. Why Delroy, anyway? It's miles from San Francisco. It's not so—well, convincing, if you want. Why not just say there was someone sick in San Mateo, or Palo Alto, or any of the near-by peninsula towns? No, they were thinking of this country, and they had to say it—it came out almost against their will. It was in their thoughts so deeply."

They left it at that.

"Maybe you're right, Dennis," Peter finally was forced to say. "Maybe even your devil can make a mistake."

"Don't call him mine," Dennis said.

The quiet words were a horror of loathing.

"Sorry!" said Peter. He drove along a little way, big hands loose on the wheel, obviously deep in thought. Then it had to come out.

"And yet, you know," he said slowly, "perhaps there's a connection. Have you thought of any, Dennis?"

Dennis looked at him with wide dark eyes of astonishment.

"Why, what could there be?" he asked.

"Well, this," said Peter, jerking his head at the surrounding sun-soaked and monotonous country through which their dirt rut of a road led. "Delroy! Doesn't it occur to you that both you and he seem to have this country in common? It's your own home stamping grounds—and yet he chooses it for a bait for Father Malletti—if he *is* playing that game. Anyway, someone summons Father Malletti to this place. Is that the someone who killed Bianca, Father Malletti's protegee, and so involved you in the case, Dennis, because he did it in your room?"

Peter turned those deep blue eyes, small-looking in their depth of eye-socket bone, on Dennis intently.

"'An enemy hath done this,'" he quoted, keen-eyed. "Do you remember saying that, Dennis, yesterday morning? What more is your enemy going to do to you? He involves you, it seems to me, whenever he can. He has plans for you. And they aren't at all nice plans. He wants you to get out of his way."

"A—a sort of sideswipe of revenge at Dennis, when he's doing his dirty work," Blake contributed breathlessly. "Oh, he is a devil! Dennis, don't you really know him?"

"I wish I did," said Dennis simply. "You make me feel as if I were standing in a lighted room with all the shades up and someone watching me from the darkness outside."

He raised his head from the comfortable leather back of the car seat, at a sudden thought.

"And if there is someone like that watching me," he said reflectively, "he knows more than you do about what's ever happened to me—down here. You'd better know, too. I've already told Blake."

Then he told Peter what he'd told Blake about the hit-and-run episode of a year ago.

Peter was silent, at the end, but not unfriendly—just thinking it over. Then he nodded.

"That was all there was to it?" he asked.

"All," said Dennis straightly. "Exactly as it happened. And it couldn't have any bearing on this thing that's happening now. It's ended for good. I just thought—you'd better know about it, Byrne."

"I see," Peter accepted it then." I'm glad you told us."

"I wanted to," said Dennis. "Before Kennedy or the police told you. Sullivan'll get onto it sometime."

They were at Hasta la Vista now. The sun was setting. It was all red and dark gray in the flat west country behind the tall elm trees around the house. The little white house had a flicker of red color on it, changing momentarily.

Wong met them. Dinner, he informed his straying master sternly, was on the table. He kept a beady eye on Dennis like a nervous hen ready to pounce on an errant and rather senseless chick. Dennis ushered his guests about.

"We," Blake said pointedly to Peter, who wanted to linger and look at things, "are starving. Dennis and I had only a couple of hot dogs, coming through San Jose."

"Wong!" yelled Dennis, at the head of the table in the small room lit by two bright oil lamps. "We're here!"

"He's not so swell at pancakes," he said modestly to Blake, of the old retainer, "but he's a shoutin' bearcat on hot biscuits and chicken."

Ten minutes later Blake looked up and caught Dennis's eye blissfully.

"Yes," she said. "He is, isn't he?"

The shoutin' bearcat cackled in delight.

"You're adopted," Dennis said to her. "That's our war cry."

"Smoke?" said Peter. He passed cigarettes around, and they lit up.

Wong fired a high-pitched and weirdly accented string of syllables at Dennis. That gentleman cocked an unaccustomed ear and finally got it.

"Man coming to see me," he announced briefly. "After dinner."

"What kind of a man?" asked Blake.

"Well, if we had any hills around here, he'd be a hillbilly," said Dennis, rather puzzled. "You know the type. Long and lean and lanky-looking, never washes, does a bit of plowing sometimes, helps out in fruit season or cattle driving. Got too much sun in him—all ambition and get-up been baked, out of him long ago Name's Bowden, I think. Lives in a sort of shack and on an acre of ground."

"Wonder what he wants to say," Peter said.

Dennis shrugged.

"I think I'll phone Kennedy," he said, getting up. "Promised to report to him. No news yet, anyway."

"Maybe," said a Peter soothed and a bit facetious from the extraordinarily good combination of hot biscuits, chicken, and cigarettes—"maybe your honest plowman can tell you a tale."

And that was the way Kennedy first got the "Honest Plowman " phrase of the later, terrible headline streamers. Dennis repeated it to Kennedy for a jest, and Kennedy remembered it—afterward.

Peter and Blake strolled out to the small front yard to finish their cigarettes in the fresh, nearly frosty air, while Dennis was inside phoning.

"What do you think of this guy, anyway?" Peter demanded.

"I don't know," said Blake, a bit troubled. "I feel as if I'd known him for a long time."

"That's the trouble," Peter grunted. "You can't get far enough away to see him good. To see what he's really like, I mean," he grumbled.

"No," said Blake. "You can't take him or leave him — he's already there."

Dennis came up to them. In the gloom of the evening his face looked white.

"I talked with Kennedy," he said. "He says—he says the police know Bianca's real name. She was Mrs. Victor Farnese!"

"What of it?" asked Peter.

Dennis's emotion seemed a bit unaccounted for.

"I forgot you didn't know," he said dully. "Victor Farnese was the man we ran over on the Salinas highway a year ago. The man they thought I killed."

He looked at them, puzzled, tortured, through the dusk.

"Things don't come to an end, do they?" he asked huskily. "They don't—ever—end."

He swayed a little. Peter put an arm around his shoulders.

"Well," Blake said, looking quizzically at the lately doubting Peter, "thunder clears the air, anyway!"

Dennis shook himself.

"It gave me a jolt," he said more practically. "What in hell is Victor Farnese's name doing here? He's been dead for the past year. What is his widow doing, getting murdered in my hotel room? I'd like an answer, please."

"Hi, Dennis," drawled a soft voice out of the dusk. A man had slouched up to them, unnoticed. An over-ailed, lanky, loosely hanging, soft-stepping man. They couldn't see his face.

"Name's Bowden—John Bowden," said the visitor. "You remember me? Ranchin' right next to you, across the south gully. Been away, haven't you?"

"Come back," said Dennis. "Hi, Bowden. Friends of mine. You wanted to see me?"

The other man nodded. "Yeah. Been wantin' to—a long time. Only you lit out of here so quick. And I had to be sorta careful around those days—was runnin' a still on my place for some fellows and didn't want too much company—po-lice, an' such. Fust thing, your trial was over, an' you'd gone. Always meant to get over here, before it was too late."

"Thanks for the kind thought," said Dennis. "But why?"

"Heard you say Farnese's name just now," said Bowden, without a direct answer. "Long's he isn't restin' right easy in his grave, or in your mind, might's well tell you now. No harm in it. You got probation, anyway—and they wouldn't never have been able to do anything about it, prob-ly, if I *had* told 'em "

"Told 'em what?" asked Dennis.

"What I saw that night," said their visitor very simply. "I was goin' along the highway on foot—on some business I wouldn't tell to the district attorney or the sheriff of this here county—and along just about that time you come along, drivin' like all get out. Couldn't see who was in the car—saw your headlights comin'. And just for a minute—just for a bare minute—saw somethin' in the road, in your headlights. It looked like a man on the highway. He was layin' down."

"You mean—you saw us hit Farnese?" Dennis said quietly, from a dry throat.

"No," Bowden drawled. "I mean when your head-lights was on ahead. Say thutty feet ahead of you. Looked like somethin' was laying there—like a big shadow—before you ever got on to it. Then you came by, hell-for-leather, and passed me, an'—whatever it was, and I heard your girl screamin' out."

Dennis couldn't speak. He was thinking of shadows— of another dark shadow he'd seen in a hotel room—on a floor. . . .

Peter cleared his throat. "Dark night?" he asked.

"Dark as hell," said Bowden. "No moon, ner fog. If you didn't want to be seen . . . Dark as tonight's goin' to be."

"Listen," said Dennis desperately. "Listen. Do you mean—we ran into a *dead* man on that highway?"

His visitor shrugged, faintly seen.

"I ain't sayin'," he said. "Only—it looked like a man might, layin' down."

"Did you touch it—afterwards?" asked Peter. "Was it—Farnese?"

Bowden shrugged again, less clearly seen than ever.

"No use," he said. "Figured whatever it was, you'd hit it square. People'd be comin', right away, and I didn't want to be there. Less *I* knew— "

"But you came and told us," said Blake. "Why?"

"Always meant to," said Bowden lazily, "sometime. Never got over here till now. Heard you was back. Last year Hell, nobody'd care now. You wouldn't spill it. Thought you'd like to know, though. Might be —sort of restless in your mind."

"Well," said Peter dryly, "we've got news for you, too. Mrs. Victor Farnese was murdered night before last in Dennis's hotel room in San Francisco!"

For a minute their self-invited guest stood motionless, soundless. As if Peter's words had cracked a hard-baked crust of indifference, were slowly entering his mind, becoming sensible, believable. . . .

He cried out once, a hoarse cry, astonishment, denial, belief— They heard him; then he was gone, swifter than shadows.

X. THE REST IS SILENCE

They hadn't expected to get such action on that single remark of Peter's; Peter last of all. For a minute they stood there, the two men lost in the darkness, only Blake in her cream-colored dress a dimly seen ghost.

Bowden's curious cry still rang in their ears. Now that he was gone, it took on another quality—the quality of fear. The man had been terribly afraid. They knew it. They'd loosed something on him—fear. The hounds of fear.

Then Dennis broke the charm of stillness. He moved into swift and startled action.

"He knows something!" he cried furiously. "What does he know?"

He started to run, and Peter caught him by the arm.

"Hey, Dennis!" he said. "Gently—"

Dennis was beyond all that. He wrenched himself from the cumbering big hands.

"Gently?" said Dennis. "The hell with that! I asked a question and I want an answer! And I'm going to get one! You'd better stay here—this isn't your mix-up."

"Blake," said Peter, quickly, as his host disappeared down the path to the open fields, "you stay here."

He ran after Dennis, as well as he could see to follow him.

"Blake," said Blake to herself, breathlessly, "you stay here."

Then Blake started to run, too. She and Peter and Dennis ran smoothly, recklessly, over sandy ground, stumbled over heavy plowed ground broken beneath their feet, ran breakneck down a little rounded hill to halt, half-sobbing for breath, at the shelter of its valley. The keen night air had turned warm and heavy to their bodies, the breaths they labored to draw into their aching lungs were unbelievably heavy and smothering.

Dennis grasped each one by the arm to get their attention, and then pointed up to the opposite slope.

"House," he gasped huskily. "His. This is—south gully. We go—up."

Peter groaned. "We would," he said bitterly, drawing great drafts of air into his big chest. "My legs weigh a ton."

Miraculously, all of a sudden they had their second wind. They made it to the top of the opposite hill, slowed to a more sober pace, but not suffering so much. Dennis didn't seem to mind that they'd come on against orders— even Blake, he didn't so much not notice as take for granted there. He was too keen on something else. On getting his answer. He'd sort of broken loose on his own hook at last.

The shack was set on the top of the round foothill between two humps of it, protected by some chaparral bush from the winds. It was dark. Dennis didn't even knock on the door. He pushed it, and it swung open.

"Matches?" he asked Peter. "Or a flashlight, any of you?"

Peter struck a match. Dennis looked around quickly, before it should go out, and located the oil lamp on the table. He bent over it, and it slowly flared into bloom, and Dennis's intent, stern face showed above it, the eyes veiled under level brows, the mouth grave and calm.

He looked at the one room slowly, fully—iron stove, bunk-cot, table, cooking things hung up, shelves, dirty rough clothes hung up on nails in a corner.

"He hasn't got back yet," he said. "Perhaps he's scared to yet. Meanwhile "

He went over to the clothes and began going through them methodically, gravely intent, searching with a curious abstract young sternness, as if he were a rather scornful but just young judge searching out truth from an unsavory case. He put his hands into the blue denim overall pockets, lifted out bits of twine, crumpled cigarette papers, once a pocketknife, other uninteresting odds and ends. He didn't find anything worth looking at twice. Then he looked under the soiled pillow of the bunk-like bed, under the thin mattress, ruffled the blankets— Bowden evidently had no use for sheets—and put it in order again deftly, quickly.

Peter and Blake found seats, he on the kitchen table, she on the one kitchen chair, and watched Dennis without saying anything. There really wasn't anything to say. This, as he'd told them, was his business. Tracing a year-old lie, a year-old injustice, to its hiding place. They didn't blame Dennis for making free with his neighbor's shack in his absence. Bowden, if he'd been telling the truth, had been making pretty free with a good year of Dennis's life by holding out his information. Peter privately thought he'd like Dennis and Bowden to meet again. It would be a swell fight. He'd second Dennis.

Meanwhile he waited. And Blake with him.

Dennis finished with the bed and stood in the center of the room, looking around. He ran one hand through his already ruffled head and surveyed the ground with a certain puzzlement. Then he turned to the interested witnesses watching him.

"It must be here," he said. "Don't you see?" appealing to them as a judge would instruct a jury, patiently. "He didn't come over to tell me about Farnese's death out of kindness. He wasn't that kind of a guy. He had something to get out of it. What? I've got to find something—or make him tell "

He turned suddenly to the kitchen table where Peter was throned, and ordered him off peremptorily.

"Beat it," he said, and was hauling out the one battered drawer, shallow but filled with odds and ends of untidy things, with the industry of a terrier after a promising rat, before Peter was halfway off his perch. The drawer was the record of a rather messy sort of life—a

futile, unpathetic sort of life. It had kitchen knives and
forks and spoons of tin and of thin cheap silver plate worn
through, mixed up with a couple of *Love Nest* magazines
on cheap rough yellowed paper that had been handled a
great deal by unwashed hands, and there were a few
letters on cheap blue-lined stationery written by women
who had evidently joined the Love Nest Letter Writers'
Club and could find nothing better in life for a romance
than a correspondence with such men as Bowden, and he
with them. Dennis's very hands expressed a disdainful
distaste, looking over the scrawled things, but he didn't
neglect them. He read them and then put them by
silently, and then rummaged around among the string
and paper and magazines, to come up with a crumpled bit
of blue paper. He held this out, curiously, with a different
look dawning on his intent face.

"Hullo!" he said. "Recognize this?"

"Money-order receipts," confirmed Peter.

"Look at the dates," ordered Dennis. He passed two or
three of the crumpled things over. Peter looked at the
dates and place of buying them, stamped in a round circle
on the scraps of paper. He looked at the amounts. They
were, as far as he looked from the collection in his hand,
all for ten dollars, even. They were all sent from the post
office at San Francisco. He whistled. . . .

Dennis was tearing things apart in the drawer and
bringing up more of them for inspection.

"Why, we've stumbled onto a little fortune," said
Blake, eagerly. "Or does your plowman send these home
to his old mother, Dennis?"

Peter and Dennis began spreading the receipts out on
the table. They sorted them out. They counted them.
There were eight. They were all for ten dollars. They were
all from San Francisco. It didn't make much sense.
Bowden wouldn't have gone up to the city to send these.
Where'd he ever get the money, anyway? And he didn't
have anyone to send them to, at that. Dennis only
laughed a bit scornfully and harshly at the idea of that

sun-scorched, wind-beaten person sending ten of his precious dollars out every month to a dear old white-haired mother. He just couldn't see it somehow, he told Blake.

Then they began looking at dates again. There was something funny about those dates. They weren't recent.

"Why'd he keep these?" Blake asked them, her eyes going wide and bluer in the flare of the oil-lamp light. Her hair caught the light like a short-haired halo around her young face. Her gold-touched hair got in Dennis's eyes like a light. He couldn't ask her to move away from the lamp, though. That would be silly. He said:

"Bowden was the kind of person who didn't throw anything away, Blake. For one thing, he was too lazy — just stuffed things in drawers and kept 'em. Too stingy, another thing. I guess he always had a sneaking idea any little bit of string or paper or anything was worth something. He was the kind of person that can't make a clean sweep of things anyway—sort of clutters up his life with truck all the time, until he dies."

None of them noticed that they were speaking of the absent owner of the shack as though he were himself in the past tense. They had such a disdain of the man that they simply didn't accept him among them there. They knew he wouldn't come in while they were there, anyway. They were sure of it. He was too mean-spirited. They'd seen him, He was afraid.

"Got it!" said Peter triumphantly.

The big head bent over the tidy rows of blue slips. He put out one big finger and pointed as he explained along the rows.

"Got the dates—see?" he said. The finger moved along the rows as he spoke. "They're a month apart, except for a gap of one here and here, and over here and here. The first one is for August, of a year ago. It's not too improbable to assume that the gaps represent missing receipts that are lost, I think. He must have lost some, in this rather careless system of book-keeping. In other words, there were twelve receipts for ten dollars each, covering a period of exactly a year. They began, you see, about a year ago, and ended this July."

He looked up then at the funny sound that came from Dennis.

"That mean anything to you?" he asked. "Think, Dennis."

"Think?" cried Dennis furiously, hopelessly. "I don't have to think! I know damn' well what it means—do you think I'd forget those dates so easily? They were last year, the year I was convicted of manslaughter and put on probation for Farnese's killing!"

Silence quivered about them. Peter broke through it.

"Well, what does it mean, Dennis?" he asked hoarsely.

Dennis stared at them, his face white and bitter as the bitter and unbelieving hurt in his voice when he spoke, slowly:

"Don't you see? Don't you see? Someone—must have known he was there on the highway when I ran over Farnese that night. They knew Bowden was there—and they didn't know how much he'd seen, maybe. And they approached him—and he sold me out for ten dollars a month—someone sent him the blackmail price of his silence all the time my sentence was due to run. Then I was free—this July—and they quit sending any more money—and he thought he'd get even on them, and waited—he waited for four months to tell me, when I finally came back here."

The slow, hurt voice stopped. They stared in silence at the silent blue slips of paper.

XI. THE HOUNDS OF FEAR

"Then what?" said Peter. "Then what?"

He wanted to be doing something, to be in action. The muscles of his big body tensed, relaxed, like a man stretching himself after sleep. It was hard to be sitting there when something was going on—outside. He wanted to be in on it.

He went to the door and opened it, and Dennis and Blake came to stand at his elbow. In the dark night they heard the rising wind charging up the hillside, rustling the bushes near the shack, dying down again—and getting up again.

Somewhere out there was Bowden, in the dark and windy night, a man afraid—running, perhaps, or hiding —Dennis couldn't forget the way he'd cried out, the way he'd run.

They couldn't hope to find him now. They didn't know where he'd gone. They could only wait, hoping he'd come back at last.

The wind tore around the corner of the hill, and the night came alive again with its rush.

"The hounds of fear!" said Dennis softly. "The hounds of fear out night-running. You sicked them on him, Peter. He won't come here. He's—running."

Peter let the door slam shut, and they turned back to the table and the oil lamp again.

"No, he didn't expect to hear that Farnese's wife was dead," Dennis went on in that same soft voice, as though he trod down a dangerous trail warily. He seated himself at the table and put his elbows on it, resting his head on his two fists. He lifted his head and put his chin on his hands at rest instead, and grinned a crooked, unamused grin at the other two.

"Professor Dennis in his famous seance performance," he remarked. "Shall I give it to you now?"

"All you've got," grunted Peter, dropping down onto the side of the bunk. He drew Blake down beside him, and they sat facing Dennis like an attentive audience.

"Here it is, then, as far as we've gone," Dennis said. "We think we're almost as much in the dark as before. Maybe so. But do you realize that every time we find out something—even a trail that goes blind on us—we find out something more about the man who put it there? Our devil who killed Bianca.

"This is the plot. And you were right, Peter, this evening when you said it did involve me. It's getting clearer now all the time. It begins 'way back a year ago last July. Farnese was killed. I think our devil killed him. Why? We don't know that. Maybe it's not important. A local quarrel. Anyway, it happened here, and I was the fall guy. Only Bowden saw him lying on the highway, before I hit him. Bowden was paid blackmail to keep quiet, and I went on trial for the killing. Okay so far?"

He cocked an eyebrow at his audience. Blake nodded, quickly, beyond speech. Peter nodded a massive head slowly.

"Neat," he said. "I give him that, anyway."

"Is that all?" asked Dennis. "Wait till you hear what I give him. That guy's good—in his way.

"Now we come to recent events. Bianca was killed by our devil. Very coolly, very systematically. I told you what I thought about him then. She was killed because she was Farnese's widow, and she'd heard at last that he didn't die—of an accident. The same man who killed him found out he had to kill her, to keep the first murder quiet. Otherwise, why the long wait? It doesn't make sense. If he was just finishing off the family, why didn't he do it all at once, a year ago? He was a friend of hers—a lover— and she was about to find out he killed her husband. So she was killed. In my room. If it ever came out that Farnese was dead before I hit him, people would think, maybe, that I'd killed him on purpose a year ago, then run over him to disguise it as a manslaughter accident, and that I'd killed his widow to keep her quiet about it afterwards. See? Our murderer saw that. He was a neat guy, at that, Peter. He didn't want to leave any loose ends if he could help it. And he thought he could help it along by adding me to the cast once more. The police would suspect too much of a coincidence like that, maybe, he'd think. I give him a swell mark on that. At first I thought he was a loose performer, letting me in for that without any seeming motive to back me up.

"Then,"—Dennis dropped that dark head down to his hands again, and that determinedly light voice went dark on him, too—"then Father Malletti came into it. Have you forgotten him? I haven't, for a second, all this night—not even when we were running after Bowden, across the fields in the dark and the wind. He's been at the back of my mind. I can't help it—I think I'm going to meet him sometime. I'm going to meet him," he repeated, and stayed for a second lost in some dark dream. "It's a funny thing—I even seem to know what he looks like. And I've never seen him, either. Maybe I've just made up a picture of him out of my mind. An old man, going into darkness— I can't get him out of my mind."

Dennis shivered, once, sharply, then stayed still.

"*What* does he look like, Dennis?" Peter said quietly.

"He's got dark eyes that go right through you," Dennis said. "They're very stern eyes. I'd be afraid, only—there's his mouth, and his smile. It lights up his face, when he smiles. He's got a thin face, and a great beak of a thin nose, beautifully arched, and a thin mouth. I think he had a quick temper, when he was a young man, but he's gotten over that now. He's worn down past the flesh and the passions to the light of the spirit. It burns in him like this oil lamp burning here in the dark. He's got thin white hair, too.

"For the rest," said Dennis thoughtfully, face propped in both his hands, staring ahead of him, "he's a rather tall, thin old man in a long black robe. That's all, I think. All I see of him."

Peter whistled, softly, like a long-held breath coming out at last.

"All!" he said, respectfully.

"I told you," pointed out Dennis, "that I couldn't tell whether that's just my idea of Father Malletti, or whether I really do see him, and he does look like that. Only—I think I'd be able to know him, if I met him, and without knowing his name."

"Dennis," Blake put in, hushed of voice, "will they— What do they want of Father Malletti?"

She'd put into actual solid words the thing they'd kept thinking around, not daring to approach too closely.

Dennis went forward to it.

"They want silence," he said straightly. "The way Father Malletti comes into this is because he knew Bianca Farnese. He was her confidant. She found out something that would have put her on the track of her husband's murderer—and Bianca, whatever she was, wasn't an accomplice to such a thing. I bet she had a kind of loyalty as splendid as she was—nothing small about her build or make-up. A home-grown goddess, Kennedy said. Well, she probably told Father Malletti what she knew, or suspected, and what she was going to do to find out more. That was the time she saw him last, when she went away crying. Someone knew she'd been to see him. They had to have his silence."

"What d'you mean—silence?" Peter said hoarsely, in a cold and drafty sort of voice. "You mean—he's dead?"

Dennis shook his head.

"I don't see anyone killing Father Malletti," he said simply. "It wouldn't do any good to them. He'd be with them all the rest of their life. It would be too much like killing themselves. And they can't buy or beg his silence. He'd speak out anything he thought should be spoken out, if he were free. No, I bet they're sort of puzzled what to do about it themselves—whoever 'they' are. I bet they're—just waiting."

He spoke with an assurance that, strangely enough, Peter and Blake didn't contest. He was like someone who knew the path, in a strange country, and led the way unhesitatingly. In a bit of a hurry, in fact, anxious to arrive at some unknown destination.

"That's it so far," he explained to them again. "I told you we know a lot more about our unknown than we did!"

"What, for instance?" Peter suggested.

"Well," Dennis considered, "I told you before that he had hell's own nerve, and that he was a cool, canny customer; I'm not taking any of that back. Only he's canny this way—he wants to let someone else take the credit for him. Me, for one. He's got nerve, but he's not taking any risks he can avoid. Then—you're right about this, Pete—he's got Delroy as a well-known country to work in. Farnese was killed in Delroy; Father Malletti was lured to Delroy; Bowden lives in Delroy; he knows something about me, and I come from Delroy. But he sent his money orders from San Francisco; he's not a native here. He lives up in San Francisco, where Bianca lived. And—he's someone who's got free access to my hotel floor, and can get to my room easily from where he lives—in my hotel. That narrow it down a bit? Think of a guy like that we know."

"I will," said Peter grimly.

"He *is* a devil," said Blake softly, passionately.

"I don't know," said Dennis thoughtfully. "He's pretty bad, sure; but I don't think he's so inhuman any more, the more I know about him. I think he's very humanly puzzled, say, about what to do about Father Malletti; if he's of the faith of Father Malletti, as he may be—Bianca was—he's probably thinking he's got a lot more than he can handle now with a priest on his hands. I think there's things he'd stick at, and this is one of them. You know, the more I see of life,"—Dennis regarded them very thoughtfully indeed—"the more I'm inclined to think there aren't any stage 'villains' in that sense of being what I'd call 'rapiers of wickedness,' that have a delight in evil and in their skill in it —like keen blades made only for fighting, and for being wicked. I think perhaps there're only two really wicked classes of people in the world, though—and those are the cruelly stupid, and the stupidly cruel. They aren't rapiers, they're bludgeons. They smash things in the first place because they're clumsily wicked, not really meaning to act like the rapiers of wickedness."

"Is this a bludgeon's work or a rapier's, Dennis?" asked Blake with fascinated attention. "This case?"

"Rapier's." That was Peter's judicial opinion, briefly.

"I vote bludgeon," Dennis said.; "Look at the case already! We've spotted holes in it as big as our heads! There's Father Malletti, for one. He can't be held silenced forever. The other way—well, our human devil doesn't want to take it. Then there's Bowden—he's a big gap in the defense. When we get Bowden, we'll make a hole in it you can see through! Those are two gaps that ought to be plugged, and aren't. And, if he'd been a rapier, he'd have done for Farnese more skillfully. All these later events, my sentence and Bianca's murder, have been the outcome of him smashing around regardless, trying to cover up his own traces through the general wreckage of lives he's made. He's cruelly stupid. And he's failed."

"What about Bowden?" Peter asked. "Where does he belong?"

"Bowden belongs to the stupidly cruel, I think," Dennis answered. "He's the kind that would set dogs onto a stray cat for the fun of it. That's the way he felt about setting us onto the trail of a man who'd been paying him money for silence, and who thought his safety was bought a year ago for good. Bowden wanted to have some fun with him, harrying him out of safety."

"Well," said Peter grimly, heavily, "he sure started something."

Dennis nodded his dark head gravely.

"Yes," he replied. "More than he wanted, or meant to. He's the one who's being hunted now. He's afraid."

And on the silent chill of that last word, they heard the, wind rising around the top of their hill, and, in the night, the hounds of fear baying in the windy dark outside.

XII. THE PLUGGED GAP

"So you see—" Dennis made a gesture with one hand that spread the whole case before them on the worn kitchen table like a pack of cards, or like the blue money-order receipts that lay spread out there already.

"And here's another gap he left, our devil," he said as afterthought. "How'd these receipts get here? They should have been left with the sender. But the murderer didn't want to have anything to do with them—even to tear 'em off and then throw them away, or burn them. He was afraid he'd get careless about one of them one day, and maybe the orders would be traced and one receipt found in his possession. He was, you see, always afraid, even though he reasoned to himself that he'd made everything safe. So he left 'em on the original orders, and they were preserved through Bowden's shiftlessness, or craftiness, and came to us. He couldn't, really, make anything safe, no matter how hard he tried. It's all coming up again. Like earth on a restless grave. Poor devil!"

Blake shuddered—she couldn't help it. Peter considered Dennis thoughtfully, deeply.

"You talk as if you were getting to know him—to be sorry for him," he said at last. "Even for Bowden, too, with his hounds of fear pursuing him. You make them too—humanly frail, Dennis, for us to have much anger left for them. Only pity. Is there anyone on God's earth you couldn't make friends with, Dennis?"

Dennis grinned. "I don't care much for the police," he said. "Or for Sullivan, if it comes to that. Or for that hotel manager."

He got up and went to the door again and stood listening to the wind outside.

"It's getting cold here," he said. "No reason why you should have to stay here all night. You and Blake go back to my house; you can stay there all night, if you want, or drive back to San Francisco if you have to be there in the morning. Bowden won't come back here as long as there's a light in this place. I'll go back across the gully with you to the house—if he's watching, he'll know we're all gone. Then I'll leave you there and come back here quietly and maybe catch him. And if I do, he'll tell what he knows."

He opened the door a little, and the keen, damp night air came like earthy darkness into the lighted room.

"You'll get cold, Blake," he said. "You'd better have something over your dress."

"She can have my coat," Peter growled and began getting out of one sleeve.

"I *am* cold," Blake admitted. "Talking of graves—" and promptly shivered again.

"Here, take my coat," Dennis said. "It'll fit you better—it's not a circus tent like Peter's."

He had it off and slung it around her, draping it over her shoulders, while Peter was still getting his off. He did it up carefully, putting the lifted collar up to Blake's cool round chin.

"Dennis," Blake said impulsively, "I think you're wonderful, the way you don't fuss about my being here. You don't treat me like a girl in that way. You let me in for things like you do Peter. I love it. Most girls miss these sort of things. But you don't treat me like that—like a *mere* girl."

"How else would I treat you?" asked Dennis, surprised.

Something faintly demure come over Blake's vivid face.

"I've been told," she said softly, "there're—other ways."

"Not by me," boomed Peter. "I need a kid sister as long as I can keep one—they're handy things to have in a house."

"You old Victorian!" scoffed Blake.

They stepped out into the night and waited while Dennis turned the lamp down and it flickered into darkness. For a second, it was totally dark around them. Then the shapes of things came out a little, darker bushes and the hill against a paler sky. Bright points of stars appeared overhead. They got their bearings and began to walk away, down the hill. Blake put her hands through Peter's and Dennis's arms, and they walked in step, stumbling once in a while over shadows that turned out to be solid clumps.

As they went down into the gully the sweet, frosty air of November came around them; the earthy smell, the smell of wet winter coming on, and the smell of dead dry grass rotting on the fields, and of leaves turning to mold, was in their nostrils. It was like a sort of nostalgia; it was a season smell they all loved, for the same reason. Peter said it wistfully, lovingly, the stolid giant made articulate.

"Football weather," Peter said, drawing the keen and fragrant air deep into his capacious chest like a loved draft. The other two sighed wordlessly.

Then Dennis began to sing absently, not caring how much noise they made to let Bowden know they were gone. . . .

"*Sweet—and lovely . . .*"

Dennis heard himself singing softly, in the starry night beside Blake wrapped in his coat.

After a few seconds—"Radio singer!" said Blake bitingly, under her breath.

Dennis stopped. Then:

"How do you like this?" he said expressionlessly. He began again. The cold night flowered into beauty. Something sharp of point as a needle went through Blake's heart.

"Drink to me only with thine eyes"

sang Dennis,

"And I will pledge with mine . . ."

It was like being kissed. Only Dennis had done it to hurt her.
"I sent thee late a rosy wreath"

—the old song was like a record that couldn't die, so beautiful it was, all these hundred years—

"Not so much honoring thee,
As giving it a hope that there,
It could not withered be."

You couldn't withstand beauty like that. It was a knife at your heart. It was someone you loved singing to you. It was something that wouldn't ever die. How could Dennis be so unmoved by it, making it so beautiful? He sang as if his love were on his lips, as if all the tenderness of the song were on his warm, young mouth, and his arm through hers didn't even tremble. He was happy, making such sorrow of love, such a havoc in the hearts of others listening to him. Was that what it was to be an artist? Blake was learning.

"But thou thereon didst only breathe,"

sang Dennis,

"And sent'st it back to me-e-e;
Since when it grows and smells, I swear,"

the deathless love song rose triumphantly,

"Not of itself but thee!"

And suddenly, it was all right again. She was Blake Byrne, walking across a frosty dark field, and Dennis was Dennis and not the disembodied spirit of deathless love seeking utterance. For Dennis had pressed her arm against his, once, closely, comfortingly, roughly, a friendly gesture, a careless gesture.

"Not of itself but thee!"

he sang over again, very softly, letting the song shatter itself against the silence.

He wasn't an artist any more, punishing others but not being punished himself by his song. He hadn't been angry. He was just Dennis again. Blake was silent. She was learning.

"Swell!" said Peter approvingly. "That's pretty."

"You think so?" said Dennis. "Pretty, nothing—hell, that was perfect! That reminds me, Peter, I have a bone to pick with you. Or I would have if I didn't have this unfortunate idea of picking opponents that could give Dempsey weight and height. You damn' near called me an Abou Ben Adhem back there in the shack —you said I was a little friend of all the world. Take back those words—or else."

"What's the matter with 'em?" asked Peter warily.

"It isn't like that at all with me," protested Dennis hotly. "It isn't that I love my fellow man ... go around with a smirk on my face loving 'em! It's just that—I don't know what it's all about. What anything's about. Half the time I think my fellow man is the lowest form of worm," said Dennis pensively, "only—then I'll remember what even worms come to in time. Dust. And then I can't help thinking how brave men must be, so casually brave, to go on living and to love life so much, knowing that at the end of it there's—nothing. Dust again. Some people have consolation. They think there's something more. Maybe there is. I don't know. I do know, though, that we have to die in this life, and that's a terrible thing to have to happen when it's a life like this. And they're so brave. They accept it so casually. How can I think they're so rotten, even the worst of them, when I see them going on to that? I don't know," said Dennis carefully, "what *it's* all about, but I think *they're*—splendid, anyway.

"Oh, Peter," Dennis went on with a quiet passion, "think how you'd feel knowing things are going to end for you. No more days like today, no more nights like tonight, for you ever! No more the sun shining in your face and the wind in your hair, and you driving along the dusty warm roads of Delroy. No more running down the fields in the cool autumn night, and the smell of the earth in your face, and the black frost rising to touch your cheeks as you run!"

Peter gave a deep murmur of sound and drew a deep, deep breath, earthy of frost and autumn, into his lungs.

"When I think of that," said Dennis, "I doubt if I could kill a fly. I'd want to give everything a chance. Even a murderer, who doesn't give anyone a chance. It's just that—I don't know what it's all about," he repeated.

At that suddenly forlorn note in his voice, it was Blake's turn to press her arm against his, hard, once.

"Only," said Dennis more cheerfully, "it's splendid, all of it. I wouldn't want to miss any of it. And when I think of that, and that our murderer made Bianca miss a lot of it, and Farnese, too, whatever kind of a guy he was, why then I feel like asking Sullivan for an invitation to see the hanging at San Quentin—the private showing. Bianca— she wasn't meant to miss any of it. She loved all this, too—every day, every hour. I don't care what she was, or what she did—she didn't deserve —death. I don't think anyone really does. Peter, you don't want to die?"

Peter murmured, like a cello string plucked hard, as if Dennis had picked out a chord on his heart.

"Well, that's the way I feel about this," said Dennis. "There may be other worlds, other faiths—I think there must be. You can see some of 'em up there now, all these bright stars. And maybe there are other lives, too, but all I know and love is this one. Maybe there are others, though. Perhaps," said Dennis lazily, the wind in his face bringing the smell of smoldering dead-leaf smoke— "perhaps God lets us out on a long leash, after all, and this life is it."

They went on a little silently; then, after a while, they began to talk softly together, in comfortable pauses. But they could feel that they were friends now truly, because they had talked of immortality together.

Blake and Dennis began to bicker, idly, as two players will toss a tennis ball back and forth across a net, purely for practice and enjoyment.

"You scrap so beautifully, Blake," sighed Dennis. "I almost wish we'd never get home."

"Good God, are we only going to your place, Dennis?" Peter boomed. "I thought we were halfway to San Jose by now!"

He brought up short in the dark and stood drawing great deep breaths, half puffing them out and in again. The others stood waiting for him.

"It only looks farther than it did," said Dennis helpfully, peering at the dark earth around them. "Coming back always does. Besides, you didn't notice landmarks before—you didn't have time, anyway. You were just about flying. The house is right around the dark clump of things to the left, and you can see the tops of the elm trees around it mixing in with the stars up there. And there's the light from the kitchen window. We're here."

"Well, if Bowden doesn't know we're out of his place and back here again, he must be deaf," said Peter contentedly, as they came through the yard and around by the lighted kitchen doorway.

"He knows, all right," Dennis said grimly. "And I'll know some more too, when I get back there. I'm going to get an overcoat—that shack's darned chilly, and it'll get colder later on in the night."

Blake slipped out of his coat and handed it over.

"Thanks a lot, Dennis," she said casually. "What was that bumpy thing in your side pocket—a gun?"

"Cigarette case." Dennis showed it to her, grinning. "Think I want to shoot myself accidentally some day? I can get someone else to do it for nothing!"

"D-Dennis," Blake said, wide-eyed, "don't you think I mean, hadn't you better let us come back with you? If there's sh-shooting—"

"The perfect host," said Dennis. "I'd invite you all for it, only—there's not going to be any. You must come down when the duck season's on, or when Wong and I are out for the jack rabbits and ground squirrels. Don't let me forget." He grinned again and opened the door to the dark hallway.

"Wong sleeps in his own place, that lean-to beyond the kitchen," he said. "There's room here, if you're staying. I'd like to have you. Wait'll I get my other coat—it's in the hall closet—" He broke off suddenly, with an almost ludicrous expression of astonishment on his face.

"Why, no, it isn't!" he said, bewilderedly. "It's in the hotel with all the rest of my things, waiting to be packed off by me, I suppose. I bet that hotel bird's hopping! You know, I keep forgetting—that it's a year since I've been here. I suppose—I suppose things do change. Even here. I would have thought—if I'd thought about it at all—that I could have gone in the dark to any place on this ground and picked up my stuff where I used to leave it. My coat in the hall closet, my car in the garage, the bumpy place where it leaves the garage floor for the dirt road, the squirrel gun standing in its place in the tool shack outside—it all comes back so clearly, as if nothing had happened in between to push it back into dimness. Only—a lot's happened. Well, I don't get my coat, but maybe there's chicken and stuff in the icebox like there used to be."

"Philosopher!" said Blake warmly, approaching the icebox cordially. "Maybe there is."

There was.

"Help yourself," said Dennis, waving his hand largely. "Wong won't mind, and if he does, why, who's the boss here, anyway?"

"Wong," said Peter.

Dennis laughed. "Right the first time. I'm only the young master. I forgot you had a Louie in your lives. He'd die for me if he thought I needed it, but he wouldn't let me put on any airs in my own house."

"He probably knows what's good for you," Peter observed.

"And you," said Dennis, "with your mouth full of my chicken!"

He looked at his watch and got up.

"Make wassail," he said hospitably. "It's five to eleven now, and I'm going back to get Bowden. He's had lots of time to come in by now."

"Want us?" Peter rumbled. Dennis shook his head, smiling.

"I think we'll take you up on spending the night here then, and make an early start back to the city in the morning. There's an inquest due there tomorrow—it may have slipped your mind—and if the chief witness doesn't show up there'll be ructions, especially in the detective bureau. As your lawyer, Dennis," Peter sighed, "I feel as if I were just hanging onto the tail of a kite!"

"This is our only chance," Dennis reminded him, "to do anything on our own hook. It's the long leash, and I'm going to take advantage of it. Otherwise—I may be watching you hopefully through a nice thickness of wire mesh up at the jail while you say that while there's life there's hope, and you'll carry it up to the State Supreme Court, and other polite things "like that to cheer me up! No, thank you. We'll do what we can on our own first."

"Sure you don't want company?" Peter tried again.

"Quite sure," Dennis said. "Thanks. It may scare him off if he sees or hears a crowd of us coming. I've got a

better chance of getting him, going alone this way. So
long—"

He stopped at the doorway and turned halfway back.

"—rather, *hasta la vista*," he said, smiling at them. A
curious gracious courtesy fell on him all at once, like the
mantle of the old dons who had lived in his sunny county,
who had listened to the gentle stately courtesy of the
Little San Ramon River rippling through the long sunny
afternoons. As though the sight of guests reminded him,
for a brief second, of other, more gracious days.

"My house is yours," said Dennis gravely in the old
formula and was gone, armed only with the cigarette case
bumpy against his side pocket.

"Dennis—" Blake began, a bit lost.

Peter shook his big head at her and laid a big brown
hand reprovingly for a second on her arm.

"His play," he said. "Don't spoil it."

So Blake—she didn't forgive herself for that—stayed
back for once, and Dennis went on alone.

He went down the yard, through the dark fields,
across the south gully—and as he looked up he saw a dim
red glow in the sky, beginning at the top of the hill. So he
began to run, and he reached Bowden's shack as the
flames took hold of the wooden walls and began to roar in
the wind. He went in and saw the broken oil lamp on the
floor and Bowden sprawling in an attitude of surprise,
arms thrown out. He knelt beside Bowden, and saw, in
that second before the flames drove him out again, that
the top was blown off from Bowden's head and the greater
part of his face with it. That gap had been effectively
plugged.

XIII. AMONG THOSE PRESENT

About one o'clock that morning Dennis got Kennedy on the phone in the press room of the Hall of Justice.

"Shoot," invited that debonair gentleman cheerfully, when his caller announced himself.

"Don't be funny," said Dennis. "I've got a lot to tell you."

"Well, my ears are still in working order," said that slightly exhilarated person still more airily. "I guess they must work automatically. The rest of me has signed off for the night—eyes see red and black spots in front of 'em, complicated by red, white, and blue round things that look to me like poker chips. Hands can't handle a pencil any more—they make funny motions like shuffling—"

"Kennedy," said Dennis hoarsely, "do you *have* to be drunk just now, when I need you sober?"

It was just a last shot, but it seemed to work. There was a slight but electric pause at the other end of the line. Then Kennedy's voice again, crisper.

"Not," said that cool voice, "if you need me that bad. I'm as sober as a judge, Dennis. Spill it."

Reassured, Dennis went on talking. He told about Bowden's visit to Dennis's garden, of the visit to the shack, and the finding of the blue money-order receipts — and the conclusions drawn therefrom.

"Blackmail, eh?" Kennedy commented. "You're shattering my illusions, Dennis. I thought all rustics who had anything to do with the soil were one hundred per cent pure at heart before they came to the big city."

"You wouldn't think that," said Dennis grimly, "if you'd ever lived around in the country, as I have. Your 'simple' sons of the soil can be mean as dirt, some of 'em.

They get a lot of time to think up things to do, I guess. Well, anyway, Bowden was blackmailing this bird—we found that out."

"Go on—he didn't come in?" Kennedy murmured, as though he were writing it all down at the other end of the line.

"Not till I went out with the others," Dennis said. He kept his voice steady, along a monotonous tone, for fear it would shatter itself to pieces. He didn't let himself think, he just went on talking to Kennedy, as though oral contact with him even at that distance kept him from seeing the fearful cliffs of danger plunging down on either side of his path. "Then I came back— alone. It was about eleven o'clock. He was there. He was there, Kennedy— lying on the floor. Someone'd shot him—so close it blew off most of his head. And the oil lamp had broken, and fired the place. It all went up."

"Whew!" said an appreciative Kennedy. "It's lucky I'm talking from a private booth! I took the call here instead of on my press-room phone as soon as I heard it was a long-distance call. I had a hunch, all right. Besides, it was too noisy there—the press room's a merry hell tonight, a dozen extra reporters sent in to cover the Hall, and the Hall is humming from top to bottom like a wasp's nest that someone's kicked open. Dennis, the Farnese and Malletti cases look like the biggest thing since the Trojan War! If these rats around here thought I was holding anything like this out on them, they'd mob me. About this Honest Plowman accepting money for silence,"—Kennedy was talking now as though he were writing it down straight for the hot metal of the print.

"He was a dirty blackmailer!" said Dennis hotly. "What's the idea?"

"Under your hat, Dennis. Sure he was. Only he's dead now, and this case is very, very alive. And we're not going to impeach our only good witness, since he's dead, by implying that he was a pretty worthless sort of skunk. We're going to play him up for a martyr. His testimony may come in handy one of these days, and by that time he'll be almost canonized by the *Star*. Another thing—keep off the subject of those money orders and receipts to the sheriff and any police officers, yet. Let the federal post office at San Francisco keep the original applications in the murderer's handwriting safe there, until we get more of a line on this case. I don't want these press-room rats climbing aboard our ship—they might swamp it. And the police would grab them without a thank-you from you. They're worth something."

"Sullivan'll be here soon," said Dennis, reminded. "The sheriff's gone to head him off at Monterey, near here. He's down following some clue or other, and Henry's letting me talk to you—he's the deputy, and I told him it was important, and he knows me."

"Sullivan? Yeh, I know," Kennedy's voice grinned. "Someone saw an old man with a black gown on coming down the street, and they phoned the San Francisco police and it turns out to be Mrs. McGuire, aged eighty, widow woman who's lived there all her life. They're getting hundreds of calls like that that always come in on a 'missing' case like Father Malletti's disappearance. Well, good luck, Dennis, and I'll be seeing you, maybe at the inquest tomorrow. Thanks a lot for this stuff."

"Inquest?" said Dennis. "Which one—Bianca's? I'm afraid I'm unavoidably detained, Kennedy, from going to anyone's inquest unless it's for Bowden's."

"This is a previous engagement," said Kennedy. "What would keep you, anyway? Where's your friends, the Byrnes?"

"How do I know?" said Dennis wearily. "I haven't seen 'em since the sheriff and his deputy detained me in Delroy. One thing that's keeping me here is an adobe jail they've got here. That's where I'm phoning from. And the sheriff has gone in to get Sullivan to explain to him that I can't attend any inquest. I'm wanted here."

"Hey, they can't do that!" protested Kennedy. "You tell them—"

"Can't they?" said Dennis. "You tell 'em. They want a lot of telling, anyway. They want to know how come my own squirrel gun was found all dirty, and with the barrel still warm from being used, stuck up in a clump of bushes near Bowden's shack! The last time it was seen by anyone it was in my tool shed, and I knew where it was kept, too. You think up an answer to that—*I* haven't been able to satisfy them!"

And he hung up with a bang and turned round to the desk of the sheriff's office in the Delroy jail.

"Thanks, Henry," he said. "I'll go back to the cell now and catch up on some sleep, if you're through for the night."

Only he didn't sleep. That was bravado. He kept seeing it all again—a red glare of fire, and a faceless thing. . . .

Peter and Blake weren't doing much sleeping, either. They sat up around the wood stove in the kitchen, with blankets wrapped Indian fashion around them and their sleepless heads sticking out at the top, their eyes tired and heavy and their voices hoarse as a crow's croak from weary talking. And yet they couldn't stop. They had to keep on.

Their host had left them, in the custody of the lanky and rather embarrassed undersheriff, who'd known Dennis when they were kids together, it seemed, and the sheriff who'd hastily come up at his undersheriff's phone call. The undersheriff and a deputy had driven up in a flivver around twelve o'clock in response to Dennis's call from his place, backed by a horrified and silent Blake and Peter, listening. Dennis after that hadn't been able to talk much about what had happened on the knoll of Bowden's shack. They'd got the main line of it from his phone call. It was too late to do much about it. The shack was nothing but hot wood ashes in a few minutes, and the main fire had already died down when Dennis had come back to them. The undersheriff and his deputy had come and looked over the place where the shack had stood, and raked over the pyre of hot wood ashes, and the two of them had searched the surrounding ground pretty thoroughly by lamp and torchlight, without saying much, but, like good hunting dogs, as it were, with a subtle current of silent communication between them. And then they'd found the squirrel gun, where someone'd thrown it in the bushes, roughly hidden, and they'd shown it to Dennis, still without saying much, their eyes reserved, judgment withheld.

Dennis had identified it as his. They wanted to know where he kept it. It was usually kept in the tool shed, eh? Well, it wasn't there now. They poked around a bit to make sure.

With this observation, and still more silence, they'd phoned and got the sheriff out of his bed, and received orders. They informed Dennis that they had to hold him. Dennis went a bit wild-eyed at that and said something about its getting to be a habit with the police, and then quieted down suddenly. The lanky under-sheriff was looking at him with grieved blue eyes from a thin tanned face. He expected his acquaintances to keep their composure better when being carted off to the jail. It made for uncomfortableness otherwise. Dennis couldn't go back on him.

Only, "Have you got them?" he whispered to Peter fiercely, as the flivver engine started and all other noise was undercovered by it.

"What?" said Peter.

"Those money orders," Dennis said. "You took them."

"I put 'em in my pocket," Peter said.

"Don't give them up," Dennis said. "We may need them."

"I won't," said Peter simply as a rock.

Then Dennis looked at Blake. He hadn't before. Blake was holding onto Peter's big arm hard with both hands and not saying anything. She smiled at Dennis—a small white smile, beyond tears, beyond words, beyond anything but a sort of still white bravery. As if there weren't anything left of her but that smile.

And the undersheriff and his deputy drove off in their flivver and took Dennis away with them, leaving a rather wild-eyed Peter and Blake behind . . . talking . . . talking . . . till their voices husked on them.

They didn't get anywhere, at that. They went over and over it again, past the ground that Dennis had already led them over before. They accepted that as tried territory now—that Bianca knew her husband had been killed, and she'd had suspicions—or near proof —or something—and all the rest, even Bowden's murder, followed from that.

Then Blake thought of something, from utter weariness, just as, sometimes, the tide going back on a muddy beach will uncover treasure—abalone shells shining, or an oyster with a pearl in it.

"You know, it may not be like that at all!" she said huskily, her eyes shining dark and wide. "Have you thought, Peter, we may be all wrong about these last two killings? The recent ones, Bianca's and—and this man's? The first man was killed by someone—and so we think the last two were killed by the same man. It may not be that at all!" She leaned forward in her chair, and her voice dropped still lower. "Where's Wong?" she asked, in a curious dark voice.

"Wong? I don't get you," Peter said. "Where is he? In his lean-to, I suppose. Sound asleep. Lots of these old Chinese take a breath of the pipe before they turn in. You know that, Blake. They're used to it. He's sound asleep. We didn't make much disturbance around, you know."

"Is he?" asked Blake. "That's good."

"Why'd you think of Wong, Blake?"

"Because I don't think we've thought of him enough, Peter. Everyone will be sure that Dennis is a murderer now. They'll think it's very suspicious that as soon as he comes back, murder happens. To people he goes to see. Well, maybe it is. I grant you this—it was probably his presence here that did make that murder come about. Not, of course, that he did it. But—don't you see?— someone knew he was here, and seeing that Bowden person, and that caused Bowden's murder."

"Yes, I see that," Peter said.

"Well, I think we're wrong about that someone. We think he's a San Francisco man who killed Bianca, too. And who killed her husband, Victor Farnese. Suppose he isn't? Suppose he was here in Delroy all the time? Suppose he is someone who knew Dennis's movements, who'd do anything for Dennis, who knew Farnese was murdered, and that Dennis might be accused of murder instead of just plain manslaughter about that? So—he killed Bianca to protect Dennis from the charge of murdering her husband. He killed Bowden for the same reason. Suppose Bianca was going to put it on Dennis? And suppose Bowden was in on it, too?—perhaps she'd paid him for saying it was Dennis killed him. He'd have turned traitor or liar for money. We know that. Maybe he thought it up himself, and put Bianca onto Dennis, thinking he could blackmail Dennis over it later!"

"The honest plowman!" murmured Peter in admiration. "Well, grant that—for the sake of argument. It was going to be a put-up job on Bowden's part to get money from Dennis, scare him on threats of this faked evidence to buy his silence. Who was the obliging friend who put out Dennis's enemy, Bowden, and his danger, Bianca?"

Blake was white and blazing now. She didn't need a blanket about her. She was on fire, whitely.

"Who," she retorted, "knew as much about Dennis's affairs as he did himself? Who loved Dennis so much he'd take anything on himself to get him out of a thing like that? Who lived in Delroy? Who knew where Dennis kept a squirrel gun here? Who knew that he'd come back again today? Wong."

"Prove it," said Peter quietly. "How'd he know anything about Dennis, up in San Francisco, away from here for a year?"

"Of course he did," Blake said. "You know yourself what a grapevine system these old Chinese have, all up and down the state. I bet he didn't miss a thing about Dennis. Why, when Dennis wanted to find out if Father Malletti'd been around here, this afternoon, he sent Wong out to gather the news from the other old heathen here. They know everything that goes on. You know that."

Peter nodded.

"And he knew Bianca was going to meet Dennis— maybe he'd been approached by Bowden and had arranged a meeting. I can see him double-crossing Bowden blandly, and then going up and doing for Bianca—swiftly—silently—that night—"

"In Dennis's room!"

Blake shrugged. "He had to. He couldn't pick his spot very much. Bianca may have known it was Dennis's room, thought she was going to see Dennis there and get the truth about Farnese's killing—sent off at that tangent by Bowden, you see—and met Wong instead. He may have reasoned that the short time between Dennis going up to his room, and giving the alarm, would clear Dennis. It practically has."

"Yes—until *this* came up," Peter said. "You can't blame Sullivan and those birds for giving him the cold eye on this."

"If he'd had witnesses—Dennis, I mean—tonight when he went back there, or if he hadn't gone back, he'd have been safe, with Bowden dead," Blake said swiftly. "It was chance, just chance, that we didn't all go back with Dennis."

"Chance," said Peter heavily, "and his own insistence."

"Don't blame yourself for that, Peter."

"I'm a fine lawyer! I let him walk right into it!"

He raised his massive head and tried to smile at her.

"All right, go on. Why did Bowden get his tonight, after we'd gone there to see him? Explain that, Sherlock, if it wasn't our First Murderer."

"Because," said Blake, "Wong was afraid—of what would happen when Dennis and Bowden did meet. He'd heard Dennis say tonight he was going to get an answer from Bowden. He knew that Bowden was a lot more dangerous than Dennis imagined. He had a picture of the two of them meeting, and Dennis flaring up, and Bowden cool as a rattlesnake, and as nasty-tempered— he thought Bowden was a danger to Dennis, and so he put him out of Dennis's way. That's one way of showing your love for a man—killing his enemies off."

"With Dennis's squirrel gun?"

"With Wong's squirrel gun," corrected Blake. "He'd been using it for a year by himself. He probably didn't even think of it as Dennis's any more. He took it because it was handy, and he was used to it. That's all."

"And now he's sleeping it off while young master's in jail?" asked Peter. "A—a sort of communistic crime, you might say. Wong commits it, and Dennis goes to jail for it. You might call that an involuntary act of brotherly love on Dennis's part, too, Blake."

Blake smiled, a curious little smile.

"I don't think you'll find him asleep," she said. "I don't think you'll find him there. I think he's going to hide himself in the nearest big Chinese city quarter. He thinks they'll be after him, not Dennis."

"So you think there's a First and a Second Murderer, do you?" asked Peter grimly. "The First Murderer killed Farnese, and the Second Murderer killed Bianca and Bowden, and skipped. Well, we'll see about that skipping part right now, anyway."

He went out, and Blake sat by the stove and shivered in spite of the fire until he returned, a few minutes later.

"Gone," he said, nodding his head in a heavy sort of gloomy satisfaction. "You're right about that, Blake.

Hadn't slept in his bed, either." He shivered. "Gosh, it's bitter outside—that damp frost."

He took up a bit of rolled newspaper from the wood box and opened the lid of the stove to begin stoking again.

"Local paper," he said, talking idly to take Blake's mind off things. "News of all the county. Want to read? It's yesterday's. Here's a shipping column, from the Monterey Bay harbor. 'Among those in today from San Francisco—' let's see whom we know who has a boat in— Blake! Blake, do you remember Morgan? The guy on Dennis's hotel floor? His yacht *Margarita* came in yesterday. William Morgan, of the Hotel Ancaster. Must be him."

Peter gave a harsh croak of laughter. His hair was wild on his head; his eyes were deep storm blue.

"Among those present," he said grimly. "Do you get it, Blake? This man was in San Francisco when Bianca was killed—he was at Delroy when Bowden got his, in this county. He had access to those places. He's at home in Delroy. You've got competition for the post of Second Murderer. He might even be the First one, too, if our original theory holds. He was here tonight. You see, Blake, among those present tonight was also—the murderer!"

XIV: BUT NOT FOR LOVE

Dennis was writing to Blake. He sat on the edge of his cot in his little cell in the Delroy jail, and put a blunt-pointed pencil to lined paper, industriously. The light came in shyly from among piled-up gray clouds rapidly getting darker and grayer outside, in the early morning.

"Darling," wrote Dennis, dark head bowed closely over his inadequate tools, "do you wish me to be serious? At six o'clock on a cloudy November morning? I belong to a generation that would cheerfully die for you, but won't be serious for you. We aren't Hemingway's ' Lost Generation' of the war and post-war period, which was so deadly serious about everything, including the road to ruin. We're the generation after that, and we don't think they left anything that's worth taking so seriously. There's the third post-war generation coming up now, of course; my young brother and sister would belong to it, if I had them, it's about nineteen years old now and it's going back to the old ways. They believe in girls with long skirts and little shining topknots of hair done up on the backs of their necks, with a few silky straggles at the ears and the nape. They believe in love at first sight, and in lots of things that we thought died with the war, and the years afterward, and that perhaps didn't. Perhaps all those things are coming up again, like flowers out of fire-blackened ruins. Perhaps that young third generation's right, and things like that don't die . . . and radio tenors sing true things, about everlasting and extremely sentimental love. Wouldn't that be funny, if true? I'd have to revise my life, Blake. Or all that's left of it. It may be shorter than I think, at that. I had a talk with Sullivan this morning, earlier. Yes, Inspector Sullivan, of the homicide bureau. He was down here chasing a line on Father Malletti's disappearance, and naturally was interested in the recent events on my place. He seems to connect them.

"He came charging in with fire in his eyes and a shotgun in one large beefy hand, and I thought for a minute he was carrying out his own private economy program and was going to save the city the expense of a trial for me. Then he asked me if I recognized the gun, so I said, 'Sure, I recognize it. It's the one Wong uses to shoot jack rabbits and ground squirrels with. It's twelve-gauge, with a hand-carved walnut stock I made myself. It used to be mine.'

"'Sure you didn't borrow it?' he says, very quiet and sarcastic. 'And that it wasn't yours again—for an hour last night? I'm going to warn you anything you say can be used against you, Devore.'

"'Do you mean I'm under arrest?' I said.

"'I mean you'd better be careful what you say.'

"That was a fine incentive to open my heart to him! Peter would have been proud of the way his client clammed up on this occasion—I think he thinks I'm too talkative, anyway. I can see your large and laconic brother eyeing me with approval for once, Blake. My communication with Sullivan after that consisted chiefly of 'Yea, yea' and 'Nay, nay,' and not so much of them, either. I did unbend enough to inquire if this was to be my rather permanent address, so you'd know where to send mail to me, and it seems we are going up to San Francisco this morning (business as usual) for the inquest on Bianca, may she rest in peace, with Sullivan for my guard, and I'm not to be charged here until that's over. So we've got a few minutes of time, tell Peter. And tell him how funny it seems that time stretches out to hours and years sometimes, and then contracts to a few minutes, like an elastic band. It always seems to be doing that, lately. Most confusing. Since last night— (Last night? No, it must have been about a million years ago, Blake.

And now I'm the last man on earth, remembering it, and you coming across the fields, and 'Drink to me only.' Surely you've forgotten?). Anyway, ask Peter if he remembers such a very long time ago. He'll be a famous judge yet. (That's in the future, and the future seems very close to me. Time has contracted again, and I can reach out and touch tomorrow with my fingers.) But he's getting some swell practice on my case! Everything seems to happen while I'm around, doesn't it?

"(Yes, that's what Sullivan commented on very freely this morning, around three o'clock. It seems he's been riding up and down this coast line on wild clues since yesterday, in a police car from San Francisco, and it hasn't improved his temper any. He knows I've got a manslaughter record here too, now—they can always identify me by a scar on my right wrist, and they did.)

"You know, I've been thinking about Father Malletti—and other things—all night. Do you remember I said that about 'an old man, going into darkness'? I nearly had the horrors last night, thinking of that and other things, and then I thought how that was wrong. It wasn't darkness, where he was. Father Malletti carries his own light with him, where he goes. So don't worry about that too much, Blake. I'm sure it's all right! I wish I could be as sure, about myself. Only I'm not exactly a saint.

"Sullivan'll come back soon, and then we'll go back to San Francisco in the police car. I'm writing this to keep from thinking of anything more after last night. Henry— the undersheriff here—has promised to smuggle this out to you. I told him he could read it first—he ought to, you know, being an officer. He doesn't say much, but he's a good guy. We used to play baseball and go swimming and hunting, before I went to college. We were in the same grades in grammar school and at Delroy High School.

"So now we're going to say good-bye to Bianca. She was beautiful, she reminded me of a gorgeous Venetian sunset painted by Turner in the '8o's. She was like a foreign country. But you, Blake, are like a picture by our own William Keith, of a California hillside by the sea, all tawny gold sand and orange poppies and deep blue lupin. You're home, to me.

"Dennis.

"P.S. Thanks for your note. Henry brought it to me. You're all wrong about Wong, you know. 'Men have died, from time to time, and worms have eaten them—but not for love.' I ought to know. Tell Peter—'Why don't you try this guy Morgan?' Adios.

"Dennis."

He looked up then at the swift first patter of rain outside the barred window and saw the darkened day.

XV. THE BEAUTIFUL AND BLONDE

Blake and Peter sat at breakfast under the electric lights of the depressing Delroy hotel dining room at seven o'clock that same rainy morning. Blake was reading a letter, and Peter sat watching the landscape of her face where sun and windy clouds chased by changingly.

"Love letter?" he asked.

"Not nowadays," said Blake. "It's from Dennis, and he says I remind him of a William Keith painting of a field, and he calls me 'darling' once."

Peter shook his head.

"Nothing to that," he admitted. "You haven't got a case. What else does he say?"

"Dennis has discovered the Einsteinian theory of the relativity of time," Blake reported. "He says it's like a rubber elastic band."

"Does he, by any chance," Peter asked, "come down to current events?"

He looked up from his coffee to see Blake's blue eyes brimming deeply.

"He's going up to San Francisco with Inspector Sullivan," she said, trying to be casual about it. She helped herself to coffee. "They've started by now." Her voice went suddenly gruff on her. She took a too hot sip hastily. "He says you're mistaken about Wong, and to get onto Morgan as soon as you can."

"We will," said Peter, very satisfyingly solid about it. He sat back, thinking it over. "Blake," he said, "what about Dennis, anyway? Does he mean so much?"

Blake's eyes were two blue meadows, abloom with lupin.

"I used to have a picture of Dennis in his football uniform," she said simply. "I cut it out of the rotogravure part of the Sunday paper, and stuck it up in my mirror when I was in high school. I'd forgotten his name, but not him when I saw him."

"No!" said Peter, surprised. "I didn't know girls really did things like that."

"You'd be surprised," Blake said, grinning. "I'll bet there was many a damsel about my age or even in their later teens who had your picture, Peter, up in their mirrors. You looked keen with your football uniform on and your hair all mussed up, and your eyes frowning."

"No!" breathed Peter again, uneasily. "You don't say so!"

"I do say so," Blake retorted. "Don't be so bashful about your snapshots going into so many boudoirs, Peter. You and Dennis seem to have missed all this bleacher stuff—you must have played football for the fun of it. And what a lad Dennis is for getting his picture in the paper, isn't he? I don't wonder he didn't want to give Kennedy another shot at it. I suppose the papers simply spilled it all over their pages when he was on trial here for killing Farnese. Poor Dennis!"

"Sullivan knows," Peter said glumly. He set down his cup and eyed it with disfavor. " I don't mind drinking brown boots," he said mildly, "but I do draw the line at burnt rubber in my coffee. I loathe the taste of burnt rubber!"

He got up. His broad shoulders made the depressing little small-town dining room look littler and grayer than ever.

"Sullivan knows," he repeated, "that Dennis has a record here. That he's been going under a partly assumed name—Devore—instead of his own, whatever it is. That he's made the San Francisco police look more or less foolish by not yielding up all his information about his past to their first hurried vacuum-cleaning method. I don't blame him much for that—he thought he could get away with it, and maybe he would have, if *this* hadn't occurred just now. But with Bowden's killing, and the burning of the shack, the police have just that much more reason to suspect Dennis's holding out on them at first. Oh, I don't envy Dennis when Sullivan and the rest of them ask him frankly and fully for any stray bits of information they think he's still got up his sleeve!"

"What can *we* do?" Blake asked, pushing away her almost untouched cup of coffee. It may have been made partly of burnt rubber and brown boots, but it was tasteless to her.

Peter shrugged. He got into his overcoat and helped her into her brown tweed coat with the tall spiky fur Dennis had liked about her face. Only her cheeks weren't so fresh and pink now, nor her eyes so freshly blue. She was pale under her brownness, and her eyes were more deeply purple—blue, but older and tireder and bigger.

"What can we do?" Peter said. "Nothing much. I went to the jail before breakfast, Blake, and they wouldn't let me see him. Sullivan must have been in there then. Wait till the inquest's over—I can do more then, as his lawyer. He's in Sullivan's hands now."

Blake shivered and drew the fur up around her chin. "'Large beefy hands,'" she quoted distastefully. "Oh, Peter—you don't suppose—"

Peter laughed mirthlessly.

"Listen," he said. "I may not know much about Dennis, not even his last name, but I'm learning. Think of this, Blake—we've known him, man and boy, for just about forty-eight hours, or two days and nearly three nights, and already we've pretty well torn up our routine by the roots for him. We've chased down here to Delroy with him, we've gone man-hunting with him, and we've spent a nearly sleepless night over him. Kennedy's a police reporter, as tough-hearted as they make them, and he's bunked Dennis and kept his record from the police as long as he could. And, from the indications, his friend Henry at the jail here is running a free-delivery mail service for him, and I'll bet the sheriff's wife has probably cooked him a better breakfast this morning than we got here at the hotel. No, I don't know what's going to happen to Dennis, but I wouldn't worry over him. I'd do all my worrying over his guardian angel, trying to keep up with him nowadays."

Blake smiled mistily.

"Peter, you *are* a dear," she said with conviction. She laid one brown-gloved hand on Peter's overcoat arm. "Where do we go from here?"

"To see Morgan and his yacht," said Peter staunchly, "before that guy can pull up his anchor and beat it back to the city. Let's go!"

They went.

By the time their car came into Monterey the sun was shining, and the marvelous blue bay, deeply blue as the sort of stuff in bluing bottles, and edged by a snowy line of white surf breaking on a white sand beach, lay incredibly lovely before them. Big white clouds sailed by in a blue sky. Smaller white yachts, slim and graceful, danced on the deep blue bay. A little gay wind ruffled the waters. It was the sort of day when nothing dark and terrible could happen. It made them, as a final magic, believe in it ... in spite of everything they knew.

They walked down past the old customhouse, and the old and mellow adobe houses left over from the Spanish California days, a hundred years and more ago. Time was gracious in this little sunlit city by the bay. A hundred years ago, *senor*, was only yesterday here. One slept in the sun, and when one awakened, the sun was as warm, the air as clear, the bay as blue, as— yesterday, under another flag and another people. *Vaya con Dios*, said Monterey softly, watching other cities rise to the skies, and foreign wars being fought, and airplanes landing on pontoons in its bay—and then turned over and slept again. It didn't really change. Blake felt it, too. Her eyes cleared, her face lightened, she gave a little joyful skip or two as they walked on down to the fishing pier and the white yachts.

"The *Margarita?*" Peter asked, of a brown-skinned fisherman.

The other pointed. "End o' the wharf, there. She come in yesterday morning."

Nets, brown like dried seaweed, were drying along the beach and the wharf. The pungent, salty scent of them with its reminiscent sardine smell clinging on, too, reminded them of seaweed brought home from its native element after a day's picnic, and hung proudly at first, then forlorn and forgotten, in their rooms when they were children, to be thrown out ignominiously at last. These scents had memory's dear and devastating power. They were by the sea again, and they were children again. . . . No, they weren't. They were Blake and Peter grown up, and their friend was in jail, and they were going to see a man they suspected of being a murderer. How did things happen that way, anyway? The bright blue-and-gold day clouded like sunshine threatened by dark storm clouds. Things turned out so differently from what you expected they'd be, when you grew up. Blake sighed.

Peter had halted before one of the slim white launches, tied up close to the wharf.

"Hello on board!" he boomed. "The Margar—"

A man's sunburnt blond head had popped up out of the companionway. Peter's voice died, then it picked up again to a roar.

"—Billy Morgan!" he shouted world-shakingly. "How in—"

The *Margarita's* owner showed more of himself. He was simply dressed in white duck pants and a white sweatshirt and a fine coat of brown skin. He stared at Peter from ingenuously frank blue eyes. The eyes wrinkled into a grin, that spread over his pleasant young sunburnt face.

"Hey, it's Pete Byrne!" he yelled back. He leaped out of the companionway to the deck, and thence clambered up to the wharf. He thumped Peter recklessly. "Hey, Pete! I haven't seen you since we left Stanford, you old sourdough! And you never looked me up afterward—I told you to. What's the idea?"

"Always meant to," mumbled Peter. He looked around a bit sheepishly, to find Morgan staring at Blake like a friendly pup waiting to be spoken to. "My sister, Blake," he muttered. Blake smiled. She'd been standing back, hands in her pockets, head on one side, gauging this affecting reunion of two old college pals. It seemed to be genuine. She was horribly disappointed, but she smiled generously, and young Morgan responded beautifully, like a friendly pup who's had the kind word thrown to him at last. He liked pretty girls. It was written on his admiring and extremely frank face.

"Your boat?" inquired Peter, going ahead grimly with his duty anyway. He eyed it stolidly, deep eyes steady. "Nice," he said. "Any objections—"

"Sure she's mine," said Billy Morgan. "She's a beauty, too. Came down from Frisco yesterday—just getting ready to pull out again this morning."

"I'd love to see it," said Blake softly.

She was surprised at the reaction she got. A red tide of hot crimson, red as a rose, swept over young Billy Morgan's face. His eyes went hotly bluer than ever with discomfort.

"I'd like to show you over," he said hurriedly. "Love to, Miss Byrne, but—you see, the old tub isn't quite in showing shape just now." His miserable eyes pleaded with her surprised cool ones. "I've just come down from the city in her, and—er—I'd love to show you over some other time. Will you? When I get back?"

"Of course," said Blake, holding him there. At the corner of her eye, beyond him, she saw Peter going into action. He dropped down lightly, for all his bulk, to the white holystoned hardwood deck, and from there addressed his involuntary host nonchalantly.

"You don't mind if *I* go over it?" he asked offhandedly and disappeared down the companionway to the cabin.

Billy Morgan, to Blake's secret surprise, seemed rather relieved at that. If she'd been he, and if he were hiding anything pertaining to Bianca's or Bowden's murders that he'd rather they didn't see, she wouldn't have taken a chance on Peter's passing it up. This man Morgan had been with Peter at Stanford, on the football squad with him—he should have known that Peter on attack was dangerously quick, even with his apparent rocklike stolidity. His mind worked quicker than most people thought it did. That was partly why he was dangerous to go up against, apart from the way he handled his bulk.

Meanwhile she chatted agreeably with the unsuspecting suspect, until Peter, a bit more flushed of face, came running up again to the deck and, jumping off again, made it to the wharf. Here he wrung his host's hand in his own large brown paw enthusiastically, accepted invitations for a visit and a yacht trip in the near future, swept Blake under his wing again, and beat it in an atmosphere of all-around good-fellowship.

"Well?" said a tense Blake, at the end of the wharf.

Peter leaned against a barrel and began to laugh.

"She is blonde and beautiful," he said, grinning. "What else did you expect her to be?"

"Was *that* why he wouldn't let me—"

Peter nodded. "She came down with Billy from San Francisco, and naturally it embarrassed the poor fellow—he's been raised right, Blake—when another fellow's sister was going to find her there."

Blake sighed. "Anyway, he didn't look like Dennis's 'devil.' What happened?"

"She's beautiful and blonde," reported Peter obediently, "and when I saw her I was struck dumb. She was in a blue satin wrapper sort of thing, and they'd been having breakfast there. Her hair was down over her shoulders, and her mouth was very red. She smiled at me. So I hissed at her, 'What's your name?' and she hissed back, 'June Oliver! I'm with the Honeyblossoms at the Columbia'—and she put out one delectable finger, all pink and pointed and shiny at the top, and put it to a ravishing red mouth and disappeared through a doorway, as we heard poor Billy's voice making valiant conversation above. She's bored with him already, I bet."

"So that's how it's done," mused Blake. "These girls have a great advantage over us. If any nice-looking male hissed at me, instead of hissing back my name and address I'd be obliged by a long line of scandalized Byrne ancestors to smack him down; or else you'd do it for me, I suppose. I've half a mind to join the chorus and see life."

"Yes, you will!" growled Peter.

Blake dropped the subject—for the time being.

"Well, what's Morgan like, really?" she demanded. "Apart from being a nice young man with a taste for chorus girls. Is he—could he be—our murderer?"

Peter shook his head positively.

"No chance," he said briefly. "I knew him when—and all that. He may have blondes in his past, but nothing else dangerous, I'll swear. You saw him, Blake. You can guess what he is. Father's head of a big stock company, Billy plays at the business, sort of ten-o'clock-to-three-o'clock hours with three hours off for lunch and the afternoon for golf stuff. He doesn't need to work, so he plays."

"You ought to know him," said Blake with a sigh. "You were a dear old college pal of his, if what I heard was true—or the half of it."

"Sure I was," said Peter, grinning again. "Sure he's a good guy."

"What do you think of him compared to Dennis? He's an old friend of yours, served a four-year stretch with you, and Dennis is a dear old pal of exactly two days' existence, as far as we are concerned with him. How does Dennis stack up with him? Would you back either of them as a murderer?"

Blake was a bit tense, but determined to see this through. She had to know.

"Morgan?" said Peter slowly, thinking this over. "He's a good guy. I told you that. How do I know if he'd be a murderer? I don't think it would ever occur to a guy like that that you could ever solve a problem, or have an out from a hard situation, by murder. He isn't conditioned to such violent responses to situations. Let me tell you, half of their living, with birds like Morgan, is being conditioned to things in a certain way —the conventional way. Dennis, on the other hand,"—Peter gave his slow, deep-eyed grin again—"Dennis, you might say, is a streak of lightning. I don't think anyone's ever thought of lightning as being conditioned to anything except lightning rods. Dennis's particular genius is that no one will ever quite know what Dennis will do in a particular situation. Not even Dennis. But I do think he's got a lightning rod somewhere around in his spirit that would keep him from murder."

"Peter, darling," said Blake softly, "sometimes you frighten me. You say things that are so extraordinarily true. The sort of thing that Dennis might say, just like that. Only you're not Dennis. You're not clever—but you're deep. You're what Dennis means when he says cleverness is such an overrated quality. He's talking about simplicity and depth—like a clear pool."

"Someone's been kidding you," said Peter, with that untroubled smile of his.

"So," said Blake, "we cross one more suspect off our list. Bowden, Bianca, Morgan, and Dennis says to cross off Wong. He says men don't die for love any more. Don't they? Maybe he's right, after all."

"I don't know about Wong, but we're right about Morgan, I'll tell you that," said Peter. "For one thing, he wouldn't have knifed a woman in the back."

"He might have," said Blake stubbornly. Peter shrugged.

"The *Margarita's* moving!" he said. "He's got the engine warmed up. I guess he's going to make the run back now."

They gazed at the slim white launch slipping off its moorings, edging slowly out from the pier, barely adrift in the crowded harbor.

Blake laughed suddenly. "Do you remember those rotten puns Dennis made?" she asked, a bit wistfully but with her eyes shining. "They were so terrible I liked them! I was thinking how true one of them was— the Morgan-Attic one. It did turn out to be that sort of a menage."

"He ought to be hung for them," Peter agreed, with a fatal absent-minded facility of phrase.

Then Blake broke down. For a terrible moment, tears reached as high as her heart. She couldn't help it.

She heard Peter's voice from a long way away, while she stood there drowning in that dreadful slow tide.

She stood there looking—not seeing anything—until her eyes caught the white *Margarita* as that shining thing put to sea, lightly as a feather floating on the blue water.

The tide receded. It might come again—would, she knew—like a sort of terrible awareness of what was happening, was going to happen, to Dennis, to herself, to life. But for the moment she was King Canute, and the wave *had* obeyed her.

She looked out to sea and grabbed Peter by the arm. The *Margarita* was curtsying to the harbor, putting about in a graceful arc of a gesture, her wake white-trained behind her. A woman was on the deck now, looking about her. Her gilt head was bright above a slimly wrapped heavy Spanish shawl, fringed and covered with embroidered red roses.

"Peter," said Blake, "look! She's wearing a shawl—a Spanish shawl!"

"What of it?" asked Peter, following that gay slim figure in the heavy silk with his leveled blue gaze.

"This!" said Blake huskily. "Don't you remember? Bianca had a shawl, too—and it was a white one, with red roses on it! He couldn't get rid of it—so he gave it to her to wear, thinking no one would connect him to it!"

"Lots of girls wear those kind of shawls," said Peter.

"White—with red roses?" asked Blake swiftly. "How come it's the same colors?"

"Listen," Peter said, "you may be right—they never found the shawl. But Morgan never gave it to this girl. You may be right about his being a murderer—Billy Morgan—and I may be wrong about that. He may have knifed Bianca. I don't know what devils a man may have in him; I don't think anyone really knows. But I am sure—I'm dead sure—that Morgan, even if he was a murderer, would never on this earth give another girl a shawl that he'd swiped from dead Bianca. I'll lay anything on that."

When Peter spoke like that, it was so. It had reached a far integrity inside him incorruptible as gold, unshakable and earthquake-proof as the center of the earth.

"But," said Peter grimly, "I practically made a date with her, and I'll get the truth out of her. I've got her name and theatrical company, and I'll look her up."

"Peter," Blake said suddenly, in a curious husky gasp, "of course! Don't you see it—her theatrical address? She's a member of the *Honeyblossom* company— and don't you remember, we found that among the people on Dennis's hotel corridor, right across the hall from his door, were a musical-comedy couple from the *Honeyblossom* company? These people were all—Dennis's neighbors that night."

XVI. GOOD-BYE TO BIANCA

Morgan might or might not be a murderer; but Wong wasn't. Dennis knew that as unshakenly as ever Peter reached rock-bottom truth in himself.

Then where was Wong?

To Blake, in his note, Dennis made light of Wong's going; but he couldn't make light of it to himself. He sat in the back seat of the big police touring car, going up the peninsula highway to San Francisco at a sixty-mile clip, and he went over and over that in his mind. Sullivan sat beside him, twice as large as life in a big rough overcoat. Could he tell him about Wong? He didn't know. He might think—what Peter and Blake had already figured out. That Wong was a killer. Or that Dennis himself had put Wong up to killing Bowden, if not Bianca.

So Dennis sat a bit huddled, and silent, in his corner of the car and thought, "Where's Wong?"

Father Malletti had disappeared; now Wong had gone. Was there any connection? Had Wong gone willingly? Or had he gone—as Father Malletti had gone? He didn't know; but he'd have given five years of his life, or his good right arm, to know that Wong was all right. Dennis had stayed away from him for one forgetful-seeming year; he'd come back as casually as if it hadn't had much meaning for him, to be greeted by Wong again; but Blake had known, what Dennis now knew, that every Odysseus wants to find home unchanged when he comes back to it after one or many years. Dennis loved his place and all that was in it, though, like Odysseus, he'd been loving it at a distance, and he knew that Wong was his family. He didn't want him to be mixed up in murder. He wanted him in his proper place, wherever young master roamed and whatever he got mixed up in. And he wasn't in that place now. It was disturbing.

He could take care of himself and take what was coming to him, Dennis thought—but he couldn't take care of Wong. Darn families! They were the dickens of a responsibility. They took the half of your curse upon them, whether you wanted them to or not.

Only he couldn't quite still that queer ache in his heart.

So they came up the straight white road through the rain-clouded peninsula towns, past the Stanford fields, brown turning to a spring green in the November rains, past the tall avenue of eucalyptus trees at the deserted track of Tanforan, past the fields of the flower growers, the round hills of South San Francisco and the green graveyards there, into the wet gray streets and the gray hills of San Francisco, and the rain-washed purple violets and the dull burning of chrysanthemums on the corners under the big umbrellas, and the hurrying crowds, like the waves of the sea coming up from the foot of the shining gray streets.

Their siren cut through noise and traffic like the bow of a big liner through a choppy sea; they raced across the city in a shriek of sound that assaulted the populace as physically as ever the weight of their big dark touring car could.

Dennis saw blurred things he knew flash by—the clock on the corner as they crossed Third and Market, at Kennedy's place of business, the *Star* Building; slim copper-brown flash of Lotta's fountain, as they crossed the busiest corner in San Francisco, and the traffic held back for them on both sides; faces looking up, all along the sidewalk, startled, pale, seen and passed in a second; Kearny Street, the Hall of Justice tall and gray on their right-hand side; the Italian quarter beyond, as the hills began to climb to the north; the narrow gray hill streets, the gay-awninged restaurants, the children, brown-faced and beautiful, playing shrilly all along the streets, the fruit stores spilling over with bright oranges and red apples and bananas, lavish Florentine style—this was Bianca's country. Even the furtive little places with close-shut doors and blank windows, the soft-drink places, the pool parlors—these were Bianca's sort of things. She was a home-grown goddess, and the patroness of such places; the petty bootleggers as well as the gay restaurants flourished under the protection of her heavy-fringed shawl. Ceres for grain, the goddess of the harvest; but Bianca Farnese for red wine, the goddess of the grapes, Dennis thought, in California.

Her people were out to do her honor; it was more like the winter festival of the death of a goddess than a real funeral, Dennis thought. Perhaps it was incredible that Bianca could die, or that she wouldn't come again, in the spring, out of the hillside vineyards of Napa, out of the warm brown dust of the Santa Clara Valley, when the fruit trees were white in April like great sheets spread out over the brown earth. This was solemnity, but it wasn't really a funeral; it was a form.

Yet she'd been killed. Didn't any of these beautiful brown-faced children with the dark hair and the great dark eyes, didn't any of the bovine-eyed beautiful madonnas, the sleek fat men, the thin, keen men—didn't any of 'em know how Bianca died, by whose hand? Wasn't there a whisper of the murderer's name running through the quarter? It seemed incredible, incredible as Bianca's being dead, that they had no suspicion of her murderer. In a case like this, there were always whispers of names—among one's own people.

But none of them knew. If they had, they'd have told the police, in this one case. For Father Malletti was missing, and he was concerned in it, too. Dennis saw how quiet they were, standing in the streets, filling the street before the place where Bianca lay dead. He saw the storm-hush over them, and he knew then why it was that they weren't mourning Bianca more. For Father Malletti was missing. They were attending Bianca's funeral and her inquest, but they were thinking of Father Malletti. There would be women as beautiful as Bianca with every spring, and like pagan goddesses they might die with every winter, but Father Malletti and his faith didn't change with the seasons.

Dennis went up the steps between Sullivan and his partner Cassidy, and the crowd parted to let them go by. They walked into the overpowering sweetness of flowers, the sort of flowers that go with funerals—roses and carnations and lilies, too sweet and close. He had to breathe them in, like heavy perfume. There wasn't any other air in the place.

Dennis didn't like to see dead people. Yet he'd already seen two or three of them dead by violence, disordered, with the marks of their deaths on them. It wasn't as bad as now deliberately going to see the dead laid out in order. He found that he was shaking—little shivers of cold nervousness that ran over him like wind in the leaves of a slim aspen tree, never quite dying down to calm. This was worse than the first finding of her dead— because he knew what was coming. He was going to look at her again. The other time, he hadn't known—he'd just stepped in and found her lying there, the eyes open—now he had to do it all over again, deliberately. That terrible half-superstitious dread of the dead came over him again. It was like looking at creatures from another world. They were dead. Let them go in peace, without looking at them!

He stood with his head bowed a little, swayed, felt Sullivan's hand hard on his arm.

"Confession of guilt," he thought, dazed. "Murderer overcome by view of victim. I mustn't."

There'd be reporters here, police detectives, too—all watching him to see how he took it. Brace up, Dennis! Only—he'd had no sleep the night before, he'd kept seeing terrible things, and he was tired, and the heavy drenched air dazed him, sickened him with its sweetness. He was deeply afraid of death, of the dead, a primitive fear far inside of him.

But fear saved him. He was drugged by it. He moved forward dully, automatically, to the heap of flowers in the center of the expensively decorous, carpeted room. Guided by Sullivan's hand on his arm, he came to the side of the flowers, spilled in a rug of red and white over the casket, and raised his eyes and looked at dead Bianca's face.

There wasn't any shock. There was only, after a second, a sort of blessed relief. She was dead, but she wasn't—different. Her eyes were closed. But the beautiful lines of brow and cheek and chin remained, the lips were folded in marble calmness, her hair was as red as red gold. Was this what he'd feared? All the panoply of death, yes; all the paraphernalia and the majesty of death; he'd feared these. But the paraphernalia and the majesty of death led only to this—to sleep.

The utter peace of untroubled sleep was on that calm face. She wouldn't ever wake. She was done with them all.

Dennis looked at her fully, took leave of her, unhurried, at peace himself again. You couldn't be afraid —of her. He didn't know whether she was in a far country, or whether she had gone out for good like a light blown, out, but he knew that there was nothing to fear in what she had left behind her. She had no more use for it.

She had cast off beauty, the beauty of red hair and sea-blue eyes and a goddess's mouth, the beauty of a long white neck, of a walk that men remembered, a body like a goddess's braced against the wind—it was all here, like a shawl she'd never use again. She'd left it behind her. That was all.

Dennis sighed. It was all right. She'd gone. She had her peace.

Sullivan touched him. "Recognize her?"

"Oh, yes," Dennis said.

"That's all right then. We're through here."

He went away from that room in peace, wrapped in calm.

The coroner was holding his inquest in another sort of a room entirely—no thick gray carpets here, and rugs of red roses and white lilies, and suave attendants. The room was bare-floored, businesslike: long center table, chairs around it, other chairs lined up in rows for the jury and the spectators, a table for the press, windows dingy with the grime of officialdom's drabness.

They came in late. The inquest had begun. They had to push their way through the crowd before the door, and the room inside was crowded. The coroner's jury was in the row of chairs up front, the press table was jammed with men like the press box at a Big Game, Dennis thought fleetingly, and the witnesses sat around the center table with some lawyers. They couldn't be anything else. Lawyers! The word gave him a shock. Peter was more than twenty miles away—he was nearer two hundred, if he was still at Delroy or at Monterey Bay.

And the inquest might decide whether the police would hold his client or not.

Sullivan and Dennis emerged from the spectators like divers coming through the breakers. They came out at the center table. Sullivan began whispering to the coroner, after he'd put Dennis at a chair a bit apart from the other witnesses. The jury, a group of respectable-looking citizens, gazed at him with intense curiosity. The press table began whispering and writing furiously. Dennis felt fearfully and terribly conspicuous. Peter would have made a darned good windbreak then.

Sullivan came back and dropped heavily into the vacant chair between him and the rest of the witnesses and lawyers. The coroner, a small round man, partly bald, with a clever, round face, turned to the witness he'd been questioning in the stand. This was a fresh-faced young man, with very blue eyes and very sooty brows and lashes, and a very rugged sort of chin and tenderly humorous, cynical mouth. His cheap suit was all right, quiet and brown, and his tie was something terrible. Dennis liked him. He thought he knew him.

"Who's that?" he whispered hoarsely to Sullivan. "What're they doing?" Sullivan, he thought, might as well make himself useful as a guide as well as the guard for Dennis that he evidently was.

"Filling up time until we came," Sullivan informed him behind one huge hand. "He's taking all the hotel people now. That's the elevator chauffeur, Malloy."

In the jury row a motherly looking large matron gazed at Dennis with mingled emotions on her usually placid face. She felt that this dark-eyed and desperate, white-faced young man appealed to her natural kindliness—and yet she'd heard that he might be a criminal, and it was perplexing. You couldn't feel motherly toward a murderer, she thought.

"Er—Mr. Malloy," said the coroner dryly, "you've heard the testimony given by the clerk at your hotel. He says that Bianca Farnese—the deceased—came directly through the lobby to the elevator."

"Yes, sir."

"You were on duty at the elevator then?"

"Yes, sir."

"Did you notice the time then?"

"No, sir, but it must have been jist before twelve o'clock, I'd say."

"You can't fix a more definite time when you took the deceased up in your elevator?" the dry, precise voice persisted.

Dennis began to feel sweaty hot and then too cold. He knew that a lot hung on this question of time, not to make a pun of it, either. He didn't know how long it took to do a murder, but he knew the jury'd think it took several minutes at least to work up to an unpremeditated killing, a quarrel first, probably, and a bit of argument to heat the blood. Cold-blooded killing was different. That took a question of seconds. He knew, and Peter and Blake knew, that that was what had actually happened that night in his hotel room. It had been a cold-blooded killing. But the jury, and everybody else who thought Dennis might have done it, would think it had been preceded by enough argument to make it unpremeditated. A man didn't come home from a radio station and stab the woman he found in his room just like that. There had to be preliminaries.

Had there, in this case then, been time for those preliminaries between the coming of Dennis and the alarm he'd turned in? He fervently hoped not.

They were getting to it now, though.

Malloy couldn't fix the arrival of Bianca definitely, more than "jist before twelve, sir. The theayter and dancing crowds hadn't gone up from the ristaurants and hotel ballrooms yet, and they came around anywheres from twelve o'clock on. It was the quiet sort of time, sir, for the elevators, though the lobby was full."

"All right. You saw Bianca Farnese at the funeral parlors earlier this morning?"

"Y-yes, sir." Malloy moved his tough big hands in his lap. His eyes were dark.

Dennis thought, "He feels the same way about her as I do."

"Do you identify her—the deceased—as the same woman you took up in the elevator that night—three evenings ago—at about eleven forty-five?"

"Yes, sir!"

"You couldn't make a mistake from among a million women, with her," thought Dennis.

"What directions did she give you? Did she ask for any room number, or floor?"

"She jist said 'Fourth, please,'" Malloy remembered in a low voice.

"There was no further conversation between you?"

"No, sir. There was not."

"How was she dressed?"

"She had on one of them white shawl things, with her hair coming down to her shoulders," Malloy said.

"Did she wear any jewels?"

"Sure, she might have, sir. I wouldn't know," Malloy said in a troubled voice.

"Her hair was shining right in your eyes," thought Dennis. "You wouldn't have seen them if she had been wearing diamonds."

He rested his arm on the rather dusty oak table and regarded Malloy intently with his chin resting in the palm of his hand.

"Well, what happened then? Did you take her up to the fourth floor?"

"Of course," said Malloy a bit blankly, looking at the coroner with frank surprise. "Why wouldn't I?"

The shadow of a grin went around the room.

"I didn't think you'd take a guest to the basement if she asked for the fourth floor," explained the coroner a bit testily. His baldness turned a bit pink, too. "I'm asking you this merely for the purpose of the records. We must have a definite statement of events. Suppose you tell us just what happened when you took the deceased up to the fourth floor."

"I stopped the car, opened the door, and the lady got out," Malloy said. The big hands moved again, uneasily, in his lap. "That was all, sir."

"How long did you stay with the car up there after she got out?"

"Not a second, sir. I shut the door and went downstairs again—the light was on from the lobby."

"Did you notice anyone—anything unusual at all—in the hotel corridor as you opened the door for her, and in the time she took stepping from the car?"

"No, sir. There wasn't anything."

"Where was she when you went down again? Had she stopped in the hall, or had she kept on walking down the corridor, do you know?"

"She walked right off, sir. To the right. I could see that. She didn't have to stop at all to look around."

"You didn't notice any room doors open, or ajar? Were the lights in the hall on as usual?"

Malloy paused briefly, to answer both questions. He raised his dark blue eyes, sooty-lashed, in a level look at the waiting room.

"The doors were all shut, sir, as far as I could notice. The lights were on jist like they always were—are. The last I saw of her, she was going down the corridor, and I saw the back of her red hair and her white shawl going away down the hall."

Dennis caught his breath. It made a harsh sound like a rasp in his throat, and he hoped Sullivan and the others hadn't noticed. He couldn't help it. He thought somberly, "Down the hall—into darkness. Into—my room . . ."

That was the last anyone had seen of her—except the murderer. The red hair shining, and the slim white-shawled back, walking like a goddess—into darkness, in that soft-lit corridor.

The others hadn't noticed the sound he made. Only Malloy with his grave dark blue eyes looked at Dennis briefly, and the two of them held that look level for a second.

The coroner was asking, "Did you see what time it was when you got down to the lobby again?"

"No, sir. I did not. There was a party—a lady—could tell you—"

"We'll call her later. Let's get on with your testimony. You took the deceased up to the fourth floor, had no communication with her except the words 'Fourth floor, please,' and left her there walking away to the right-hand side corridor. Then you immediately brought the car down to the main floor level again, as you saw the light signal on your board. That right?"

"Yes, sir."

"No communication!" thought Dennis scornfully, of the little dry-voiced coroner. "You fool! She didn't have to say things to you. She stepped into that guy's elevator and out again, and he'll never forget her as long as he lives. There'll be a sort of brightness dazzling him all the rest of his life."

However, you couldn't say things like that to a coroner. Dennis sighed, and shifted his elbow more comfortably, and dug his chin in, and followed events closely.

They were coming to him now.

"You took these people up to the seventh floor," the coroner was repeating. "You passed the fourth floor twice, once coming up and once going down. Did you stop on the return trip going down?"

"No, sir, I did not."

"At any floor?"

"No, sir," Malloy said patiently.

"Did you hear or see anything on the fourth floor on either occasion you passed it?"

"No, sir."

"Or on any further trip you made?"

"No, sir."

It was like a patient litany, in a gray Celtic voice.

The coroner gave up.

"Well, we come to the arrival of the hotel guest in whose room the deceased was found," he commented. "At what time, Mr. Malloy, was it, should you say, that Mr. Devore entered the hotel lobby?"

"It was afther twelve o'clock a bit—more than a bit," Malloy answered, consideringly. "I'd say—around twelve-fifteen, sir."

"You've heard the testimony of the manager of Station KDO, the broadcasting station," the coroner reminded the jury and the interested room, "that Mr. Devore's program ended at twelve o'clock, and that he left promptly."

"Oh, my cat's whiskers," commented the equally interested Dennis gleefully to himself. "They had to drag that guy in. I bet he was about ripe for murder himself, being hauled away from the studio like that on a busy morning."

"Leaving the broadcasting studio, which is situated in the Market Street district," the coroner went on precisely, "and arriving at the Hotel Ancaster, on the hill district to the north of Market Street, would be a trip of about five minutes on a street car, or about fifteen minutes' uphill walk, that is, if the walker were a young man and brisk."

He shuffled papers for a second.

"That is, the times twelve o'clock at the broadcasting station and twelve-fifteen arrival at the hotel would agree, if Mr. Devore had walked from the studio. We have the hotel clerk's testimony, you'll remember, that it was actually 'some time' after twelve—that is, not directly after twelve—that Mr. Devore came in, although he didn't know the exact time. He did not stop at the desk for his key—he apparently had it with him. Mr. Malloy, will you tell us anything you remember about his arrival? Anything—you can think of?"

"You mean," Dennis thought grimly, "did I come in all wild-eyed and ready to kill any visitor I had."

Malloy didn't look at him.

"He come in—well, prompt," he replied, echoing the. manager of the studio unconsciously. "Like he always does—as if he was going places, and in a hurry."

"Indeed?" said the coroner. "What was his appearance? His clothes?"

"He didn't have a hat," Malloy said. The room leaned forward at that. It sounded promising—coming in in a hurry and without a hat on a foggy midnight. Malloy disappointed them, and so, to a degree, did Dennis.

"He hardly ever wears a hat," that honest young man informed them. "At least, I've never seen him with one, all the times I've took him up and down in the car."

"Was he wearing an overcoat?" the coroner asked.

"No, sir," Malloy said. "Sometimes he wears one and sometimes he don't, but he wasn't that night. That's why I thought he'd been walking, let alone the time he come in. He wasn't cold-looking, he was briskcolored like he'd been walking up the hills in the fog."

"That's why I walked," said Dennis to himself. "It was a swell way to get warm that night."

"All right. Then what happened?" The coroner made his favorite move again. "Tell us just what happened, what was said, everything."

"Well, Mr. Devore, he come—came—charging in like he does, and walked across the lobby, and into the car. There were two others, a couple, came in then, and I took them all up together. They got off at the third, and he went on to his floor, and just said 'Thanks' when I opened the door for him to get out there. He walked off down the right-hand side of the corridor, to his room, I guess."

"Oh, yes," thought Dennis. "It was—to my room, all right."

He wanted to bury his head in his hands at that memory. He'd been feeling swell, a sitting-on-top-of-the-world sort of feeling that comes to brisk young men who've been walking up San Francisco hills at midnight in the fog and lights and sounds of a city in their eyes and ears, and then he'd opened the door of his room—onto darkness and murder and nightmare happenings. He wanted to bury his head in his hands and shut it all out. He couldn't. He sat there with his eyes dark, no reflections at all in them.

There was the slight stir of concluding testimony through the crowded room—a shuffle of movement, a murmur of whispers.

"Er—one moment, Mr. Malloy," said the coroner, looking up dryly as the witness moved tentatively, too. "One more question: Do you recognize Mr. Devore from among those in the room now?"

Malloy's deep Irish eyes rested on Dennis for a second.

"Sure I do," he said. "That's Mr. Devore there," and he half pointed at him. The room made that stir again, as everyone turned to look in Dennis's direction.

He stood up, automatically. The coroner seemed to expect it of him. He felt like Exhibit A being shown off.

"Is Mr. Devore wearing the same suit he was wearing three nights ago, when he came into the hotel just after twelve o'clock, can you tell me?" the coroner asked hopefully.

"I think so, sir," Malloy answered conservatively.

He looked at it intently. Dennis looked down at it fondly. He liked that suit. He'd paid a lot more for it than he should have, and it didn't look aggressively expensive, and it stood up under hard wear like a thoroughbred. It was dark, almost black stuff, but with a little pattern of white running through it like light on a black night. It had been his constant companion these past three days and nights, too—he'd gone to two jails in it, gone man-hunting in it, he hadn't had it off him now since he'd dressed at Kennedy's and borrowed shorts and socks and things from that elephant-memoried gentleman yesterday morning, and it was still good enough to stand the gaze of the coroner's jury and the spectators. He loved it. He always felt for it as a man does who has paid more than he should have paid for a good dog or any thoroughbred who is worth the money—that he'd got a lot more than his money out of it.

So Dennis looked down at it fondly, and the coroner's jury and the crowd and the press table looked at it with more varied emotions, among them fascinated horror. This might be . . .

"Looking for bloodstains," Dennis thought. "I suppose they'll call it the 'death suit.'"

"Thank you, Mr. Malloy," said the coroner now. "That will do."

There was the slight stir, more decisive now, of a concluding witness. Malloy stepped down and came to the long oak table and dropped down heavily at his chair up near the front. The hotel clerk, a dapper gentleman who, Dennis had always felt, should have been a radio announcer, got up when his name was called again, went up and was sworn in again and briefly asked the same questions that had preceded Malloy's dismissal.

"Do you recognize the man who came into the lobby at a few minutes after twelve that night?" He did, and pointed Dennis out, by name.

"Is he, do you know, wearing the same suit he was wearing when you saw him come in that night at that time?" The hotel clerk thought he was. He hadn't noticed him especially. Thank you, that was all. He stepped down, dapperly.

XVII. DANGER NEARER TO DENNIS

They called the lady who'd looked at her little diamond-set wrist watch as the elevator with Malloy and Bianca in it had reached the fourth floor that night. She was slim and cool and blonde and very well dressed, with nice make-up, a small blue hat, a tailored dark blue suit, and a brown fur that even Dennis thought might be a couple of sables around her shoulders.

"And what time was it, Mrs. Armstrong, when you looked at your watch that night?"

"It was—just—three minutes of twelve."

Her voice was cool and low and somehow amusedly detached in spite of its levelness. She didn't look at Dennis all the while she was on the witness stand. She carried her good manners and her breeding into even the distasteful duty of an inquest on murder, and she extended her manners even to a person suspected of that murder. Dennis wanted to thank her for that.

The coroner did, but not for that. He thanked her for adding another link to the evidence which might form a chain to snap around Dennis or around some "person unknown."

"Thank you, Mrs. Armstrong."

"Not at all."

She stepped down and sat quietly at her place again, gloved hand against her chin, listening.

"Madam Chairman," thought Dennis. "Or Madam President. She'd listened to meetings a lot."

They called the hotel manager next.

Dennis didn't know much about him, except that his name was Fersen, he was a Swiss of some sort, and he didn't have any use for Dennis at all.

Dennis didn't blame him much for that last. No hotel manager wants to see his hotel in the papers with an "X Marks the Spot" caption on it.

He was a rather pleasant-looking sort of man, brown done in tones of autumn coloring—face a bit full, but nice easy smile, brown well-brushed hair with a mere hint of red in it, brown shining eyes with a bit more red in them, figure square and very well dressed, square hands that he occasionally used to gesture with. A man who wanted to be pleasant, ordinarily—to get along with people. Yet a man accustomed to getting his own way, to being a bit of a disciplinarian, as a good hotel manager had to be. He could be, as Dennis had found out, brusque.

"You know this man—Devore?" the coroner asked as a form of beginning, indicating Dennis.

"I know him—yes," Fersen said guardedly.

"As a guest of your hotel?"

"He was." The answer was brief but somehow pretty comprehensive.

It sounded, thought Dennis uneasily, as if he hadn't quite realized what he was implying. It sounded as if he'd fired Dennis out of the hotel, wouldn't have him on any terms—as if he'd found out something about him— murder, maybe.

"He isn't there now?" the coroner followed that up quickly.

"I haven't seen Mr. Devore," the hotel manager stated distinctly, "since the night—the body of Mrs. Farnese was found in his room. He apparently hasn't returned to claim his luggage or any personal belongings awaiting him."

That was that. It did sound bad.

"He thinks I was scared to come back to a place where I'd killed a woman," thought Dennis resentfully. "He knows better than that! I didn't kill her! Only—he's making everyone else think that, on purpose. Why?"

It wasn't tangible. Nothing definite. The man was answering questions—yes, and truthfully. It was only in the way he was answering them—giving Dennis the worst kind of breaks, the worst implications.

It wasn't only unfriendliness: he was being deliberately nasty about it, in his pleasant way. The very way he said "Mr. Devore" in quotes was a sort of sneer. He didn't believe in the name, and he made everyone else see that Dennis had a last name that sounded like a chorus boy's dream.

He told of the hotel's brief but too lasting relations with Dennis. Mr. Devore had come in about three months ago—he didn't say from where, or if anyone had recommended the hotel to him. He'd registered from Los Angeles. That wasn't a crime in itself, of course, but unidentified lone gentlemen with pasts might very well come from Los Angeles. Every San Franciscan in the coroner's room knew that the best murders of past years had, in fact, taken place in Los Angeles. Even New York columnists had commented on it. A round half a dozen could come to mind—the Phillips hammer murder, the terrible Hickman crime, the chicken-farm murders, Mrs. Patty's killing, whose murderer is still being hunted—oh, there was quite a list to choose from. And Los Angeles was a swell place to come from if you had to come from somewhere, so to speak. In that big, sprawling, tourist center of a city, trails and the beginnings of trails might be conveniently lost and never traced back.

Mr.—er—Devore, in fact, had conveniently come from Los Angeles out of nowhere, with no friends, and had established himself at the Ancaster with no further recommendations. They all got that.

They were meant to get it, Dennis discovered in a helpless anger. It was put that way deliberately. Good Lord, did this man, this respectable man, hate him, the unrespectable, so much? It was like a class war. He knew why I.W.W.'s went blind with rage and surged to burn and destroy. It was a helpless feeling, seeing society, respectable society, down on you like that. It was the anger of the cornered.

They were told further about Mr. Devore. In strict answer to the questions put by the coroner, the hotel manager told them that he had no friends visiting him, that he paid his bills promptly, gave extremely little trouble—"sitting quiet because he didn't want to be noticed" was the version Dennis gave this, with the courtroom following suit—and that he hadn't been seen with any woman. This was given reluctantly, though honestly, and everyone got the reservation in Fersen's mind, that just because he hadn't been seen with any woman at his hotel didn't mean he didn't know any. He probably wanted to keep his woman friends out of the hotel to avoid talk about him there. He sure kept to himself in his room there, eh? Not exactly hiding—just "giving no trouble" to the hotel staff. Unobtrusive.

They went into the events of the night of the murder. The hotel manager acknowledged that he'd heard that Dennis sang over the radio. He hadn't heard him himself, he believed. He'd just heard that was what Mr. Devore did. He hadn't seen him come in that night, either. The office, where he was working late that evening, was on the ground floor of the hotel, but on a back corridor, away from the lobby and public dining and ball rooms. It was accessible to the kitchens and the chefs offices and the hotel garage, which were in the basement, and connected of course with all departments of the hotel by telephone through the switchboard in the lobby. It also had a back stairs near it, and a service elevator.

"You didn't see either Mr. Devore or the deceased—Bianca Farnese—enter or leave the hotel then, Mr. Fersen?"

"No."

"Could you tell us about when you were in your office that evening—the approximate times?"

"I was working there from about eleven o'clock on—until I was interrupted by news of what had happened on the fourth floor."

"Did you leave the office for any extended time during that time—between eleven o'clock and, let us say, the interruption?" the coroner asked briskly.

A slow red began to creep up the well-fleshed cheeks of the hotel manager. His hands fiddled a second with each other, then one of them began to turn a solid signet ring around his third left finger. The coroner hastened to turn away any coming signs of a storm.

"I'm asking this," he explained precisely, "in order to get everyone's action quite clearly set out during that evening—everyone of whom we have any definite knowledge, or whose actions might interest or influence the murderer. If, for instance, you had left your office open during quite a period of time, might not someone have passed unseen by your hallway, taken the service elevator or even the stairs, to the fourth floor, and there committed the killing?"

The hotel manager quieted down at this.

"He's a hot-tempered bird," diagnosed Dennis. "Not used to having to explain himself or what he does."

"I see," he was saying more graciously. He smiled, that easy and, in other circumstances to Dennis, rather charming smile. He was making himself pleasant. He unbent to explain:

"I didn't, at any time during that evening, leave the office for a long period of time. Twice I stepped into the lobby, once in response to a telephone call from the desk clerk to meet a friend and greet him, once to listen to the music from the dining room. Anyone who used the corridor to my office would have had to pass me then. No one did."

"Thank you, Mr. Fersen. How about someone coming up from the basement offices to use the back elevator or the stairs?"

"It's impossible for a guest of the hotel"—those brown eyes with the red shining in them lit on Dennis briefly for a second—"to wander into the basement unnoticed. Any stranger would have been seen at once."

"There are only two ways to get to these stairs and the elevators, I understand from the chart of the hotel —by the corridor running past your offices on the ground floor, and by entering them at the basement level?"

"That is so. And one other way. You could enter them from the higher floors."

"You suggest?"

"I don't suggest anything." The hotel manager spread those hands of his briefly in depreciation. "But it has occurred to me that one might get off from the front elevator at some floor—say the second, the seventh, any of them—and walk the length of the hotel to use, not the service elevator which is run by an employee, but the service stairs, in order to go up—or down—as he chooses, unnoticed. It would be less conspicuous than using the front stairs, which are for guests and are more likely to be noticed."

The coroner digested this for a moment. Then:

"You said 'down,'" he pointed out. "Do you think anyone, on the night of the murder, used those stairs to go—down, from Mr. Devore's room on the fourth floor? He would have had to go, assuming he was a guest and not an employee of the hotel, past your office to reach the lobby. You have pointed out that the basement descent would have been too perilous for a stranger or one obviously out of place there."

The hotel manager shrugged—a pleasant shrug.

"I don't know," he pointed out in his turn. "It's too mysterious for me to say that."

"He's got something up his sleeve," Dennis thought to himself, watching that well-tailored part of his clothing instinctively. "Wonder what it is."

The coroner went back to events instead of surmises.

But for a second Dennis didn't hear what he was asking. He was sick and cold with a wave of sudden fear that had swept over him. He knew what the hotel manager had been doing, what he'd had up his sleeve. The whole room had known. He had cut anyone—anyone not a recognized employee of his hotel—off from using the back elevator and the service stairs. The murderer had gone up—must have gone up—by way of the lobby and the front elevators, in full view of anyone there.

Dennis had gone up like that.

There wasn't, it seemed, any "unknown" in this case who could have slipped in conveniently.

A hotel, even a crowded popular one, was like a safe. It was pretty well guarded at its strategic points, under a casual exterior of smooth service.

That put it up to Dennis. He'd gone up to his room and then said he'd found a murdered woman in it. Had he had time to do the killing? He hadn't done it *before* he left for the radio station—Bianca, according to most competent witnesses, had come in at about five minutes to twelve. Dennis had been in the radio station then. That ran like clockwork. No question of false time there. Bianca had been walking along the corridor to Dennis's room then. Malloy had been bringing the elevator down to the lobby. Well. . .

That left the problem of time and Dennis to the period *after* he'd left the station. Bianca'd been in his room all that time. Waiting for him? He knew she'd been killed then. But no one else—no one except the murderer—knew that. She might have been waiting for him. He came back, and it was about fifteen minutes past twelve, and she was dead. Somewhere in that time it had been done—it had taken only a minute or two. But no one knew that, except Dennis and the murderer. Even his friends didn't know that. They just took it on faith. . . .

Dennis's eyes darkened there, thinking a second of Peter and Blake—and of Kennedy. He wished Peter could have been here with him. It wasn't any use wishing that, though. And at that, it was a pretty selfish wish. Peter might not want to be standing by with a suspected murderer in the full light of an inquest. It was asking a lot.

Well, then (his thoughts scurried briefly like mice surprised in the dark by a light flashing on them), Bianca had been dead at twelve-fifteen, even if only he and the murderer knew that. What time had Dennis come up to his room, and what time was it that he'd phoned for the police? It sort of hung on that, he thought.

He wasn't counting on anyone's malignity to corner him there especially. He'd underrated the contemptuous hatred felt by one sort of man for another, a different type—the hatred of the respectable for the patently unrespectable artist, the substantial for the unsubstantial, the man of property for the man to whom property was something binding, who didn't, deliberately, want any ties like that.

He'd underrated the hotel manager.

The coroner asked the hotel manager:

"Mr. Fersen, you were, you say, in your office when the telephone girl from the public switchboard rang for you. Will you tell us just what was said in that call, and what time you received it?"

"I don't know," Fersen said deliberately, "that I can put an exact time to it. Doubtless, as it went to the police station, the police noted the time, I should say. however, it was about twenty-five minutes past twelve that the telephone girl notified me that Mr. Devore had put in a call for the Central Police Station, and that he seemed to be having some trouble in making his meaning clear to the officer answering."

The room sort of rose in a whisper of sound, like a wind getting up among trees.

"Er—we'll go into that message more exactly," said the coroner. "Twenty-five minutes past twelve, you said? Thank you!"

"Satisfied," thought Dennis a bit dully. "They all are. Was it that late when I phoned? Must have been. I must have just stood there, looking at her . . ."

He remembered, from a long, long way off, how it had been that night. He'd held onto the edge of the table and gone 'way under for a while. Then he'd thought of telling someone—the police. Then he'd got onto himself and made himself walk across the room, away from Bianca's body, conscious of it—at his back. It must have been around that time that he finally phoned, and got through to that deep-voiced, question-asking officer. Then he'd stammered it out—there was someone dead here, in his room—at the Ancaster—how'd he know what it was about? She was dead— maybe he'd said "murdered," but, funny, he didn't remember that, quite.

Anyway, the hotel manager was saying that. The phone girl had told him that Mr. Devore was ringing up the police and claiming that battle, murder, and sudden death were prevalent in his room. She'd immediately rung up the manager and told him. The manager's instinctive reaction had been to safeguard the good name of his hotel. He'd wondered about calling the hotel physician, decided against it until he knew more about just what had happened, he'd gone up by the service elevator run by a hotel employee, and left that interested man at Dennis's door while he knocked on it, wondered at the silence behind it, and in a sudden spurt of unease had thrust his passkey into the lock and had opened the door—on Dennis and Bianca's corpse, there on the floor.

"What did Mr. Devore have to say about this discovery?" asked the coroner keenly.

"Why—he didn't say much, as I remember it now," Fersen hesitated. "He seemed—dazed."

"Dazed, eh?" Everyone looked at Dennis, dark head bent a little, gaze on his hands locked idly together, lips set tight.

"Why wouldn't I be?" thought Dennis furiously. "D'you think I see murder's work every day? It's your callous guy you ought to suspect, not the man who's bowled over by a glimpse of the body."

"Then what happened?"

"Mr. Devore began to tell me—to protest—that he'd never seen the woman—the deceased—in his life before,"

Fersen said smoothly. Too smoothly. The coroner's jury and the crowd caught it. There was a little whispering sound like a laugh going over the room. It was—funny, at that, maybe. My Most Embarrassing Moment! He'd found a strange woman in his room, murdered. It didn't sound true, somehow. A protest seemed faintly farcical. Sure, he must have known her.

The hotel manager obviously hadn't believed Dennis, and he'd made the room see the impossible side of the crime—that Dennis hadn't known Bianca, even as a casual acquaintance. It didn't sound true, told like that. It sounded as if Dennis had just lost his head then and had protested too much. If he'd come out and said it was an accident—or that they'd both been drinking—or that they'd had a scuffle . . .

Only he hadn't. He'd tried to get out of it, to hush it up. Dennis saw the coroner and his jury and the whole room going away from him, its belief or sympathy or even will to comprehension withdrawing like a tide that left him stranded there. He felt defenseless and very lonely, rather like a mussel left exposed at low tide.

He bent his head and stared studiously at the lower knuckle of the third finger of his left hand. He knew without looking about him what was going on. Sullivan was shifting his heavy bulk in the chair next to him, preparatory to taking the witness stand soon. The motherly-looking lady juror with the placid face and the comfortable width had decided that he was a murderer— that white-faced, desperate young man, poor thing!—and was staring at him with interest and repulsion mingled in her kindly, rather faded blue eyes. The hotel manager Fersen, having done his duty nobly by the city and by his hotel, was stepping down jauntily, sure that everyone knew that the Ancaster had cast out Dennis even before the police had decided to take him in among themselves.

The coroner decided to go catch minnows for bait for a while, and the bigger fellows could lie unmolested on the bottom of the stream with their tails waving gently, facing upstream in position. He called the service elevator man who'd accompanied Fersen upstairs to Dennis's door. That obviously thrilled person, exhilarated by his brief contact with the live wires of a murder case, gave negative information. He'd taken no one up or down that evening except a few employees, all of whom had accounted for every minute of their time and their errands to the manager. He'd seen no one around the corridor on Dennis's floor while he waited outside until the police came. The telephone girl came, red-lipped, blonde-haired, furred, a good deal like a hotel guest— a good imitation, Dennis thought.

No, she hadn't had a call from Dennis's room all evening except—the murder call. Her voice dropped. The room swayed forward.

"Murder?" emphasized the little round coroner. His eyes were very keen behind his spectacles. He wasn't a fool, Dennis realized. He was a clever man.

"Cleverness," thought Dennis forlornly, "may be awfully overrated and a surface quality, but it sure does count, Peter. He may be able to get your client hanged on it, regardless of any deeper superiority you and I may possess."

That would be a joke on—Peter, he decided.

"Well," said the telephone girl, "he asked for the police, and when I got the police and plugged him in through the outside board he began saying there was a dead woman in his room, and would they come around right away."

"And?" prompted the coroner, head poised like a bird—a rather choosy bird selecting his worm.

"And they said they would," said the telephone girl simply.

There was a subdued snort through the room. The coroner's bald spot got pinkish again.

"I mean—what further conversation did Mr. Devore have with the police about this dead woman—did he say, actually, that she'd been killed, or murdered, or did he make any reference as to who she was?" the coroner said brittlely.

The telephone girl got brisk, too. It was the sort of manner she assumed with too impatient customers, Dennis thought.

"No, he didn't," she said a bit snippily. "He said— she was dead. She'd been killed in his room, and he'd found her there. And for them to come at once. So they did."

"Very well," said the coroner. He couldn't ask too leading questions of the witness, of course. He couldn't say suggestively, "Did he actually say she'd been killed with a knife wound in her back, done with a kitchen knife at exactly seventeen and a half minutes past twelve, by one Dennis Devore?"

He'd already tried to lead her to suggest that Dennis knew the woman was murdered as soon as he saw her. That he had accidentally shown too much knowledge of it over the phone. The hotel manager had sort of backed him up in that. But the telephone girl had on the whole thrown him down on it. And she'd had the first-hand knowledge of the call.

She'd plugged in for the hotel manager, gasped out a story that had sent him upstairs, and—that was all she knew until the police came. She hadn't taken the time of the call.

"I bet the rest of the Ancaster got rotten phone service during those minutes," Dennis decided.

A uniformed policeman took the stand, his blue and silver spick-and-span in that rather grimy room. He had a broad face rather rarely done in pink, and a deep voice that Dennis found reminiscent. It was the sort of official voice he'd often found in policemen, especially ones with rarely done reddish broad faces.

They'd met before—over the telephone. At exactly— lemme see—twelve twenty-three p. m. on the night of the murder.

The coroner encouraged him gently. The policeman fixed his hard-boiled small blue eyes on a distant target at the other end of the room and fired words at it.

"I was on duty at the switchboard, sir, and took the call from the Hotel Ancaster. I made a note of the time when I had done so. The call was from a Mr. Dennis Devore, and asked the police to come to the hotel at once as there was a dead woman in his room. There was nothing said of killing or murder at the time by Mr. Devore." The cop took a breath and went on: "I then asked Mr. Devore what had happened. He said he didn't know. He had found the deceased there when he came home."

"Er—thank you, officer."

"I then notified the detective bureau, and Inspectors Sullivan and Cassidy, homicide squad, answered the call."

"Thank you, that'll do."

Inspector Sullivan was called next. He got up, leaving the seat next to Dennis empty, and a few more people got a good look at Dennis. Inspector Sullivan's testimony, given in a quiet voice, was depressingly familiar to Dennis. It was becoming as familiar, that story, as the well-known linked chain of his leash is to a dog. And it was closing around his neck. There'd been no one up there, around his floor and in his corridor, who hadn't had a right to be there, it seemed. There'd been nothing suspicious. Only Bianca going into his room, and Dennis calling the police. That left it up to him. Circumstantial evidence? Of course, but what else was there in this case? There was Father Malletti's disappearance, and the murder of Bowden, the "honest plowman." Murdered near Dennis's ranch, at the time when Dennis was alone near there, with a grudge against him, and with his own gun handy. There was Dennis's former record, concealed from the police.

"A bad habit—finding bodies," thought Dennis, shielding one side of his face with his hand. "They'll hold me, sure. All that about Bowden and the rest'll come out at this inquest. The police don't care if they do tip their hand all at once. They've got me, haven't they? They should worry about the surprise element. It'll all come out, and then the jury'll turn in a verdict mentioning me as recommended for further investigation, and they'll hold me. And the murderer's going loose and laughing somewhere. While Bianca's being buried. At that, I can't blame the jury. That's three killings I've already been mixed up in—Farnese's, Bianca's, and Bowden's. Three strikes and you're out, in any man's league."

He sat up suddenly, dropping his hand away from his face, at hearing the last question from the little coroner:

"Have the police, Inspector Sullivan, found out anything bearing—or that might bear—on the murder of Bianca Farnese in any events or acquaintances of her life?"

"She was a home-grown goddess," Kennedy had said. "Statue of Liberty of North Beach."

She was Bianca Farnese, from a rather bloody and gorgeous sort of fairy tale.

She had been the patroness of gay restaurants and little furtive bootlegging parlors.

Many men must have loved her.

There wasn't one of them that had come forward to say anything that might give up her murderer; there wasn't a restaurant where she'd danced and given her patronage that could tell of her true loves and hates. She'd been seen with this man and that man; she had lived in an apartment near Powell Street, on Nob Hill; she had had a pretty good bank account in the savings department of a big national bank; she might have been a light-o'-love, but to most people she had been more like a lighthouse that flashed its beams in their face, blinding them to anything behind that blazing light of her beauty, her vitality, her generousness.

Now that she was dead, that blinding, powerful light flashed off, a lot of people had scurried for cover like beetles seeking the friendly dark of an under-stone, before the fiercer light of publicity and the police would be flashed on them. Already some of their letters had been recovered, and frankly indignant and terribly respectable gentlemen had had to explain pettishly that she had been only a "friend." The letters may have mentioned money. Well, they had "loaned" Mrs. Farnese some money once when she was ill, and she had asked for it. The letters may have mentioned appointments. Yes, these suddenly frank gentlemen had replied, wiping their foreheads, Mrs. Farnese had wished to consult them about buying bonds, and had written to make an appointment at so-and-so's restaurant so they wouldn't be interrupted in their business talk. Or they had gone home with her after dinner for a cup of coffee and a quiet business talk. The city chuckled, and the police, after a long hard stare at the victims, had reluctantly given up most of the clues of the letters. None of these scared and reluctant gentlemen, dragged so painfully to light as "friends" of Mrs. Farnese, had had anything to do with her murder, they decided. Some of them had alibis, and some of them had acquired wives since their acquaintanceship with Bianca, and some of them, just plainly, weren't murderers. They were gay young men who could have afforded Bianca a lot more than they relished the publicity attending her murder.

"There wasn't," as Sullivan explained to the rather mirthful room hearing these primly official disclosures, "a murderer among them. We made sure of that."

There was a deep disgust in his voice.

"You suggest, then," said the coroner, "that although there were undoubtedly many men in Mrs. Farnese's life, there was no one affair serious enough to cause her killing?"

"I do that," said Sullivan stoutly. "She may have played some of her men friends for easy marks, but the ones she played around with could afford it. And there was no suggestion of blackmailing any of them, in any of the letters they wrote her. It was, on both sides, I should say, a casual sort of affair, a companionship more than usual in such cases."

"Friends with her victims," thought Dennis, eyes shining. "Oh, clever Bianca! She rooked 'em, and they loved it. She was civilized, and she picked civilized men for her sort. All except one. One was a wild beast in her civilized kingdom. One of them killed her. He pretended to love her—maybe he did love her. Only she found out about Farnese, and so he killed her. He didn't play the same game or the same rules as the rest. He was wild, under all his pretense of being civilized."

"Then, Inspector," the little coroner said, "can't you give us any information from Mrs. Farnese's life that might lead to a suggestion of who her murderer was?"

"The police are still investigating Mrs. Farnese's life,"—Sullivan on the witness stand crossed his knees comfortably and went on blandly—"but we have no information as yet to make public—except this: that the man who killed her probably wasn't in the limelight at any time while she lived, as a friend of hers. Otherwise he wouldn't have dared to kill her and think he could get away with it like that. He must have known that every acquaintance and incident of her life would be dragged up by the police after her death, and anyone unquestionably linked with her would be subject to a thorough questioning, if not being put actually under suspicion of the murder. For that reason, then," Sullivan took a deep breath and continued his speech, "we are inclined to think he was someone who has, so far, kept his connection with her a secret. None of the men we've questioned as friends of hers, according to the letters they wrote her, fill the bill in points of time, place, and other circumstances of the killing. Also they've been questioned by the police as to their relations with Mrs. Farnese, which questioning usually brings complete results," said Sullivan dryly. "It's only occasionally the police don't find out the whole truth of a man's story in their questioning."

His eye lit on Dennis for a moment, in passing. Was there—could there be—a sort of flicker of light deep in their small dark depths, like a passing signal? It had never occurred to Dennis before that Sullivan might be a kind of sportsman, feeling a sort of unprejudiced admiration for anyone who could beat him at his own game. But then, reflected Dennis philosophically, Sullivan could afford to feel that kind of admiration—he had, after all, finally hooked Dennis. It was easy to be a sportsman if you were on the winning side. You felt large and generous toward your opponent then.

It would be, anyway, in a split second now, Sullivan's inning. Because Sullivan's statement had put it entirely onto some "unknown," and the whole room knew that Dennis had strenuously denied any acquaintanceship whatever with Bianca Farnese. There couldn't be a more dark unknown in anyone's life than a man who protested he'd never seen the woman in his life before until the time she was found dead in his room. The more Dennis made that statement stick, the more, paradoxically, would he be under suspicion of her murder. He would fulfill Sullivan's sketch of the "unknown" then, to perfection.

Sullivan stepped down from the stand. Dennis was going to testify next.

The coroner was calling out his name.

Dennis felt the way he'd felt only once before in his comparatively carefree life—once when he was in an airplane and the darned thing had suddenly gone wonky, off balance, and begun to stagger and flounder wildly around in the blue air, about five thousand feet up; and the pilot, a friend of his, had pointed with a grin to Dennis's strapped-on parachute and then to the terrible emptiness below, which was coming up rapidly to meet them. He'd known fear then, the dreadful cold fear of utter cowardice, forced to walk off' like that onto nothing. His friend was waiting for him to jump, before he'd leave the plane himself; and he had to do it, by himself. It wasn't so bad, once he'd jumped. It was the decision over himself first that took strength. He'd thought then that if he won over the feat that weakened his physical self to the stuff of water he'd never know such fear again in all his life. It didn't come twice, that sort of thing. He'd be over it, having conquered it once. Once he'd jumped, it was all right. He'd won. He felt good, and as if nothing could ever touch him in that way again. He thought he'd won a sort of inoculation of sheer mental bravery over physical fear, forever.

But now he knew that a man could feel that same sort of fear twice. Even if he'd won the first time. Maybe he would go on feeling it, like this, whenever something extra frightening had to be done and he had to force himself to go ahead and do it. He was cold and weak again, with that fear that was almost unashamed, so strong, so crying out in him.

Things didn't ever end. You never won completely, once, for all the rest of your life. You always had to go on fighting as if every previous fight had never happened before. He knew that now.

He was standing up, one hand resting on the back of the chair, before he went up to the stand to tell away his life, his liberty—his precious liberty that meant his life. He knew now that the long leash had come to its end, that it was tightening, tangling around him. He knew the unbelievable story he was going to tell them all, and how they'd take it. It was the end of his liberty, and so of his life, because when he was in jail no one would bother to investigate any other trail but his. No one except—Peter, maybe, and Blake. What could they do? They could only follow him, and he'd come here, at last.

He didn't blame any of them. He saw now, for the first time, that his story of what had happened was unbelievable, except on the grounds of his guilt or guilty knowledge.

Things didn't happen that way, unless you made 'em happen. Men didn't get murdered all around you, and you not involved . . . unless . . . someone was involving you. No one would believe that, though. Only he and one other knew that was true.

Dennis swept weary eyes briefly over the crowded room, the jury with the shocked and kindly faces in it, the miscellaneous group of witnesses gathered around the shabby oak table. He gave up with a heavy motion of one hand and started up to the witness stand. The coroner was calling him, impatiently, repeating his name: "Devore! Devore!" Then Peter grabbed him.

XVIII. THE MARINES

"Quick," said Peter, "before the gendarmes mass. Where are we?"

"H-how'd you get here?" asked Dennis huskily, instead.

"Flew, you fool. Don't waste time. Where are we?"

"Returns coming in from all counties. Landslide against me, I guess. No final count."

"You testified yet?"

"Just going to."

"What's the coroner like?"

That gentleman was getting ready to go into action and separate the huddle into its component parts. He objected to having unannounced meetings going on in the middle of an inquest, particularly with suspected persons taking part in them.

"He's an er—er," explained Dennis quickly but satisfactorily, with a side glance at that worthy. "Not an error, though. He knows his stuff", but he's awfully slow at a getaway."

"Good enough," said Peter, taking his hands off Dennis and straightening up.

The room, which had been seething a bit like a windy sea, began to subside.

"Mr. Coroner," Peter rumbled above it, standing staunch as a rock in the midst of the excitement, "I represent Mr. Devore here, and I'd like to talk with my client and with you and Inspector Sullivan before we go on further in this inquest. We haven't had a chance to confer yet."

"Sure you can," said Sullivan. "You can begin with us, Byrne. We'd like to hear it."

"Good enough," said Peter again and went on up front. A policeman, uniformed, moved unobtrusively to a place a bit behind Dennis's chair, as if he'd just happened to drift there in the shift of the crowd. The three men bent their heads close together over the coroner's part of the big table, where his papers were massed. You couldn't hear what they were saying, but you could hear the tone of the voices. Peter spoke first, quite a while, deep voice urgent. Then Sullivan spoke, a little shorter. The coroner snapped them up on something, dry and businesslike, as if he'd stamped an okay with his signature on a signed paper, like a formality that ended the conference. They broke it up then.

Peter came back to Dennis, with Sullivan dropping into his chair on the other side. The coroner arranged his papers, regardless of the stares and whisperings that roved around him.

"Er—," he said, raising his partly bald head again, "we'll have Mr. Devore as a witness now."

Peter laid a hand on Dennis's arm as he started to get up.

"You can claim immunity from testifying," he said in a whisper, "if you want. Or you can waive immunity, as you please. Because you're the one witness they're liable to try to pin it onto."

"Immunity?" said Dennis, widening his eyes innocently. "What's that? Do you want 'em all, to think I did it?"

He grinned at Peter, and before Peter could stop him he was up and going forward. Peter gave a subdued grunt, whether of satisfaction or of disturbance no one could tell, and leaned back to watch his client. Dennis, he thought, wasn't afraid to take it, anyway. For anyone whose previous private life bore investigation as little as Dennis's did, he wasn't backward, Peter realized, about it.

Dennis, on the other hand, walking up to the witness chair, simply felt as if the marines had come. Perhaps not in the very nick of time, but enough in time to avenge his dead body, which was satisfactory to him. A man doesn't like to go down in a crowd of enemies and be totally forgotten, and no one even know of the fight he's put up. It's even more satisfactory to have a monument of dead enemies erected over him, and he felt that Peter would attend to any details like that in an elegant manner.

He put up his right hand and was sworn in. He seated himself and waited for the opening shot. It sort of ricocheted and hit him from an unexpected angle. Yet it was only a mere routine question, after all. No one in the room, with the exception of Peter and Inspector Sullivan, and maybe Kennedy if he was there among the reporters, could have known of its unexpected effect. Even the little bald coroner couldn't know.

All he'd said was, "What is your name?"

"Er—er!" stumbled Dennis helplessly for an agonizing second. He turned red, and the room began to titter. He'd forgotten how many names he was supposed to have, and which one he went under here, anyway. They all knew him as Devore, of course. What in the devil was the proper name to give now? Spring a totally new one on them? He thought that might have a bad effect. But after all, he was under oath.

He caught Peter's eye and stopped fumbling. His mouth closed more firmly. Peter was rising from his seat.

"Mr. Coroner," said Peter massively and very respectfully, "my client's professional name is the name that he is known by on legal contracts and in business, and with your permission, the police have agreed to accept that name as his proper one in this case—that of Dennis Devore."

The coroner caught Sullivan's small but wise elephant eye. Sullivan nodded an equally massive head. Peter sat down. For a man who had no idea of what Dennis's real name might be, he'd done pretty well on the spur of the moment, he felt. Of course a broadcasting artist could have a professional name, without any rude questions arising from that fact. It wasn't, then, an alias.

Dennis gave his name. Dennis Devore. His—er— former address, the Ancaster. The coroner asked him if he was returning to that address. Dennis said yes, all his things were there. He'd had every intention of returning to it. The hotel manager stared stonily in front of him at that.

Dennis didn't care. He was still a bit stunned from one amazing fact that had just penetrated his brain: Devore! He was Dennis Devore here! The coroner kept calling him that. Sullivan didn't rise and expose him. There were no questions about his manslaughter record down at Delroy.

Dennis realized in one dizzy second that the police weren't telling all they knew. Neither was Kennedy. He must have kept it quiet, as he'd said he might unless something broke to make it worth his while to spill the whole thing. That encouraged him. It sounded as if they wanted to keep things under cover, after all. For the benefit and surprise of—some other person.

The coroner asked questions that brought Dennis step by step over the route of that night when Bianca died in his room. That journey of his had been pretty well mapped out—by the manager of the radio broadcasting station KDO, by the hotel clerk, the elevator man Malloy, the telephone girl, the hotel manager, the police. Now in Dennis's low dark voice it gained a new interest. He answered questions quietly and briefly, but the room leaned forward and saw pictures as he spoke.

He'd gone up—he'd tried his door—it was locked— he'd had his key with him—he'd put it in the lock and turned the knob, and the door opened—the room was dark—it was a bit stuffy, the windows were all closed— he'd turned on the lights.

"What did you do then, Mr. Devore?"

"I thought of opening the windows," Dennis said.

"Did you open the windows?"

"No." Sullivan slouched in his seat. Dennis went on: "I—I meant to, and then—I crossed the room, and saw — her. The body. Lying on the floor."

"Just a minute," the coroner said. "You heard nothing when you came in?"

"Nothing," Dennis said tiredly. His dark eyes looked at the breathless room without interest, as if he didn't see them all there. As if he saw things, pictures, in his mind instead.

"How was the body lying?"

"On its back. Her—the face was upward."

"Did you touch it?"

"No." It sounded like a dark wing drooping, that low word.

"Did you see any cause of death, or know she was dead?"

"I knew she was dead," Dennis said simply. "I didn't see anything—I didn't know how she died."

"You didn't know it was—murder?"

"No."

It was a dark whisper of a word again, lower.

"What did you do then, Mr. Devore?"

"I called the police."

"By telephone?"

"Yes, through the hotel board."

"There was an interval of time before you called the police, after you'd come into your room and discovered the body?"

"I didn't know it," said Dennis simply. "I—at first, you see, I didn't even know she was there. I suppose it was a minute or two before I saw—the body. Afterwards—I thought I phoned almost as soon as I saw it. Maybe I didn't."

"I see. Er—what happened before the police arrived?"

"I called the hotel clerk," Dennis said. "Then I asked for the manager. He told me the manager had already gone up. The phone girl had given him my message to the police. A few minutes later I heard a knock at my door, and Fersen came in."

"What happened then?"

"We just waited for the police to come." Dennis recalled that brief passage at arms, and decided to say nothing about it. "Inspectors Sullivan and Cassidy came, and after that some reporters and fingerprint men, and— I told them about it."

"I see. Mr. Devore, have you ever seen the deceased before, to your knowledge?"

Dennis shook his head. "No. Never."

Somehow the room didn't laugh at that statement now. It was given too gravely. There wasn't anything funny about it after all.

"You didn't know who she was?"

"No. I didn't know that until—the morning after she'd been killed."

"How did you learn it? From the police?"

"No." Dennis grinned that brief glimmer of a grin over mouth and eyes, as he looked at the press table. "I learned it from a reporter."

There was a subdued but appreciative deep chuckle from the press table. Sullivan turned the nicely done color of rare beef under his brownness of face.

"Er," said the little coroner a bit hastily. There was a polite silence, all waiting for him to speak.

"You can tell us nothing, then, of the circumstances under which the deceased was found in your room that night?"

"The circumstances," said Dennis grimly, "were that someone took her in there and killed her. That's all I know. I'd like to know more about it myself!"

"Quite so," said the coroner. "We—er—appreciate your feeling on this subject. We should all like to know more. Er—can you tell us under what circumstances you came to San Francisco, Mr. Devore?"

Dennis leaned forward in the confidential attitude of one about to tell a longer tale. The room subtly became relaxed, as those about to listen to a life story. He put his elbow on his knee and rested his chin against his fist.

"It was about three months ago," he said engagingly, taking them all into his confidence. "A friend of mine who's a radio engineer suggested that maybe I could sing over the radio. So I did." He grinned, as though it were as much of a surprise to him now as it had been then. "They offered me a contract. So I went first to Los Angeles, and then came up here, and got a try-out at KDO, and I've been here ever since."

"Until this happened," he thought.

He was a Native Son, eh? They knew all about him now. The whole room felt sort of friendly to Dennis, as though they'd known him quite a while. There wasn't anything fishy in his story. His life history was as clear as crystal. He'd explained everything, in those few simple sentences.

Only Peter, and Inspector Sullivan, and maybe the wise little coroner perceived that Dennis had offered the courtroom his whole life all wrapped up in three months, with a fine frank gesture of confidence. His history hadn't gone back beyond that.

But then, most people in the room, if they'd stopped to think about this point, wouldn't have believed that Dennis could have much of a history by now. There didn't seem time for it. The motherly-looking juroress was beaming on him. She knew that her feminine instinct had been vindicated. That nice young man a murderer! It wasn't likely, and she'd known it all along.

Dennis, however, cocked a cynical dark eye at all this sudden relaxation toward him. He didn't dare take it too much to heart.

"Fine!" he thought. "If I could break it off now— What's the use? Now comes the grand exposure. Recent events are going to trip me up so hard I'll discover a new universe. I could have made it, too, if—all those other things hadn't happened."

The little coroner was rustling papers again, with a sound as precise and dry as his own voice, in the stillness.

He looked up.

Dennis took a deep breath.

"Er—thank you, Mr. Devore," said the little coroner dryly.

Dennis stared at him.

The room rustled again, with the sound of many people suddenly alert.

The coroner looked again, a bit testily, as the witness didn't take the hint.

"That'll be all," he said briefly.

Dennis came to. "Oh—er!" he remarked a bit vaguely, but finally he got up and came down to Peter in a state of beginning excitement, eyes shining.

He dropped into his chair beside Peter.

"They didn't ask me a thing!" he protested in an excited whisper. Peter seemed asleep, almost, lying back comfortably, eyes lost in the shadows of his rock-ledge eyebrows. Dennis went on: "Not about anything that counts, Peter—such as, had I ever been in jail before or up for manslaughter, or what Bowden had to do with it, or Farnese, or Father Malletti—or those money orders we found ..."

Peter grunted a warning. The coroner was looking at them even more testily. Dennis subsided. He didn't want to take any more chances on the inquisition chair.

"Ladies and gentlemen of the jury," the coroner was saying, "you've heard these witnesses testify that the deceased, a woman known as Bianca Farnese, met her death in a hotel room on the night of the 3rd of November in this city. The circumstances leading to her arrival in that room and of her death are unfortunately, at this time, er—obscured. The manner of her death, however, was made plain to you by the physician of the police department who examined her immediately after the discovery of her body, and, as he has testified, not more than an hour after her death. The cause of death was the wound made by a knife blade entering her back in such a position, stripped of technical verbiage, as to cause almost immediate death. The knife remained in the wound and was exhibited to you. Efforts to trace it have not been, so far, successful. There seems to be no doubt, ladies and gentlemen of the jury, that this adequately describes the cause of death. The immediate cause, or agency, that is. What further cause there may be—er—you've a pretty good idea, as I've said, of how the deceased came to her death.

"Er—it's been represented to me, by officials of the police department who are working on the case, that this death of the woman Bianca Farnese which we're engaged in investigating may be—undoubtedly, I should say, was—involved with—other recent occurrences. I suggest, therefore, ladies and gentlemen, that you bear this in mind when fixing not only the immediate agency of death, but also if you wish to fix any definite responsibility for the manner of her death on any person or persons. That definite responsibility will in due time, we trust, be legally placed by—er—the courts, with the aid of the police department. I can only suggest this—you are quite free to return your own verdict under the circumstances—but at this time—er . . ."

The jury nodded gravely. That last "er" meant more to them than the whole speech together. It meant all that the coroner meant it to mean. The police had clues, and didn't want to be burdened by a ready-made defendant handed over to them. The jury, in fact, "got" the coroner neatly. He and the police wanted a free hand. All right, they'd get it.

"The long leash," whispered Dennis irrepressibly to Peter. "He wants it, too."

He got it. The coroner's jury consulted briefly, came back, announced when questioned that Bianca Farnese had come to her death through violence, specifically by a knife wound made by the hands of a person or persons unknown.

The courtroom broke up in a great rush of sound. Dennis turned to Peter.

"How'd you do it?"

"This is an inquest, not a trial," Peter reminded him. "That's all they had to do, really. Just say how she died, not who did it."

"Yes, I know," said Dennis impatiently, "but how'd you get them to fall in with that? You know Sullivan wants a definite charge on me so he can hold me."

"Ugh," grunted Peter absent-mindedly, gathering papers.

"Listen, Indian," said Dennis threateningly, "that reticent ugh-ugh stuff you've been pulling doesn't go with me. Explain in words of more than one syllable."

"I made a dicker with the police and the coroner," Peter said. "I offered to hand over the facts about the money orders and Bowden's last words. Kennedy's held all that back until he had something to follow and spring on 'em all at once. In fact, with a great price, I'm afraid, obtained I this freedom for you."

"What price?"

"We're going to have Sullivan come to lunch with us, and then we're going to Tell All."

"Well," Dennis sighed, "I don't care if I do!"

XIX. THE RESTLESS GRAVE

"In fact," said Dennis, "the more I think about it, the more I feel like a rather antiquated safe with the family jewels locked up inside of it and the fake butler, alias Sure-shot Mike, picking away at the lock, and no Rin-Tin-Tin to dash through the French windows at the last minute and rescue the diamonds. In other words, to tell the truth, Peter, we've been carrying pretty valuable information around with us, and if that 'person unknown' the jury was talking about knew that, he'd be apt to take us apart to get at it. He's already," Dennis reminded Peter, grave-eyed, as they put on their overcoats to go, "put Bianca and Bowden out of the way for that very thing—knowing too much about him."

Peter nodded. "He does know now, Dennis," he confessed. "It can't be helped. He knows we know something important. It's like this"—the logical Peter began to make his brief as exactly as if he were going to argue it out with the court listening—"he must have been here today, to see what would happen. It was too important for him to know that, let alone his unholy curiosity. He was here, then, and he knew you were going to be up for a target by the police. Then I come in and say something to Sullivan and the coroner, and the situation changes. I've brought information that lets you out. If it lets you out, it must implicate him in some way, if it's anywhere near the truth. He can't afford to have any glimmering of the truth come out. Not even the beginning of a trail to him. He's been so careful about that! The coroner and the police both let you off easily—too lightly, in view of the information they must have on your recent doings. Follows, then, that my information supersedes theirs. Therefore he knows they've got it now. Q.E.D. The family jewels are in the old safe, and the fake butler knows it now."

"Don't be so darned logical, Peter," Dennis protested. "You take away any appetite I might have had for lunch, if that's a satisfaction to you!"

The room was pretty well cleared by now. Sullivan remained by them, heavily putting on his overcoat. Dennis grinned fleetingly.

The three of them turned to go, and Dennis put a hand on Peter's arm, dragging him back.

"Where's Blake?" he asked hurriedly.

"She's bringing the car back from Monterey," Peter said. "I came up by plane from the Hotel Del Monte grounds there."

Dennis dropped his hand, freeing Peter. "Oh," he said.

"By the way," said that sisterless gentleman, following Sullivan's broad shoulders out of the room, "Morgan's a washout, Dennis."

"I thought so," Dennis said, "when you didn't say anything about him. Oh, well!"

He shrugged and went on behind the two of them, thinking what a battle-cruiser line he had in front of him now—Sullivan and Byrne, both broad-shouldered, tall, heavily built, alike in their rough-coated overcoats swinging along, in their soft felt hats jauntily pulled down over their right eye. Dennis thought the two of them were enough for any battle line.

It was sort of nice, and a relief, after all, to have Sullivan with them. It had been pretty hard on Peter, scouting alone for Dennis.

"Where'll we eat?" demanded Peter, as they stood on the outside steps beside Sullivan.

"Somewhere where it's quiet," Sullivan said. "These places around here are all crowded now. We don't want the world listening in on us."

"I know a place," Dennis remembered. That faint glimmering grin began in his eyes, but his face was grave. "It's a swell place, near here. On a roof."

They found themselves following his lead, along the narrow and crowded hill streets. Dennis climbed the stairs, nodded affably to the dark-faced proprietor in a way which chased some of the anxiety out of his large, dark, mournful eyes at seeing Sullivan there, and chose the same table among the potted plants that he'd had with Kennedy. They not only had a quiet table to themselves—they had a space around it entirely left to them, too. Peter looked all right—respectable, solid, but not official; Dennis was obviously a bosom friend of Alexandro, the boss; but no plainclothes suit could disguise Sullivan as anything but an officer of the police.

The other patrons, under the striped umbrellas and among the stranded sort of palms and things scattered about, gave them a respectful assurance of privacy and a sudden lowered tone of voices.

Dennis dropped into a chair with an air of homecoming and looked around for landmarks outside, under the blue and windy sky of a rainless November day. The warm wind ruffled his hair pleasantly, the sun was warm on his face. It was a swell day.

"What'll it be?" asked Peter.

"Some of the same," said Dennis, taking no chances with the rather illegibly written bill on the table. "And coffee," he added. The proprietor flashed him a smile, and departed, heavily, to his kitchens.

"That's the guy who saw Bianca coming out of the church there, down the street, the night Father Malletti disappeared," Dennis told them in a hushed voice.

"He told Kennedy and me about it night before last—remember? It was in the paper next day."

"All *I* know," said Sullivan bitterly, "is what I read in the papers. And at that, the little rat of a Kennedy has been holding out on us, it looks."

"Well," Dennis murmured, "there's a lot in them just now."

"Suppose," Sullivan suggested, "you tell us what isn't in them yet, Devore."

"All right," Dennis surrendered with a sigh of relief. "Here's the layout, as far as we've gone. Shall I tell 'em, Pete, or you?"

"You," said Peter briefly, beginning to eat.

So Dennis put his clenched hands on each side of his face, sunk his chin in them comfortably, and began to talk, ignoring the slowly congealing food in front of him. He told of their visit to Delroy, of Bowden's coming into their garden at dusk, and of Bowden's strange and last words about Farnese. "He said Farnese was lying on the highway, Sullivan, for a target for any car to hit. He was dead before we—I—hit him!"

"We'd know a lot more if we could get a line on Farnese," Sullivan commented. "He's been dead more than a year, though."

"But his widow," Dennis pointed out, "was killed— only the day before yesterday, Sullivan! That case is still alive, still recent. It must be. Farnese isn't resting easy in his grave, after all. Bowden was right. It's—the restless grave, betraying his murderer after all this time."

"Yeah," Sullivan said only, "but who?"

Dennis shook his head. He went on, but he couldn't get any answer to that question. He went on to the visit they'd paid Bowden—"I told you all about that, except finding the money orders and why we actually went there that night, when you saw me in the Delroy jail," Dennis commented virtuously at this point.

Peter grinned. Sullivan was turning that dull red again, under his tan. He laid down his knife and fork and looked at Dennis.

"All," he repeated. "Sure you did—all except anything that counted. We'd get somewhere, maybe, if you thought to inform the police about this case once in a while. We're in on it too, you know. It isn't your private case. We want to find out what's happened. That's our business. If I find out that you or that little squirt Kennedy have been holding out anything more on me after this, I'll shake it out of both of you at the Hall of Justice. Well, go on. Those money-order receipts—where are they?"

He picked up his knife and fork again.

"Peter's got the money-order receipts," said a more subdued Dennis. "Hand 'em over, Pete, will you?"

This ceremony was accomplished with no other formality than a grunt of acknowledgment by Sullivan. That large, solid gentleman had been shaken to his foundations by a gust of official wrath, and it took his bulk a little while to acquire calm again. He stowed the compact small packet away in his inside breast pocket carefully.

Then Dennis went on, picking his way carefully among the many pitfalls that seemed ready to trip up the unwary who went in threat of official displeasure. He told about the second trip, alone, back to Bowden's dark shack in hopes of catching him there—and its result. Its lack of result, all clues ended in that swift murder and blaze.

"Damned amateurs," observed Sullivan, still simmering, "to let Bowden go like that! Our only direct line on the case! *We* wouldn't have done that. We'd have had a squad of men spread around the shack to pick him up—and we'd have got the killer, too, at the same time."

"No," protested Dennis, "it wouldn't have done any good to wait for the police, and anyway, how could I have done that? We didn't know when we went down there we'd run into this. You had the alarm about Father Malletti being missing as soon as we did. That's what sent us down there. You had the same information on that. Then I only got onto Bowden when I was actually there. I called Kennedy up and told him—it was too late to send anyone down there then from San Francisco and have 'em get there in time."

"You or Kennedy could have called me—or the bureau."

"It wouldn't have done any good. Kennedy didn't know where you were—anywhere between here and Santa Cruz on the coast line. He knew there were cranks' tips coming in all the time along the coast. We had to go ahead and handle it ourselves."

Sullivan was slowly getting convinced. He grunted, more pleasantly this time, a softer, more lenient grunt of almost assent.

"So that was that," ended Dennis, encouraged by that grunt. "Only—it wasn't, Sullivan. I wish it had been."

Dennis's eyes looked darkly out at the bright day, from between his clenched fists. "I wish it had been," he repeated.

"What happened then?" Sullivan asked.

"Wong disappeared," said Dennis simply but rather desolately. "I told.you who Wong is, didn't I? He's a great friend of mine, anyway. He's—I've known Wong for as many years as I can remember back." Dennis's voice had suddenly thickened. He cleared it huskily and said, "You go on, Peter, and tell him. I wasn't there at the time, anyway. I was with the sheriff and Henry back at the jail then."

"There's nothing to tell," said Peter, devastatingly. "That's all that happened. I went out to look for him where he was supposed to sleep and he wasn't there. Bed hadn't been slept in. We waited—Blake and I— until morning and then got the car and went in to Delroy, to the hotel there. He hadn't come back by then."

"Why'd you go to look for him just then?" asked Sullivan keenly.

"Blake thought he wasn't there," Peter said. "So I went to look. And he wasn't. We'd been talking things over, and Blake said that Bowden was shot with a squirrel gun that Wong had been using for the past year; it wasn't Dennis's gun any more; and that Bowden was Dennis's potential enemy, and he'd been killed before he could blackmail Dennis. She—we—thought that the same person might have killed both Bianca and Bowden, because they were both dangers to Dennis—they might both have raked up that old scandal of Farnese's killing, and have blackmailed Dennis about its being a first-degree murder charge, if they knew that Farnese was dead before he was hit by an automobile. And we thought that the person who put them both out of the way was—Wong."

"Listen," said Dennis hotly, "you tell me anything about Wong that we can use against him in this case, and I'll pay you a million dollars—cash. That's what I think of Wong!"

"Then why did he skip?" demanded Peter.

"Probably so he wouldn't have to listen any longer to you two theorizing," said Dennis ungratefully.

Sullivan lifted a heavy hand, checking argument.

"This is a sweet case," he said, in heavy sarcasm. "You say the only reason you can figure out, Devore, why they ever picked on you as the fall guy is that you ran over this dead man Farnese a year ago. Hell, that's no real reason for anyone to hate you so they'd try to pin another killing, a woman's murder, and then another, Bowden's, on you. And get this—there are no direct clues to the killer, if there is only one killer, except these bits of paper in my pocket. The absence of direct clues suggests a homicidal maniac's lack of logically reached conclusions, to my mind. You see, a maniac's mind leaps ahead in gaps that a normal man's mind has to have bridged. A normal man has to have pretty good solid reasons for his acts. Or," said Sullivan meditatively, "maybe we're the crazy ones, not to bridge the gaps with significant clues, probably staring us in the face."

"This is sweet," said Dennis with interest. "Either the killer's crazy or else we are, with betting odds on us. Sullivan thinks we're cuckoo, Peter."

"I wouldn't doubt it," said Peter.

"Or else," said Dennis, "I'm a killer."

"He doesn't think that," protested Peter, as the silence from the other third of the party became a bit uncomfortable.

"What does he think, then?"

"Well," Peter said, hesitating delicately, as he seemed to be the intermediary in this affair, Sullivan smoking on easily, "this may be a little hard to take, Dennis. He doesn't think you're a murderer, I believe, but he does think you're a little cuckoo."

"Hard to take!" Dennis echoed in astonishment. "If I never had anything harder than that to take, I'd be doing swell. That's what everybody thinks, probably including you, Peter."

"Well, you see," Peter grinned, "as your lawyer, Dennis, he does include me."

Dennis turned to Sullivan. "You don't think I'm a killer, do you?" he asked a bit apprehensively.

"No, I'm beginning to get a line on the kind of birds you are," that large and lethargic gentleman answered. "You like to go ahead and do things on your own, have your fun with the bombing squad, so to speak, and let the police department do the mopping-up operations for you afterward. You do all the damage, we clean up the case. That's dangerous work. It's apt to land you in jail as— accessories to murder, perhaps, unless the police know about it in advance. You do too many things on your own."

"You don't think I know anything about Father Malletti's going away, do you?" Dennis went on. "I swear I don't—"

"Listen, Devore,"—Sullivan pointed his pipe at Dennis, all lethargy gone from him now—"if I'd thought there was any chance of you knowing where His Reverence was, you wouldn't be sitting here offering to let me know things—you'd be begging me to take the information as a free gift, down at the Hall of Justice."

"Don't you really know where he went?" Peter asked gravely.

"No," said Sullivan. "Nor who took him there. But whoever it was,"—the big man knocked his pipe out, preparing to get up—"the curse of Cromwell on him."

"It will be," said Dennis. "I'm quite sure of that. Or an even worse one on him now. The curse of—himself. Because we know one more thing about our killer now."

"What's that?" Peter asked, as they went on down the stairs again.

"We've one more thing to add to the killer's description," Dennis said, "if Sullivan's right about the gaps he's left in his crimes. The very absence of clues. We must look for a man with the light of unreason in his eyes at times. The light—"

Dennis stopped there, groping for words, on the very edge of some great discovery, he felt. There was something—he almost knew . . .

They were in the street now, and they saw the tall gray Church of Saints Peter and Paul, with a crowd in front of it, and people coming down its stairs, and automobiles driving away. Bianca's funeral—Bianca's last Mass! Glimpse of flowers piled high—a black hearse, followed by automobiles—going to the green graveyard in the hills of South San Francisco, where Dennis had come past only that morning, very early. The crowd was going away, slowly, people coming past them, jostling—swarthy faces, bright black eyes, curious glances, bursts of excited talk, sudden lowering of voices—Peter and Sullivan standing like large, steady rocks in the midst of this oncoming sea.

Dennis leaned against the wall of the house, waiting for the crowd to go by. His eyes were half closed, concentrated, intent on something in the darkness of his mind. He couldn't quite get it. He frowned a little.

"The light—of madness," he repeated.

He looked up and saw Peter's eyes, those clear and deep blue pools set in the overshadowing rock ledges of his brows, and as he looked he saw the sudden change come into Peter's clear eyes. It was like a sudden flash of sun into them, a light—of warning, danger.

Peter roared out something.

And Dennis, responding instinctively, hearing again the old signals of combat through the years, flung himself forward, in front of Sullivan, arms outstretched.

There were red rockets whirling madly in a black world of pain. Then they disappeared, and Dennis fell forward into the thick, the stifling darkness of a restless grave.

XX. DEAD MEN RISE UP

Dennis sat up and hastily held his head with both hands. He opened his eyes, and the light pierced them like a sharp bright sword. He closed his eyes. He was sitting, he'd discovered, on the edge of the curbing in a practically deserted street. Peter was the only human object looming around anywhere.

"How's your head?" Peter asked.

"It's a rotten head," Dennis said, sick and dizzy with pain. "What happened to it?"

"A bullet tried to make connections with it," Peter said, "but just missed the train. It just grazed you. You're lucky, Dennis."

"I was born to be hung, I guess," Dennis agreed.

He winced as a frightful noise began at the other end of the street and mounted to shatter his head to pieces. Sirens screamed in death agonies, and their echo beat in his brain relentlessly, against his too thin head. It made him feel sick.

"Sullivan's called out the gendarmes," Peter said. "That bullet was meant for him, Dennis, and you took it. He's very peeved."

"Well," Dennis groaned, "don't let him roar at me, Pete. I can't stand it."

He got to his feet in one swift act of will, saw the street swerving and whirling around him, and felt Peter's arm holding him up as he drooped. Funny, it was his head that was hurt, but his legs felt stiff and the world was rocketing around him. A police rifle squad in a touring car roared past them, siren sobbing and then screaming again, and Dennis shuddered.

"Do they have to do that?" he inquired piteously.

"Yes, but we don't have to listen to it," Peter said more practically. "Let's go somewhere."

Dennis became aware of a soft, insistent hissing somewhere. He opened both eyes in a heavy gaze and saw the dark-faced proprietor of the roof garden hovering around, apron anxiously clasped in both not too clean hands.

"Signor," said this person, weepingly, "this is very bad. They shoot you, yes?"

"Yes," said Dennis.

"Ah-h-h," said that somehow comforting dirty and dark person, conveying everything in one simple word: sympathy, execration, promise of brighter things to come, and dolefulness for what had happened to a patron of his. Dennis felt encouraged. He felt still more encouraged when the proprietor bolted and came back with a bottle and a glass, into which he poured some of the contents of the bottle.

Dennis drank it, and the world got more stable, his head became subdued, and he was able to take a faint interest in light and sound again.

"Thanks," he said, more firmly.

"I need some, too," said Peter grimly. "You only got shot at. I saw it being done."

"All right," said Dennis. "Only don't let go. I don't want to hit the pavement again. Where is everybody, anyway?"

"They left," said Peter, chuckling, "in a great hurry. Like spilled mercury. And our killer was among them, I'm afraid. The next thing I knew the sirens were screeching their heads off, and the streets were blockaded by cops and flying squads, and nobody dared show up till now. Here they come back again—we'll be mobbed."

"Let's get out," said Dennis. "That's Kennedy's place, that apartment house down the street. That's where I spent the night before last, remember?"

"So that's where you were hiding out!" observed Sullivan on his other hand. "If I'd known that then, you would have been down at our place instead, day before yesterday."

"Day before yesterday?" said Dennis, reviewing the events of the past hurriedly, as he went across the street partly under Peter's power and partly under his own.

He began to laugh helplessly.

"And I told Blake it was about a million years ago since last night! Things sure do move fast, don't they?" he unconsciously echoed a plaint of Peter's after he'd first met Dennis.

"They move fast when a killer's around," Sullivan said, leading the way up the stairs in the grim manner of a shotgun squad. "It's like having a mad dog loose."

Madness! Dennis stopped abruptly, racking his already aching head for something—something that eluded him. He sighed.

"How's the head?" Sullivan asked.

"I have got," said Dennis very carefully, "the father and mother of all headaches."

He sank onto Kennedy's davenport when he had the door unlocked and they came in.

"Do I look interesting?" he inquired.

"You look like a ghost," Peter said bluntly, standing over him. "The guy who shot you ought to see you now. He'd think you'd come after him to get him, and he'd probably babble it all out."

"Get some iodine and gauze," said Sullivan briefly. "We don't want to go to the Central Emergency unless we can help it. No use letting too much information out. If it's all right with you, Devore, we'll treat it right here. It's a scratch."

"It's all right with me," said Dennis. "What happened, anyway?"

"What didn't?" said Peter, sticking a cigarette in the invalid's mouth and striking a match to it. He sat down on the nearest chair arm, and his blue eyes shone joyously, reviewing battle. "One second we were ahead of you, in the crowd, and then—there was a big, dark car

coming by, slowly, from the funeral, I guess— looked that
way—and I just happened to look up at it and see—I
don't quite know what I saw." Peter's brow was puzzled,
but his eyes were very candid. "You know how it is when
something—dangerous happens and you get just a bare
glimpse of its action before you go to meet it? I saw
something," repeated Peter, "something that was bright,
like steel, and I knew it was a gun sticking out where it
hadn't any business to be—and I couldn't jump for it,
because I was too wedged in by people, and I couldn't
knock them away to get to Sullivan—the damn' thing was
aiming at him—so I yelled, and you jumped at Sullivan,
Dennis. And the gun went off, and you got it on the side
of your head and dropped down there—Sullivan left you
there for me while he went forward to get the enemy—
and in a split second all that mob had disappeared like
silver balls of mercury rolling away—you've seen it,
Dennis— and our big, dark car with them, a couple of
taxis filled with mourners almost collided going over the
hill, and the police sirens were raising hell along an
empty street. And you began moaning, so I sat you up on
the curbing, and the next thing I heard, to my great
relief, was that you were swearing heartily away under
your breath at all the noise around. So I knew you were
okay."

"Okay!" said Dennis bitterly. "My head's filled with
lead."

"It should have been," said Peter. "Or Sullivan's. I
can't make out how that guy could have missed both of
you."

"What I can't make out," said Sullivan, dabbing iodine
on Dennis's aching head, "is why he went for me at all.
I've been on the squad for a good many years, and those
birds don't usually go out gunning for an officer like that.
They'll shoot when you get 'em cornered, but they won't
go out and look for it like that."

"I told you our killer wasn't—usual," said Dennis.

He sat up suddenly, regardless of a racking pain that tried to put him off his balance. He swayed and regained control. His eyes brightened. He had an idea.

"Listen," he said. "Sullivan doesn't know why that guy shot at him and missed. But I do!"

"One reason," said Sullivan,—"why he missed, I mean—was because you shoved in and took it for me, Devore."

Dennis tried to shake his head impatiently and gave it up with a faint groan. He had to be content to sit back again and let his tongue do all the talking without any help from his eager but pain-bound self.

"I mean why you were shot at all!" he said. "You're right—people don't go around potting officers. It's against the law, or something. Inhibition, maybe. Anyway, I know I'd a sight rather take a shot at an unofficial guy than at a cop. Retribution comes too fast, I guess, when the gendarmes get used as targets. Therefore, get this—our killer wasn't shooting at you, Sullivan. This may be a blow to you, but he wasn't."

"Well," said Sullivan, with a suspicion of a grin, "he made a darn' good imitation of it. It had me going."

"No, he wasn't shooting at you," Dennis insisted, slowly, " although he probably thought he was, at that. He was right, if he only knew it."

"Listen yourself," said Peter, getting worried. "Do you want me to get a doctor, Dennis?"

"Don't you see?" Dennis urged. "I saw it myself for a second, when you were both walking out of the coroner's room ahead of me this morning. You're both alike!— you're built alike, you walk alike, you wear practically the same sort of clothes, wear 'em the same way, too—that you-be-damned way, as if someone you didn't much care for were blocking your way and you were going to knock them over. And our killer didn't know that. He saw a big man in an overcoat and a felt hat standing there, looking like the guy he wanted, and he let go at him. And the guy he wanted, Peter—was you."

Dennis sank back again, eyes brilliant in his white face. He was picturesquely decorated, with a white bandage set high up around the right side of his head, curving lower on the left. Peter stared at him, his brown rock of a face getting darker and darker and grimmer and grimmer, until his mouth was only a tight line in it. His blue and candid eyes were dark with shadows, too. He looked at Dennis as if that picturesque young man were the ghost that he'd called him. The ghost of unpleasant memories.

"Why did he want me?" Peter asked, very quietly. Only his big hands clenched and unclenched very steadily, very quietly, unconsciously.

"He wanted to get you," Dennis said jauntily, as a man demonstrating a problem in perfectly plain geometry to a rather dumb class, "because of what he thought you had either in your head or in your pocket, Peter. In *this* pocket."

He reached out a languid hand and nicked with one finger the upper left side of Peter's suit.

"The receipts!" said Sullivan, in a voice like dynamite going off.

"I told you," said Dennis, a bit wearily, "I felt like a safe when the fake butler is picking away at the lock and the family diamonds were inside. Only—I wasn't the safe this time, Peter. You were. And you nearly got burgled, at that. He was aiming, you see, at your—or Sullivan's—heart, so he'd get what you had in your valuables-carrying pocket just over it, and at the same time get what you had in your head. A thrifty guy. He darn' near made it, too."

"How'd he know?" asked Peter softly but thunderously.

"He guessed," said Dennis. "Same as I'm guessing. Only you've got to admit it's a swell guess at that. He may have been one of the customers up on the roof with us, and seen Sullivan stick the things in that pocket, but I doubt it. I just think he was at Bianca's funeral and saw us, going by, and guessed—and took a chance on it. But he mistook Sullivan for you, and not only that—he missed."

"Then that shot was meant for me, and you took it." Peter took this into the fastness of his mind, revolved it around thoroughly, and then looked at Dennis again. "I won't forget that."

"Don't be dumb," said Dennis. "What could I do?"

"All the same," said Peter, "it was fine of you—"

"No, it wasn't," Dennis interrupted firmly, in his element of argument now. "I want you to be clear on that point. It was a darn' fool thing to do, if you look at it from my point of view. Here was Sullivan, with his large, capable mind set on finding someone to hang all these murders onto, and he might very well set himself to proving my guiltiness in spite of all his reassuring words this morning. That might have been a bluff on his part, to lull my fears to rest. I should have welcomed the opportunity to remove him from among my opponents. But I didn't. And I didn't say to myself, either, in a drowning-man flash, 'If I save his life he'll be properly grateful to me and maybe think I'm innocent after all and lay off' of me.' I simply saw someone was going to go for our side, and I went for them first, that was all."

"I told you I was beginning to get you," said Sullivan.

"Well," said Peter, "after all this dissection of your motives I should say Sullivan ought to be thoroughly dead. You've got the Irish genius, Dennis, for proving that black is white if you happen to believe it at the time.

"Thank you," said Dennis, gracefully inclining his head.

Peter retired behind his cigarette, balked. Then he came out again with another remark.

"And," he said, grinning, "you've got a stiff-necked Armada pride from some black Spanish ancestor, Dennis, that's going to earn you a good working sock in the eye one of these days. If a man wants to thank you decently, why don't you let him?"

"All right, he can," Dennis said. "And if he wants to do it up properly, how about a little more of that nice red wine across the way to do it with? I could do with some of it right now."

"Got it," said Peter. "Brought it over in my coat pocket. Not the inside pocket, either."

He went to Kennedy's midget kitchen to get some glasses, leaving a Dennis considerably brighter. Dennis after a second broke into a whistle, found his head could stand it, and the thin sweet whistle broke into fuller song, as a thin brown twig breaks to flower.

"Or leave a kiss but in the cup."

Dennis sang, very thoughtfully eyes far off,

"And I'll not look for wine!"

"You bet you won't," agreed Sullivan. "Not while you're with me. You'll take it straight. Have some respect for the police."

"Do you know," said Dennis, sitting up and taking a glass from Peter's hand, "I'm beginning to!"

His tone was that of such honest astonishment that even Sullivan couldn't take offense. Peter laughed, and Dennis after a second began to laugh, too.

At last he said firmly, "I've got to get my things out of that hotel manager's clutches. But," a bit dizzily, "not just this minute. Give me a couple of hours to tear off some sleep, and I'll tackle anything. Even that fish-faced guy."

XXI. DENNIS ENTERS A CAGE

He woke up to the soft bloom of lights, stretched himself in a long, beautiful ache of sleepiness, all pain gone, and yawned with his mouth very wide, open and his eyes very tightly closed.

There was something very nice going on; it was strangely like something he knew and loved; it was just outside the edge of his mind now. It was like the Little San Ramon River singing sweetly to itself through the sunny days, down by the river banks. It came closer to his consciousness and resolved itself into Kennedy's dark-toned piano, playing "Home to Our Mountains."

Dennis decided it was the loveliest song he'd ever known, except perhaps one. He lay there listening and presently decided that he wasn't sleepy any more. He turned over to the light and lay there on Kennedy's comfortable davenport, idly drinking the music in, and watching Kennedy's lean brown fingers going over the ivory-and-black keyboard in a pool of light.

"There in our younger days"

played Kennedy,

"Peace had its reign."

The swirl of music stopped, like a pool dammed up for speckled trout to lie in, and Kennedy fingered the last phrase slowly, more pointedly, with one intent finger.

"Peace had its reign"

sang that dark and lovely piano in a final intent word.

Then Kennedy turned around on the bench to look at his guest, lighting his eternal cigarette and letting the song trickle away into silence.

He cocked an eyebrow casually at sight of the ruffled bandaged head and the general wild state of affairs in the visitor's still-white face, where even sleep hadn't smoothed out all the recent damage done there.

"Wirehaired pup," he said, "where'd you get the scratch?"

"Oh, that," said Dennis, sitting up and dismissing the subject with a casual hand to his bandage, "a guy shot at me. Where did Peter Byrne and that bird Sullivan go, Kennedy?"

Kennedy shrugged.

"They didn't tell me," he said. "All I know is that I came home for a few hours of peaceful rest, as I'm accustomed to before I go on what is now a practically twenty-four-hour shift at the Hall, and I find a big flatfoot of a cop standing guard outside my place on the stairs, and you with a souvenir of war on your brow sleeping it off inside. Where've you been, and what doing, Dennis?"

"I've been to the wars," said Dennis.

"I'll say," said Kennedy. "I hope you got the first shot in, that's all."

"Sullivan doesn't think so," said Dennis a bit grimly. "You see, it was really meant for him, only the guy thought he was Peter. So he took a shot at him when he was standing across the street, after we came out from lunch on that roof place. But he missed—he only got me."

Kennedy sat up straighter and whistled softly.

"I might have known it," he said, eyes bright. "That was what all the row was about a couple of hours ago in this district, and nobody down at the Hall would give out any dope to the press-room gang on it. We were all het up about it—thought Father Malletti's kidnaper had been found, not to mention Bianca's killer and Bowden's little shotgun pal. None of the cops would talk—they'd been told off not to. I've been chasing around on that for the afternoon. And I come home and find the story all neatly wrapped up and asleep on my couch, with a cop guarding my front door for me!"

He laughed soundlessly.

"I might have known it!" he jeered at himself. Then he eyed his visitor very pointedly indeed. "Peace," said Kennedy, "has had its reign here as far as I'm concerned. I think I'll order in a machine gun and a pair of sandbags to prop up against the windows."

"What d'you mean?" asked Dennis.

Kennedy pointed the end of his cigarette at Dennis.

"You go down to Delroy," he said, "and people get bumped off, burnt up in shacks with their faces blown off; you come up to San Francisco and someone starts shooting in the street—the Hall of Justice just about gets the lid blown off it in the excitement of having all the flying squads out with their guns cocked, and there's general hell to pay. Do you suppose," Kennedy asked himself an academic question, "he's sort of a natural force of disturbance, attracting these things? He reminds me a lot of the calm spot inside the center of a typhoon. You can't deny, Dennis, that things do happen in your vicinity, whether you want them to or not."

"It must be my head," said Dennis. "It just doesn't make sense. Oh, and by the way, Kennedy, if you want a good line on our devil—our killer—we've just about decided that he's a homicidal maniac. He leaves too many gaps in his reasoning. He doesn't make sense to any ordinary man who wants to link up his reasoning. Too much space between his bridge spans. What do you say, Kennedy?"

"If I knew just what you are talking about," that much-tried gentleman replied, "maybe I could do better. Begin at the beginning, Dennis, and—er, shoot."

"Gimme a smoke," Dennis said. He bent his damaged dark head over the flicker of light for a second and looked up, eyes lit by a deep reflected gleam from the match

before he blew it out and settled back again. "Let's see—
what d'you know?"

"All about Bowden and your squirrel gun," said
Kennedy crisply. "A lot about the inquest—I wasn't there,
our page-one guy covered it, and I got it from his story—
and why you weren't served up on toast to the coroner
there. In fact your lawyer Byrne asked me about it before
he went in there, and I told him to play those money-
order receipts. He did, eh?"

"He did," Dennis said. "He's a swell guy, Byrne is. He
played 'em like a professional card sharp. That's why I'm
here."

"Instead," said Kennedy, "of being *safely* in the city
jail."

"Oh, I don't know," said Dennis thoughtfully. "Being
shot at's no fun—at the time. But all the same, it's the
breaks of the game. The breaks," he repeated, very
thoughtfully indeed, dark eyes looking into some dimly lit
future.

"Things are beginning to break, eh?" said Kennedy.

Dennis nodded. "I think so," he replied. "I think our
killer gave a lot more away than he took. Listen!" Dennis
gave his favorite exclamation and prepared to indulge in
his favorite indoor sport of talking. "How's this look to
you? We've made an alliance with Sullivan —treaty of
peace, dancing around the council fire, and all that—up
at Alexandre's roof place at lunch. We told him
everything as far as we've gone about this case—"

"That must have been a treat to him," Kennedy
interrupted.

"He wasn't pleased at first," said Dennis pensively.
"But I persuaded him it was all for the best that we'd
kept some things dark before. Anyway, we told him
everything then, kept absolutely nothing back—Pete even
handed over the money-order receipts—by request —and
then we went downstairs, stood looking at the end of
Bianca's funeral Mass going away from the church, and
somebody going past slowly in a big, dark closed car takes

a shot at Sullivan. Peter sees it in time, yells, and I jostled Sullivan. But that shot wasn't really meant for him, anyway."

"Well," Kennedy said judiciously, eyeing his smoke circles, "I can only say it looks a lot to me, Dennis, as though you and maybe Sullivan and Byrne had included a lot of Alexandre's good red wine in your peace pow-wow. People are getting more thrifty nowadays. They don't let off shots unless they've got a pretty good bead on someone at the other end of the line."

"You wrong us," said Dennis. "All of us."

"All right," said Kennedy. "Go ahead."

Dennis elaborated on his theory of Sullivan being shot at in mistake for Peter. He had a good listener. Kennedy sat in a deceptive quietness, brown head bent, body tense.

"Yeah," said Kennedy at last, "I see."

He lit another cigarette off the end of his lighted butt. Kennedy was working again.

"I see," he said again, slowly, "and it's possible. It's darned clever, too. Dennis, just how much of all this stuff do you believe, anyway?"

"Believe?" said Dennis. "All of it. Why shouldn't I? It's my theory, isn't it?"

"Well," Kennedy said, "I just wanted to make sure. You talk a lot, you know."

"And so do you," said Dennis indignantly. "And so, for that matter, has Peter Byrne been talking—recently."

"I make my living by talking," Kennedy said briefly. "Over the phone at the press room. Phoning stuff in to men who can handle a typewriter more flossily than I can. As for Bryne—sure he talks a lot at times, but it's always a bit surprising to hear him—like the stunt Moses did with the rock, making water gush out of it. He talks, but you'll notice he always says something. Your talk reminds me of a fountain playing, purely for decorative purposes—beautiful, but not so strictly utilitarian and necessary as the water from the living rock in the desert. At that, Byrne's been putting on a few accessory jets and frills, probably influenced by you, Dennis. What I meant to say, though, was if you do believe all this stuff of yours about the killer leaping ahead so quickly in his reasoning, and if you have traced him almost as quickly as he does things, like the way you got onto this shooting, the real purpose behind it, like a flash—why don't you put on a big spurt, Dennis, and instead of being one step behind him leap ahead of him and think out his next step before he takes it, for once. You've got the brains—no one else has even kept up with him as you have, up to this time. All it takes is a little extra pace, to reason out his next move."

"You think I lack logical reasoning power, too?" said Dennis. "That's why I'll be able to do it, I suppose — because I skip a lot, too. That makes it unanimous, I must be cuckoo."

"It might work," said that cynical person, his host. "On the theory—set a nut to crack a nut."

"I'll do it!" said an aroused Dennis. "You wait and see! But first," he amended, "I've got to go over to the hotel and get my things. Coming?"

"I'd like to," said Kennedy with conviction. "Although I don't see what could possibly happen on such a peaceful errand as that. But I've got to get some sleep before I take on the night shift, if I'm not going dead on my feet. When the fire engines go by I'll know what's happening, time enough. How're you going to get past that cop on the stairs, anyway? I'll bet he's got his orders to stop you from going out, as much as to stop anyone from going in here and getting you."

"I'll walk by him," said Dennis. "He doesn't know me from Adam. With a pleasant greeting."

And he did.

The officer, brave in blue and silver, responded handsomely to a cheerful "Hullo, Sergeant," especially as Dennis sauntered down the stairs waving a nonchalant cane, wearing a raglan coat hanging loose from his shoulders, and with a felt hat sitting pretty on his head, concealing any betraying bandage there. All the accessories came from Kennedy. The officer, who'd had Dennis described to him, hadn't heard any of these things mentioned. He stood aside and let this blithe young man pursue his pleasant and apparently very casual way down the steps to the outside door.

Dennis found the disguise had been so useful in one case that he didn't discard it in another. He hailed a taxi at the corner and was driven downhill and up dale to the heights of Nob Hill and the Hotel Ancaster.

He entered the pleasant little lobby, more like a private living room than a hotel public place, at tea time, and no one noticed him especially. The clerk over at the desk was murmuring soothingly to some people there, the music from the hotel orchestra came faintly from behind the closed doors, where people were having tea in the many-windowed, lamplit, flower-decorated Etruscan Room, the soft lights of the lobby glowed enticingly. Tea time. It was a pleasant hour.

Dennis had his own key still in his pocket, and he didn't want to talk to the clerk. He crossed the lobby to the elevator, and as he felt the soft thick plushiness of the taupe carpet underfoot he thought of Bianca walking across that same carpet, under these soft lights, going up to his room, three nights ago. And he thought of the last time he had entered this hotel himself, that same night, later. And of how he'd felt then, careless, unknowing of what was to come, in a hurry.

The elevator door clicked open, and Dennis stepped in, to meet Malloy's astonished eyes.

"Whisht!" said that shaken young man.

"Whisht yourself," said Dennis, leaning against the wall of the cage in a reassuring way. "Take me up like a good fellow, and don't talk so much about it. Unless"—he looked straight into those dark and Irish blue eyes, sooty-lashed, in their rugged setting of face—"unless you think I did it."

"You mean about killing the lady?"

"Yes."

There was a short but electric silence. Then Malloy clanged the door of the elevator shut on them.

"I don't think nothing of the kind," he said with a curious kind of violence in his voice. "What floor is it—fourth?"

"Yes," said Dennis absently. Then, "Who does think so?" he inquired gently.

The elevator cage rocked a bit. Dennis put his hand on the wall and steadied himself. The cage resumed service. Dennis felt that it had been a mistake, perhaps, to spring such a question on Malloy then, but he couldn't pick his time and place.

"Why do you say that, sir?" said Malloy thickly. His nice and rough-hewn face was paler, under the electric light.

"Someone thinks so," said Dennis, "evidently. And you've been arguing with 'em—in your mind. Good egg."

"Well, it was like this, sir," said Malloy, stopping the lift at Dennis's floor but not making a move to open the door, "I never did think so—about your doing that, the way you come in all bright and gay that night —it wasn't reasonable you'd be changed so quickly into a murderer, was it?—but at the inquest, Mr. Fersen did seem to think so, sir. The way he said no one could get up here without me and him seeing them."

"You mean no one did come except me," said Dennis softly. "That was right, wasn't it?"

"Yes," said Malloy sullenly. The stubborn blue eyes stared defiantly from narrowed black lashes into Dennis's dark ones.

"He's quite right," said Dennis. "No one did, besides me. Except the murderer. What do you think?" He looked at Malloy, broad and big in his dark blue uniform, there alone in the elevator with him.

"Malloy," he said, "suppose one of us two is a murderer. What do you think then?"

The silence seemed icy cold, in that little closed cage lit by the glaring electric globe above them. They stared at each other.

"What do I think?" said the boy bleakly. "Would I risk my mortal soul to do such a thing? And would I be afther kidnaping a priest?"

"No," said Dennis. "I shouldn't think so. But—did you kill her, Malloy?"

The tired dark voice persisted. There was a feeling like an icy cold wind coming up around them, in the elevator cage, a cold from the far, inhuman spaces of the ends of the earth, from the naked North itself.

Malloy stood up to the last truth.

"No," he said. "Whatever you want me to swear by, I'll swear. I didn't kill her. I— No, I didn't."

Dennis's hand dropped away from the wall. He sighed.

"I didn't think you did," he remarked. "Then that leaves—me, doesn't it? Me and—the murderer."

"Have you got any clues on him, Misther Devore?" Malloy said humbly, still a bit shaken.

"Clues?" said Dennis. "What are clues? The kind of things any street sweeper can pick up in the streets? Bits of string, and paper, and a cigarette butt? Sure, you can have all of those you want, out of the wastepaper baskets they empty and burn down in your basement!"

He leaned against the wall again and looked in front of him darkly.

"Or are clues the things you don't do? The only reason I wasn't arrested at the first go of this was because I *didn't* open and close a window here, and a dick was bright enough to see that. Is that a clue?"

"I wouldn't call it that," offered Malloy, frankly puzzled.

Dennis grinned at him suddenly, gravity gone again. "Neither would I. The kind of things I call clues is going along a dangerous place and seeing where someone's been—someone who hasn't any business to be there, and who was there—a killer. Seeing, not from what kind of cigarettes they smoked, or stuff like that, but from what they did, what kind of people they were, what kind of things they could do—what they were capable of—and coming at last, slowly perhaps, but inevitably, to—them. A man can't help leaving a vital imprint on a thing that's as close to him as—murder. It's too much his own work, his forces have been engaged in it so."

"Is it fingerprints you'll be meaning, sir?" asked Malloy.

"It is not," said Dennis, grinning again at him. "And will you let me out of this jail and keep your mouth closed about my being here? I'm just going to clear away my stuff and then see Fersen and pay my bill here, and I don't want the whole force charging up to restrain me as a dangerous character."

"I'll do that," said Malloy, his face lighting up in relief at hearing something from Dennis that was put in straight words meaning action.

Dennis stepped out into the softly lit corridor and stood there, seeing the dark shape of his door dimmer down the hallway. This was the hallway down which Bianca had come to meet her murderer.

He opened his door and went in.

XXII. DENNIS IS TRAPPED

Dennis didn't waste any time in there; the police had evidently gone through his things pretty thoroughly, and the maid had then laid them out in order ready for his packing. He got his suitcase from the corner, stuffed in neatly arranged rows of socks, handkerchiefs, shirts, ties, threw his other suit and his dressing things into odd corners, strapped up the suitcase and turned to go.

The room seemed exactly the same as it had always been. The lights were the same, the furniture waited there, graceful and impersonal, chosen to suit almost any cultivated taste well enough. The bedclothes weren't turned back, though, with the white sheet partly covering the white counterpane as it had been —that other night. And as he crossed the room to get to the door, he saw—he couldn't help seeing, his eyes going there with a dreadful fascination-that there wasn't any stain at all, not even a slight trickle of darkness or a betraying lighter color there where it had been cleansed off, on the taupe carpet near the table. This must be an entirely new floor covering, from the Ancaster's supply department. You couldn't know that anything—anything unhappy—had ever happened there in that pleasant room. It was just the same as it always had been. Hotels were wonderful, Dennis thought a bit wryly. The minds of the people who ran them must be as impersonal, as uniform, as pleasant as—a hotel room.

He came out and closed the door behind him, hearing the lock click into place. He stooped to take his suitcase, set there beside him, and straightened up again, listening. Someone was saying, "Oh, Mr. Devore!" in that restrained but urgent voice of a well-bred person in a rather public place. He turned round.

One of the doors was open, down the hall. A woman was there, partly behind it. Dennis took his suitcase and went on toward the door, and as he came it opened a bit more and he saw an elderly woman standing there. She was imperious and tall and thin, with gray hair almost white piled up in a rather old-fashioned way over her thin hawk face. She was dressed in a fussy silk dress, with the color that Dennis thought of as lavender in it and a lot of pink, too, and an amethyst necklace around her once fine neck.

"Come in," she said more graciously, having had her way in attracting his attention so far.

Dennis hesitated.

"You're Mr. Devore, aren't you?" his hostess said a bit more sharply.

"Yes," said Dennis, "but—"

He wanted to explain that he didn't have any idea of coming in for a chat with this rather grasping person who stood at her doorway and summoned guests like that. He'd got onto who she was, as soon as he saw her clearly. She was the old lady who had the corner suite at this floor—the cornerstone of respectability of the hotel, as Blake had described her. And she wanted to chat.

"Always suspect old ladies," Dennis groaned to himself.

She was waiting for him.

"I can't come in," said Dennis nicely. "I've got to catch a train."

That inspiration didn't work, in spite of the suitcase evidence in his hand.

"Nonsense," said the dragon sharply. "Just tell your taximan you'll give him five dollars to go faster. It always turns out that you've a few minutes to spare. Come in and have some tea."

Dennis came in.

His hostess sat down on the davenport by the wide windows that gave a view of the city and, beyond gray buildings, the bay. Dennis sat down in a comfortable armchair across from her, with a small table between them.

"Lucy will bring your tea," said the dragon kindly. Dennis always did have a particular charm for old ladies. He made them feel, somehow, young again. "I've been wanting to talk to you, Mr. Devore, and as Lucy saw you going to your room just now—"

"Lucy must do a sentry go at the door," thought Dennis, taking his cup of tea obediently from the rather gaunt hands of Lucy, a ten-year-younger edition of her mistress, but in severe black and white. "I wonder if she keeps a midnight shift there? It might come in handy."

He decided he'd ask. As soon as he got a chance.

"You sing over the radio, don't you?" his hostess asked. "I think that's wonderful, Mr. Devore. Lucy and I—we have a radio here—have often heard you."

"Yes," said Dennis. "I mean I used to."

"Aren't you singing over KDO now?"

"No," said Dennis. "Not any more."

He accepted very thin and tiny sandwiches from a plate offered him by Lucy and wondered how soon he could get in his question.

"Lucy," said that gaunt person's equally gaunt mistress, breaking into Dennis's thoughts, "you've cut the sandwiches too thick again. I've told you before how I like them. Or did these come from the hotel kitchen?"

"No'm," said Lucy. "They sent the things up here for me to make, Mrs. Appleby. I can't get 'em any thinner. They won't cut."

"Nonsense," said the formidable old lady. "Give the bread to me, I'll show you."

Lucy apparently wasn't at all surprised by anything her mistress chose to do, even to giving a sandwich-making demonstration in the midst of a tea.

"Yes'm," she said only and disappeared.

Dennis went on eating the rejected sandwiches placidly. He drank his tea. It was pretty good tea. He'd had coffee and red wine and now tea since he came to San

Francisco only this morning, and he didn't despise any of them. They each had a place, he felt, and at that moment the place for tea was in him. He was hungry again. Five o'clock in the afternoon was a swell time to eat.

"Why aren't you singing over the radio now?" Mrs. Appleby came back to her guest briskly. She sat with her hands folded in her pale lavender-pink silk lap, and reminded Dennis a lot of the little coroner he'd met in the morning in her way of asking things.

"I'm going away," he explained.

"Because of that thing that happened here?" his hostess surmised even more briskly. "That woman being killed here? But I thought that was practically cleared up by now."

"It is," Dennis assured her. "Only for a few odds and ends. No, it isn't really that. I have to go on business."

"Lucy," said Mrs. Appleby as that patient servitor entered with a tray bearing bread, a bread knife, soft butter in a dish, and other paraphernalia of sandwich-making, "set those here and watch me. Stand here."

"Yes'm," said Lucy, taking her stand to the right.

"I'm sorry to hear that," said his hostess, jumping back to their conversation efficiently. "We enjoyed your singing so, Mr. Devore. Lucy and I always liked to tune in on it. You sing with such feeling."

"Yes'm," murmured Dennis. "I mean, thank you very much."

"That other night—the last night you sang," old Mrs. Appleby said, casting an aside of "Like this, Lucy" to her faithful subject as she cut slices of bread of about the same thickness as the first Lucy-made standard, "we listened to your entire program. We particularly enjoyed your singing 'Sweet and Lovely.' Didn't we, Lucy?"

"That was the last song on my program," said Dennis, remembering back. "If I ever come back here again, I've got a new program ready. Did you—did you happen to look out of your door at any time while I was singing? Or about that time, you know?"

"No," said Mrs. Appleby very decisively, "we didn't. There wasn't any occasion to go out of our rooms. Did we, Lucy?"

"No'm," said Lucy. "We were listening to the radio all through the program, Mr. Devore."

"Oh," said Dennis. "Thanks. I just wanted to know."

"The police," said Mrs. Appleby, "asked us that question, too. Didn't they, Lucy? I soon put them right. They didn't find out anything about that killing from us."

"No," sighed Dennis. "I'm afraid not. I just asked."

"There," said the old lady triumphantly. "Now you see how I mean to do it, Lucy. These are much better. I'll show you—where are the old sandwiches?"

"I've eaten them," said Dennis simply. "They were awfully good. And I don't feel hungry a bit now, I'm afraid. I really must be going."

He rose and stood waiting.

"Well," said the old lady, rising reluctantly, "if you must. I wanted to have a nice talk with you, young man. Some other day—it's been very nice to have had you."

Dennis smiled at her.

"I liked it," he said. "Some day—I may come back. I'd like very much to sing 'Sweet and Lovely' for you and Lucy if I do. May I?"

He shook hands and went away, leaving a sort of young light on two old faces, like a reflected bit of his smile.

He went on down the corridor to the front stairs, and, not being up to facing Malloy again, carried the suitcase quickly down the four flights winding around the elevator until he landed in the lobby again, by the corridor leading back to the manager's office. He set the suitcase down quietly there and turned to go down that corridor with the subdued lighting. Then he paused.

"They didn't see anything," he said softly, thinking it over to himself for a second there in the half-dusk and privacy of the hallway, a little apart from the lobby. "They were listening to their radio, and they didn't look

out or go out of their rooms. That's all right. And the
police didn't find or see anything that helped them to
solve a murder, in their rooms. But I've been up there,
and I've talked to them and gone into their rooms."

Dennis turned white at the thought.

"They're all right," he argued palely with himself. "No
one has hurt them, or tried to, since that killing. Only—
people I've talked to have died. You can't get away from
that. If someone knew I'd been up there— and they will
know—they know all about me—"

Dennis leaned up against the wall a bit faintly.

"I'll write a note to Sullivan and ask him to put a
guard on their door," he said at last, decidedly. "He'll do
it. He can take the cop he put on Kennedy's door to guard
me, and just transfer him to this suite. Although you can
get past a cop at the door—it's been done before."

He grinned and, feeling more cheerful, went on to
Fersen's office. There was a snug little anteroom with a
pretty, capable-looking tailored girl typing away behind a
big desk in one corner of it. She had violets in a fragrant
bunch in a jade-green bowl on the brown desk. She looked
up and smiled as Dennis came in. The inner door to
Fersen's private office was open, and the light lit in it. So
Dennis just grinned back at the girl before she really
knew who he was, and went on in.

Fersen was filing away some papers in a medium-
sized but grim-looking safe along the opposite side of the
office. His well-creased trousers were bent slightly at the
knees; the light shone on his smooth and well-brushed
brown hair. It was a peaceful scene—until he looked
around, at some sensation of sound, and saw Dennis
standing at the door watching him.

He came up to his full height with a slight hissing
noise reminiscent of a startled cobra shooting up its hood.
The papers actually dropped untidily from his hand and
lay at his feet, mocking the neatness of the rather good-
looking office.

Dennis smiled at him and remembered to take off the unfamiliar hat on his head. Fersen's eyes followed the gesture automatically, and widened still more as he saw the neat white wound stripe of a gauze bandage uncovered by Kennedy's concealing hat. Then those eyes began to narrow in a determined way. Fersen was over any flurry he may have felt at suddenly seeing his unannounced and troublesome visitor.

Dennis recognized that ominous narrowing of his eyes—he'd met it in other people before the storm broke —and he forestalled it.

"I've just been up to my room," he said pleasantly, "and it really looks very well now. I congratulate you on your nice, efficient organization here. Too bad you couldn't have removed any body before the police came and disturbed the place so."

"The floor covering," said the hotel manager coldly, recovering himself and sinking into his chair with no gesture of invitation to Dennis to do the same, "was handed over to the police department by their request, if that's what you're referring to. The Ancaster management has no wish to hide any clues to such a serious thing as murder, as you're evidently hinting."

"That's fine," said Dennis heartily, choosing a big chair himself. The office, he thought, was pretty well done—it looked just the club sort of place where two comfortable business men might get together over their cigars. A few posters with bright colors conveying news of conventions, black-and-white posters announcing symphony concerts and other musical events, and a few gayer resort pictures, one showing a man golfing on a green turf, supplied the only hotel-profession atmosphere around.

"I'm glad you think that," said Fersen pointedly. His square and very well-kept hands held the arms of his office chair rather hard on each side of him, though he was leaning back at his ease otherwise. His hands and his voice were the only things that gave away his distaste for his visitor. "I should have thought that under the circumstances the fewer clues left for the police the better, if I had been you perhaps."

"What circumstances?" said Dennis.

Fersen showed his nice white teeth in a surprisingly animal gesture of drawn-back thinned lips for a fleeting second. Dennis, evidently, as he'd done to other and not so well-polished persons, was getting under the top layer of civilization and culture to the more primitive person underneath the hotel manager's exterior.

"I think you know them," said Fersen, recovering himself again, but with an effort, perhaps, this time, "as well as I do. Better, should I say?"

There was a nice and calculated deadliness in his smooth voice. Dennis responded beautifully.

"If you're going around saying things like that," he said hotly, "it's about time I came back here!"

Fersen's eyes lit on the suitcase by Dennis's side.

"You don't think you're coming back here to stay, do you?" he asked coldly.

"I know I'm not!" retorted Dennis, the light of battle vivid in his eyes. "You don't think I'd stay in this dump, do you—after the way you tried to shove that killing onto me, though you were damned sure in your own mind I couldn't have done it in the time? How do I know that? Because of the way you talked when you first came up to my room that night! You weren't scared—you knew pretty well I wasn't a murderer—and you weren't alone up there with a killer— but you wanted someone to hand the killing to so the police wouldn't bother your darned old hotel any more and disturb the other guests! You didn't care about me —you only wanted a goat for the sacrifice. You'd have let the killer go without a murmur of help to the police, if you'd thought you could hush it up that way! I knew you weren't scared to be up there alone with me —you were just plain peevish at things happening! Any other guy who really thought I'd done it would have looked at me with horror in his eyes. You were just annoyed with her, and me, and the cops coming!"

He stopped to get his breath and go on.

"You don't give me credit for—overcoming any natural fears I may have had?" Fersen asked smoothly.

"Don't make me laugh!" said Dennis inelegantly. "I've seen brave men scared, and overcoming it, too —recently. Don't put yourself with them. You're just plain careful of your own skin."

He rose with an odd effect of violence in the suave room.

"Give me my bill, and I'll pay it here," he said. "I don't want any more of this hotel any more than you want me. Where's my statement?"

"Right here," said Fersen crisply. He reached among the drawers of his desk and drew out a paper. "I've made it up already. I told the clerk to let me know when you were coming, so that I could see you personally about it."

He tossed the statement carelessly and contemptuously across the broad desk in Dennis's direction. That hot-headed young man took it up and smiled, narrow-eyed, with a contempt that made the hotel manager's look like Grade C, slightly rancid.

"Don't worry," he said. "You weren't going to miss me. I was going to ask to see you personally and tell you to go to hell, anyway."

Fersen made a sound slightly like a strangled snarl in his throat.

"That covers it," said Dennis, putting a bill on the paper and shoving them both back across the smooth wood desk. "Do you mind signing for it?"

His voice was bland and innocent again. Fersen took out his fountain pen, shook it slightly, scribbled his signature across the paid bill. The second of action had given him back his poise again. He was the man of business, the older and much more suave man of the world regarding unpolished youth again. He looked at Dennis with veiled and slightly shining brown eyes in a pleasantly blank and fleshy face. His lips even smiled, slightly, showing a white edge of teeth behind them.

Dennis had regained some of his own poise again. He felt that perhaps he'd been a bit uncouth.

His eye fell on one of the brighter posters along the wall, the poster with the blue-sky background and the man in white knickers swinging at a golf ball on the green turf, with the ocean in the distance behind him.

"I see you've got the golf-tournament poster there," he said chattily. "That was for last week-end, wasn't it? Saturday and Sunday—let's see"—he leaned forward, making bright conversation with his unwilling host, "November 1st and 2nd, it says. At Del Monte. Do you like golf?"

"Do you mind getting out of here?" asked Fersen, restrainedly. "I might remind you that you're no longer a guest of this hotel. I'll have to ask you to leave at once."

"Or you'll call the police," said Dennis, but with an absent air of near-hostility that didn't do him justice. He was thinking to himself behind the light words. Something had caught like a jagged bit of torn silk at the corner of his mind. Some word had awakened a memory—a wonder—a puzzled effort at remembrance. He had it. Del Monte, of course. He'd heard the name before today. From Peter. Peter had flown up from Del Monte grounds, he'd said, in time for the inquest. Peter must know Del Monte pretty well. He wondered if Peter played golf much. If he was there often—for week-ends, as lots of sportsmen were. It was a swell hotel for a week-end.

He rose reluctantly and took up his receipted bill and looked at the signature across the bottom of it. In spite of all the hotel manager's wrath at the time of writing, the letters were small and distinct and beautifully written. "A. Fersen" said the neat and lovely signature there. "Paid. November 6th."

But Dennis saw it through a darkness and a coldness that made him feel physically sick. It was November 6th,

and a Thursday. Bianca had been killed on a Monday.
This last Monday, November 3rd. The golf tournament at
Del Monte—Peter's Del Monte—had begun on a
Saturday, November 1st. Two days before Bianca'd been
killed here. It was on the evening of the 1st of November,
a Saturday, that someone had taken Father Malletti
away, in a big, dark car. Down to Delroy, they'd said.
Delroy was in the same county as Del Monte. Anyone who
knew Del Monte pretty well would have known the
county about there well, too, on drives and trips. Dennis
stood there staring at the comfortable, well-furnished,
dark-shining brown walnut office, with the big,
overstuffed armchairs and the taupe carpet and the
brown-shining head of the hotel manager across the desk
from him. But his dark eyes didn't see any of it. He was
cold. This was the ultimate fear. He'd reached it at last.
His eyes were dark with emptiness beyond any shadows.
Something'd burnt out in him. He was cold, and sick, and
shaken, and weary to death of the wickedness he'd caught
a glimpse of, had been trailing all this time.

Nothing mattered. Nothing really mattered. He
wanted to turn his head to the wall and die quietly. His
spirit was already dead. Only it was so damned cold. As
long as he could feel that awful cold, he supposed he was
alive, and ought to be grateful to it.

He had to go on, anyway. He knew that, dimly, 'way
down in him. You had to go on even when you were
knocked out, and beaten by this glimpse of the terrific,
implacable casualness of life—that had led them to this
conclusion, through such deviating ways.

He felt the need of a clear space about him, a clear
second of time to recover his bearings, as a man staggers
up in the ring.

He wished he had Peter now with him, helping him.
Peter would have helped him, cleared his head, given him
a second of grace. No, he wouldn't, either. He wouldn't
have had Peter ever, backing him up. Peter and he were
opposing forces. They'd always been enemies, friendly

enemies, and now it was real. He'd forgotten that. He couldn't have Peter now.

He fought for time himself, in a harmless ruse. He looked at the statement in his hand, and asked idly:

"What does the 'A' stand for?"

"Adam," snapped the hotel manager.

Dennis took a deep breath. He didn't feel quite so dumb and dazed now. His head was getting clearer, and the objects in the room were coming out of the almost total darkness that had enveloped them. He could go into action again.

"Good-bye," he said amiably, going toward the door. "I always seem to be saying good-bye to people lately. There was Bianca—Bianca Farnese. I said good-bye to her this morning. Just before her funeral."

"That woman!" said the hotel manager, and the words were somehow spitting with his unconcealed contempt.

"Her name," said Dennis, "was Bianca Farnese, and she was a human being, and she's dead now. You're the second person I've met today who's called her 'that woman.' Her name was Bianca."

Fersen's nerves, under the strain of the past few minutes of sparring, suddenly snapped.

"Don't call her name in here!" he ordered brusquely.

"Bianca—Bianca—Bianca," said Dennis very distinctly, and vanished suddenly—indeed, to the somewhat distraught hotel manager, like a light blown out. That sorely tried gentleman wiped a wet and well-fleshed face with an immaculate white handkerchief wielded by a square, well-kept but slightly trembling hand, and gave a hearty Swiss curse.

Out in the corridor again, Dennis leaned against the wall and grinned a fleeting grin. He felt a lot better. That last rally had done him good.

"That was a low brawl!" he rebuked himself. "It reminded me a lot of two cats spitting at each other. Here, of all places. Peter wouldn't have approved of it. All the same . . ."

The glow of brief battle began to fade again. Dennis felt as though his teeth were going to chatter. He felt entirely defenseless and extremely cold again—that sick cold that made him craven. He wanted to hide from what he knew was coming.

"All the same," he said steadily, to himself, "you'll have to face it. Peter or no Peter. He could have done it. He knows Del Monte. His car is red and a roadster —he would have taken one just the opposite from his, dark and big and closed. He c-could have done it. He went down to Delroy, to meet us. He knew what Bowden told us. He knew where my squirrel gun was—I told him. He and Blake weren't together in the house all the time I left them there—he said he went upstairs. It fits in. Oh, damn it, it fits in! He d-defended me when he didn't have to "

Dennis broke off. "I feel like a cur trying to bite a man who's given him a good dinner," he told himself soberly. "But I've got to go on. I've got to."

He went on, there in the dim corridor.

"He may have known Bianca," he reasoned. "Peter's been around town for a year since he left college, and he knows plenty of people in this town. He may have met her—the most beautiful and rather notorious woman here. And if she did treat him a bit lightly, he wouldn't take it like the others did. He's got more to him. He won't take too rough treatment. Pete's— dangerous."

Dennis sighed and changed his place against the wall.

"He knows the Ancaster," he went on, very monotonously now, as though dulled by emotion. "He's gone to dinner with people who live on my floor—the Anstruthers. They're—very respectable people. I count them out. They haven't the feeling for murder, or for much else. He knows the Ancaster, and he saw me singing one evening in the studio, and knew I was there on a scheduled time every evening. He happened to think of that—when he wanted to. Only—Farnese? How does he come into it?"

Dennis was frightfully tired. He hardly felt that he wanted to go back a whole year, yet he had to. He moved his head restlessly against the sustaining wall.

"He comes," he said to himself meticulously, "because Peter loved Bianca, maybe. 'Way back. It was such a strong passion it lasted. He may have hit Farnese rather hard—and Farnese died of it. He may not have meant to kill Farnese at all. Just to hit him. A man could die of Peter's blow, if Peter was very angry."

That faint grin flickered up through unimaginable deeps again to Dennis's haggard face and dark eyes. It lingered a second, and then went out, for good.

"He would be," said Dennis simply, "if he knew I was standing here and trying to trace back his life so I could swear it away. I could hardly blame him for that."

He let his breath out again in a long shallow sigh, as though his life were slipping easily away there with it.

"Farnese's skull was fractured," he went back relentlessly like a tired ghost driven back and back again to a scene. "They said the automobile had done it. I thought he'd been hit by a club, or something. But a man hit by Peter, hard, and falling on a cement highway, could have his skull fractured, very easily. Far- nese might have been down at Del Monte when Peter was there, a year ago, and Bianca too probably, and he may have tried to blackmail Peter. Or threatened him. Anyway, he got his skull fractured. Then it would have been very easy to dump him into an automobile and go along the highway with him out from Del Monte until the road was lonely enough to let him out and leave him there on the highway. Then I came along."

His mind cut ahead again. The field opened up, all of it, so damnably easy. He almost hated that clear mind of his now. It saw too much.

"Morgan was a friend of Peter's, and Peter clears him," he thought, dragging the thought out almost against his will. "I'm nearly charged with murder, and Peter defends me. He doesn't want anyone else charged

with it. I'll say that for him. He doesn't want to put
murder onto anyone else. Manslaughter's—different, of
course. And there was Blake. He didn't want Blake to be
in on a murder case a year ago, with her brother involved.
No, that all fits in, too."

But at the thought of Blake, such an agony seized him
that he couldn't go on. Not to any conclusion. He just
stood and suffered in a dumb stricture of agony like an
animal's, with no means of expression or of relief for
himself. It was hardly endurable. You just held on as best
you could. It was like something dying, very slowly, very
painfully, inside of you. You couldn't do anything. You
just endured—and after a while it became better. You'd
lived through that, at least.

Dennis gasped. His face was wet. He became aware
that he'd passed through something like a mortal
sickness and was on the other side of it for the present.
He was better. He felt a bit more alive again. He lifted his
head.

He hadn't moved. He was standing in the corridor of
the Hotel Ancaster, in the dimly lit dusk apart from the
lobby, and he'd gone through all that without any
movement of his body except that of his drooping head
against the wall. Funny, how you could travel in spirit
such strange and terrible ways, while your own material
self didn't even budge a step. He felt—convalescent, now.
Terribly weak, but not so bad. He felt more alive. Even—
hopeful, with the irresistible if unstable hopefulness of a
man who'd just passed through a serious illness and was
getting better. His head was clear and bright, if he did
feel a bit weak.

He'd go on.

Maybe something would happen—

That irrepressible hopefulness urged him on, like life
springing up again from a recently frozen, hard winter
ground.

But he had only the blind, unreasoning conviction
that it couldn't be like that. Peter Byrne couldn't be a

murderer. All the same, his clear mind pulled him that way; something blind and dark and stubborn tried to pull him the other way. He couldn't give in to it. He wanted to too much.

He came into the lobby again, and a young man in a dinner suit, with a fair sunburnt head, turned away from the desk and saw him at the same minute. Dennis knew him, but slightly. He was Morgan, on the same floor with him. The man Peter'd traced to Monterey Bay, near Del Monte, this morning, and the man Peter'd let go clear of the case with the explanation that he was a friend of his and out of it.

Morgan nodded to Dennis, saw his suitcase, and crossed over to intercept him.

"Hello," he said, being sociable in his nice way that made Dennis feel about a million years older than this fair-haired boy who always seemed just out of college. "Leaving us?"

He took out his cigarette case and offered Dennis a smoke.

"Thanks," said Dennis. "Yes. I'm on my way. I think maybe I'll rest up a bit—at Del Monte, maybe."

"A swell place," said young Morgan. "I was down there this morning—near there, anyway. Ran into Pete Byrne and his sister Blake down there. She's a pretty kid."

"Yes," said Dennis carefully. "Very."

"Which is lucky," Morgan said, "because Peter likes to have pretty girls around him." He grinned, frankly.

"Oh," said Dennis, "does he?"

"Well, he's in there now with a very golden-haired girl," Morgan indicated the doors of the Etruscan Room with his head. "She's in the chorus of a musical play here. At the Columbia. Pete's squiring her."

"There's a very pretty girl in Fersen's office." Dennis made conversation automatically, while his mind digested this information about Peter liking pretty women. "I saw her just now."

"And that's all," said Morgan disgustedly. "She goes home promptly at six every day. Never stays in the evenings."

"Why don't you offer to take her home?" Dennis retorted.

"I have," said young Morgan simply. "I offer to nearly every night. I even offer to talk business—hotel business—with her while we're going home. It doesn't work."

Dennis cocked an impolite and incredulous eyebrow at that black and white and gold butterfly with the nice grin talking hotel business. "Business?" he said.

"My dad's buying in," Morgan said. "Syndicate, you know. Fersen's managed this place for years for some old birds who never bother their heads about it much. He's a darn' good manager. We'll keep him on. The Ancaster'll just join a chain of hotels under the syndicate, that's all. And I'm sort of keen to start in here. Funny, isn't it? I think I'd be pretty good at it, though. I like playing host, you know. Of course, to start with I'd be in a 'way-down-under job and work up. I wouldn't mind that."

"No, I think it'd be okay for you," Dennis agreed. "If you like this kind of work, you'd be swell at it. Playing host."

"Oh, as a host," said Morgan, "or nearly so—I'd like to tell you we liked your singing here the other night, Devore. Monday night, it was."

Dennis stared at him in a sort of whiteness.

"I wasn't here," he said stiffly. "I was at the studio most of Monday night."

"Sure you were," Morgan said. "We tuned in on you in the Etruscan Room—by request. Our party wanted to hear your program. That was about just before twelve."

That was the night that Bianca had been killed here, Dennis thought dizzily. Monday night. November the third. Bianca had been here.

"I'm glad you liked it," he said, carefully. "Fersen wouldn't have liked it, if he'd known. He doesn't care much for me as a guest or any other way. I've just come from his office now."

"Oh-h-h," said young Morgan, with an understanding, long-drawn-out drawl, "you mean because of that killing up there, in your room? You can't blame him —much—for not liking that. That guy's goofy about his hotel, of course. No reason why he should put the blame for all this publicity on you, though. Listen—if he acted up—I mean there's no reason—" Young Morgan floundered in a stiff, choppy sea of embarrassment. "I mean," he brought it out, red-faced and looking at the end of his cigarette instead of at Dennis, "my dad's buying in here—and I've got a say—if you

want to stay here—"

"That's white of you," Dennis said softly. "But all the same, I'd rather go—down to Del Monte. No, Fersen's not driving me out. We just don't jibe, that's all. Lucky for him he couldn't hear me when I was singing here the other night. He doesn't like radio singers, especially me."

"Oh, he heard you!" said Morgan, puzzled, but polite. "He must have heard you. I asked the orchestra leader to stop playing for a few minutes while we got KDO on the loud speaker, and they did. The orchestra leader's got a phone there, connects with the hotel switchboard—people sometimes phone him for programs and to arrange parties, you know—and I used it to call Fersen in his office and see if he minded my cutting the orchestra off. I knew he wouldn't, of course —it was just a formality. But he didn't answer—so he must have been in the lobby at that time, and I guess he didn't object to it—he didn't say anything about it, anyway, to me."

"He probably didn't know who was on," Dennis said.

"Sure he did. He didn't mind," young Morgan said reassuringly. "The doors to the Etruscan Room were open to the lobby then. And they announced you between every song, by name. He must have heard you, but he didn't mind. You're seeing things."

"Yes," said Dennis. "I guess I am. I thought he'd be ready to bite me, even hearing me over a radio like that. Of course, that was before—before things really happened, that night."

"That's right!" said Morgan, getting interested. "That was the night of the murder here, wasn't it? We all missed that—didn't know a thing about it until the police came in. None of us, in my party at least, left the Etruscan Room until the cops came. We were all listening in on you."

"It seems to be a habit around here," said Dennis a bit dryly. "That night, anyway."

"Oh, you're famous," Morgan grinned. "The Ancaster claims you—or did. Say, Peter Byrne's your lawyer, isn't he? He's one grand guy, isn't he?"

"Yes," said Dennis in a muffled voice. "You know him well?"

"Stanford together—met him around town a bit afterward," Morgan said.

"He used to play football a lot, didn't he?" said Dennis, hating himself a lot. "What does he play now —any golf?"

"I think so," Morgan said. "I've seen him down at Del Monte sometimes, going round."

"Did you get to the tournament last week-end?" asked Dennis very casually. "Or did Pete?"

"No," said young Morgan regretfully. "I stayed here, like a good boy. School's beginning already for me, though I'm not officially here in any position yet, you know. But there was some sort of a convention here that winded up at Del Monte, and Fersen was pretty busy shuttling around just then between here and there, so I stayed here as sort of assistant manager. No, I don't know if Pete was down there or not last weekend. He probably was, if he could get off."

"You had a pretty girl to help you," Dennis consoled him. "I suppose the assistant manager inherited the office and all its fixings."

"A lot of good that did me with her," said young Morgan frankly. "She still went home promptly at 6 p. m. every evening, very businesslike."

"I hope she didn't get into this mess the other night," Dennis said. "It was sort of ghastly for anyone, let alone a girl."

"No, she didn't," Morgan said. "She went home as usual that night, too. Say, Devore—it's a funny case, isn't it? Is it—would it be too frightfully indiscreet to ask you if you or Peter have a line on it? Clues, you know, and all that? Or do you know now who did it? I know you and Byrne have been working on it."

Dennis looked down at his cigarette.

"We're—beginning to know," Dennis said slowly and very softly, almost as though he were speaking to himself. "We're dealing with two people—persons. One of them is out in the pleasant light of day during the entire time. We know him. He may be a friend. He may be a casual acquaintance. Anyway, we know him. Perhaps we like him. He may be—a friend of ours. The other's —a bit mad. If you c-call it mad—to kill and hide behind—the first person."

He raised desolate eyes to young Morgan's friendly, sunburnt fair face and attentive blue eyes.

"You see, they're—the same person," Dennis said. "That makes it—d-difficult."

He rose and threw away his cigarette into the nearest ashtray.

"It must," said young Morgan sympathetically and quite uncomprehendingly.

"It does," said Dennis briefly. He was himself again. "Difficult as hell. I've got to get on. I'll be seeing you."

"Driving down?" asked Morgan.

Dennis shook his head. "Train. Got no car."

"I could arrange for one," his near-host informed him eagerly, professional hotel instinct aroused at seeing a guest go forth into the night carless. "I've got a big old hack here, keep it in the hotel garage as sort of common property. I use my roadster a lot of the time myself, but I keep this thing here in case I've got a big party to take around places. It's old, but comfortable—got a powerful engine, too. Wait a second, I'll see. Phone the garage."

His fair head crossed the lobby quickly, leaned over the black phone on the room clerk's desk. He talked into the mouthpiece for a few minutes, put the phone down, and came back again to where Dennis waited, with a more rueful expression on his extremely candid young countenance.

"Washout," he said. "Sorry. After all I said about it, too. It's out of the garage now. It's sort of common property, you know. Anyone in the hotel who's responsible, like you if I vouched for you, or me, or the manager, or the chef, could use it, on hotel business. I'm frightfully sorry, you'll have to take the train."

He spoke as if it were a misfortune that couldn't be equaled. As if he'd said, "Sorry, here's a parachute, you'll have to go overboard." Dennis smiled.

"I was going to, anyway," he pointed out. "I'm not out anything. Thanks for thinking about it, anyway. I suppose you've let Pete Byrne have it sometimes?"

"Any time he wanted it, he could have it," said Morgan. "I've been down there in the garage with him, and they know he's a friend of mine. I think he has had it out, once or twice."

"Well, I thank you for him, too," said Dennis, "as he's my lawyer. I'll be going. Got to phone first, though."

He crossed over to the telephone room, just off the room clerk's desk space, shut himself into a booth, dropped a nickel in the slot, and said, when he had his number, "Sullivan there?"

"No, he isn't," the deep voice at the other end of the line answered. "Who's calling him?"

"Devore speaking," Dennis said. "Know where I can get him in a hurry?"

"Well, he left word," the cop at the other end in the Hall of Justice said. "He's at the post office—he was, anyway, when he phoned here. He's tracing them receipts, he said to tell you if you called up, and he wants samples of your handwriting. He's getting them from everybody. He also left some kind of a message about an officer at a door—he wants to know why in heck there was or wasn't one, at some door when he called there on his way to the post office this afternoon."

"Oh, yes," Dennis murmured, while his mind worked busily. "There was one, officer. Only it was at the wrong door. That's what he meant. He wanted you to send one good stout officer over pronto to the Hotel Ancaster and station him outside the door of old Mrs. Appleby's suite, fourth floor—got that?—and take notice of every- one going in or out of that door. It's very important. And I'm in a frightful hurry."

"Yeah," said the cop, evidently writing this down in earnest heaviness. "I got that. What else?"

"Tell Sullivan," said Dennis more sweetly, "that I've been at the Hotel Ancaster, and I've found out practically all about it. All he has to do is arrest the man I tell him to. Got that?"

He hung up the phone, stood ruffling his hair impatiently for a second with the flat of his hand, came out of the booth and considered.

"A frightful hurry," he repeated absently. His eyes were darkly worried, crowded with thoughts. "Only I can't move—until I've made them safe. To go away like that—and leave them here unguarded—it just can't be done. Not anyhow. Not though—I know all about it."

And all of a sudden his eyes cleared of thought, became once more dark and untroubled and luminous, as though he smiled deep within them. A clear pool, in the dark of a calm evening, when even the night wind was hushed, Dennis's eyes reminded one of, then. Peter's eyes were clear pools in the daylight, reflecting calm blue sky, but Dennis's dark eyes reflected stars at night when they were calm and at peace.

Dennis thought to himself, standing there, hands in his overcoat pockets, hat on as a disguise for his bandaged head, waiting for promised relief from the Hall of Justice:

"Peter's in there with a gold-headed chorus girl. Peter likes pretty girls. Peter had access to a big, dark closed car. Peter knew Delroy country pretty well. Peter this and Peter that. Morgan let me drag it all out of him. Sure, Peter did this and that and had ac- cess to this hotel and to Delroy. And if I saw Pete Byrne with the bloody knife in his large brown hand coming out of my room two seconds after Bianca'd died there, I'd know he hadn't done it! And thank God," said Dennis very sincerely, "that I had sense enough not to really believe that—and the hell with split infinitives—in spite of Morgan and my own eyes and my very clever mind figuring it all out! I was—just being clever, that's all. Peter was right. I'm too apt to be."

Dennis laughed, soundlessly but very keenly, eyes very bright, face eager again. He felt like a too eager pup on the trail who thought for a while he'd scared up a mountain lion instead of a rabbit, and who knows now to his great and inexpressible pleasure that it was just a rabbit after all. He bounded forward again.

"Now," he said, "from what I know of him, what would he do with Father Malletti? Where would he take him? And—what did he want with Wong?"

He thought acutely for a second. His mind leaped forward in great bounds, like an eager dog clearing obstacles that ordinarily are too much for him. He was, so to speak, playing 'way over his head for a moment, caught up by the fire of chase and of battle. His mind caught up with—something. Began to worry it. Like a too eager dog, wouldn't let go. . . .

"Oh, no," said Dennis, in a very small voice, without any feeling at all in it. As if horror had dulled it. As if he were looking at something he wished he hadn't had to look at. He'd caught up with it. "No," he said, in a futile

defiance again. "It couldn't—he couldn't do that. Not with
Wong. That's why he wanted—"

He made a gesture, a forward movement to fling this
thought away from him. It wouldn't go. Dennis's face was
white again, as white as the bandage over his dark head.
He had to move—to move quickly—his face was ablaze
with a sort of white impatience and fear.

Only he couldn't go—yet. He had to stay. He didn't
know where Sullivan was, either. He had to wait in this
dim corridor away from the too lighted lobby, away from
Peter, from young Bill Morgan, from any too curious eyes,
until the promised policeman came, to station himself at
that door he'd promised protection.

Only he couldn't wait. There wasn't any time. This
was Thursday, and Father Malletti had been gone since
Saturday. An old man—he couldn't hold out. Not any
longer. And Wong was there, too.

Dennis at this moment saw with rather abstracted
eyes something that said "For Fire Only" on the wall
beside him. It seemed to be the sort of thing you pulled
down, like a hook. It reminded him of something.

"Kennedy said this would be a nice friendly visit
here," he thought. "He didn't see what could possibly
happen here. I didn't, either. At the time. But now—if
he's listening, he'll be able to hear the fire engines going
by, all right."

He then knocked out a small pane of glass, pulled
some sort of a small lever down, and released it again.
Then he waited, leaning stilly up against the alarm box.
He fished around for pencil and paper and began writing.

Pretty soon he heard the fire engines outside. They
seemed to be making quite a bit of noise as they stopped
outside the hotel. There'd be a great deal of noise and
confusion within and without, firemen rushing around in
odd places where they usually weren't, and perhaps a
little water spilled around. There'd be protection. No one
would go stealthily around—he couldn't—when there
were firemen rushing around each corridor rescuing

people. There'd be guests' heads popping out of doors with inquiring expressions. It wouldn't be any time for a killer who liked the shade and quietness to pick for another killing. Dennis thought he'd arranged it quite neatly, after all.

The first of the firemen rushed into the lobby. They had oilskin coats and long drooping-looking hats on, and one of them had an axe. Dennis stepped out to meet them.

"I'm expecting Inspector Sullivan around here in a minute," he said. "Would you mind giving him this note?"

He walked on quietly out of the lobby, leaving behind him a folded note which, when opened five minutes later by a white-faced Sullivan, turned out to be a hotel statement, marked "Paid. November 6th" and signed in a small and lovely handwriting by A. Fersen. Under that Dennis had written hastily in pencil, "This is a sample of my handwriting. Dennis Devore," in a much more sprawling hand, as requested.

Dennis was nothing if not obliging.

XXIII. SO THEY CAME OUT—

Dennis came out to the sidewalk and said to himself:

"He may be dead! And if they find him there—I can't take any chances. I've discovered too many bodies already. Oh, it's damned clever! Even Peter would say so. If they found Father Malletti—dead—or dying—in my house at Delroy, I'd lose my last friend on that. And someone meant me to. And break my neck over it, too, into the bargain."

He was walking down the steep hill street now, going like a river unconsciously with the descent down into Market Street, at a pretty stiff pace. All the street lamps were lit, soft gold globes in the dark and misty night, and the Path of Gold flared softly and brilliantly and beautifully high overhead all down Market Street to the Ferry Building and the bay. Dennis felt as though he were an invisible ghost walking among all these people going by, hearing bursts of laughter, sounds of brief conversation, noise of cars and traffic whistles and street cars rushing by. He thought: "I can't go to Sullivan or Kennedy or anyone—for if they find Father Malletti dead in my house, I'm done for. Someone has seen to that. And I haven't much money—I paid out my hotel bill, and I'm pretty short, and the banks aren't open now. What'll I do?"

He halted at a particularly busy corner, staring about him as one awakened, and saw the slim copper shaft of Lotta's fountain in the middle of the intersection where three streets met, and across the street the clock, and Kennedy's tall gray *Star* building with lights in every window shining through the evening.

"There!" thought Dennis with a wild relief. He plunged into the traffic with an abandon which whitened several more hairs in the head of an already iron-gray traffic officer there, made it to the opposite side unscathed, coming up to the sidewalk again like a dog who has breasted a strong current, and disappeared around the corner of the building before any official action could be taken.

Here he stopped and caught his breath in a great sigh, almost a sob, of relief. It was the alleyway where he'd come out with Kennedy the other day—days ago—and there was the discreet taxi hovering, or rather sleeping near, its entrance, the driver huddled over the wheel reading a newspaper.

Dennis wrenched the door open and said:

"Quick! Get her going, will you? I've got to get down country to Delroy tonight!"

The driver raised a dispassionate thin face and surveyed his uninvited passenger.

"Can't be done," he said. "This cab belongs to the *Star*."

"But this is on *Star* business!" said Dennis crisply. "Step on it, guy."

"Got a press badge? Or an order from the desk?" the man inquired more alertly but still suspiciously, not stirring.

"Listen," said Dennis calmly but desperately, "you know me. I came here with Kennedy, the man on police, the other morning. You took me to Kennedy's house. I haven't got time to get any orders—this is urgent."

"Yeh, but—'way down to Delroy!" the driver demurred.

"I'm with Kennedy, I tell you!" Dennis insisted.

"Yeh, but how do I know if Kennedy is good for a long ride like this?"

"You'll know!" said Dennis ominously. He reached forward and picked the man out of his seat with one hand clamped on his shoulder, and as he'd heave a javelin on a long throw he sent him sprawling through the opposite door. The driver spoke, once.

"Things," said Dennis to him, "are just beginning to happen. That was nothing at all."

He drove away with the startled driver's expressions of astonishment half heard above the roaring shift into high. That was at San Francisco, at the beginning of night. Say six o'clock. Afterwards Dennis couldn't remember much about that ride except the way the engine droned so monotonously, so reassuringly, and the way his right foot got still and numb on the accelerator. Sometimes he was conscious of the towns going through, the little wayside towns with the lights in the streets and the houses, and sometimes he knew there were wide fields on either side of him, and the wind blowing past the windshield to his hair and face. But mostly he just drove in a suspension of thought. There wasn't anything to think about, any more. That was all over. All he had to do was to get down to Delroy, and there wasn't any use sending his mind ahead of him down there. He was so damned tired of thinking. He was so damned tired.

He lay back and drove on, without any thought or feeling. Occasional stray thoughts went by in the wide spaces of his mind, and out again, like birds flying through a dark night. . . .

Night was the best time to drive. Not so much traffic on the road then—and what there was, was making time. What was he doing, anyway, driving on and on like this? He didn't know—didn't want to know. He'd had a good reason at the beginning, anyway, and he couldn't be bothered to look it up and sort it all out again. Just keep on going. *"What country, love, is this?" "This is Illyria, stranger."* That was wrong, he knew, but he couldn't be bothered to straighten it out now. The sense was the same. The words sang themselves to him over and over— *"What country, love . . ."""Illyria, stranger."* That was a very far-away country, too. Things happened in it.

He half checked the big car involuntarily at a remembered landmark—a white stone bridge showing up out of the black night. He swung it forward again, full speed ahead, through country that even in the dark was familiar to him now. Here a slight grade, going up — around the corner of a mountain—there straightening out, a curve on level ground again—he followed the white road in the dark, headlights shining on ahead. Here Farnese had died—Victor Farnese—killed by his car once. No, Farnese had been dead before the car hit him. He'd lain there on that stretch of road for Dennis to come along and hit again. Oh, you couldn't let ghosts reach out and grab your hands from the wheel now! Get going, guy. Dennis was miles past the place where Farnese had lain in the road a year ago. He'd laid that ghost.

He was on the dirt road to his place, off the highway. He had to slow up. It was nearing midnight, from the looks of the stars. It was deep midnight, and the stars were very bright. There were no lights in his house at all. There wouldn't be. He had matches.

He left the car before the house and went on up to the front steps. There was no sound from the silent and dark house. He tried the front door. It was locked. He listened. Whatever else there was was listening, too.

There wasn't any sound at all.

"What country, love, is this?"

It went through his head like sign and countersign.

"This is Illyria, stranger."

Illyria—the place where strange, where terrible things could happen. He was on its threshold. Should he go in?

It had already drawn him in. He was an inhabitant of that strange country. Whether he wanted to be or not. He was unlocking the front door with his key, and the noise grated in the quiet night. The door swung open. The house waited for him.

Dennis went up the inside stairs in the dark, the house creaking and protesting about him. He tried doors. They opened. He went into one room and held a lighted match up, and found nothing—only the usual furniture, bulky and dark in the dim room—bed and bureau and chairs.

The frost mist of November over the fields outside made the old house desperately chilly. Dennis was glad he had Kennedy's coat on. He couldn't help shivering a lot, at that. His teeth wouldn't clamp together tightly. — they insisted on trying to chatter. It was horribly cold here.

He left that room and tried the next, and another match flared up into his eyes for a second of confusing light. And he looked on the narrow bed and saw Father Malletti laid out there, a thin, long line of black against the white cover. Dennis's hand shook uncontrollably. The match flickered and went out. He lit another, set it to the oil lamp on the bureau there. Then he turned around and looked at the bed again. His eyes were blinded with darkness before them and in them. He couldn't see for a second.

The light caught, slowly, slowly, and grew in the room. Dennis watched things coming clearer. He looked at Father Malletti again.

Someone had closed his eyes. The thin face, white as the white bedcover, sunken and calm as a death mask, had his sweet life written on it in deep lines of nostrils and straight-set thin mouth.

Dennis found himself on his knees, beside the bed.

"O God," he said to himself intensely, "if he's dead— let him into his heaven."

He laid a tentative hand on Father Malletti's, lying there so frail. It was warm. Faintly warm. Like the merest flicker of life hanging on. Father Malletti had come to the end of the long leash of life, with very little farther left for him to go. Dennis recognized that.

The sunken eyelids opened, heavily, slowly. Father Malletti's deep eyes looked out at him, from great distances. They were dark eyes, like Dennis's, but deep-set in the arched caverns of their sockets.

"Alive!" thought Dennis. "Alive. Alive."

He hardly dared breathe for fear of blowing out that flickering bit of life before him, deep in the depths of Father Malletti's dark eyes. He feared that the pounding of his heart would be too gusty for the frail craft of Father Malletti's life, when he touched him with hammering pulses beating through his fingers.

He got up, a bit unsteadily, and went out through the door quickly. He left the lamp in Father Malletti's room, and lit matches, groping his way to the stairs again. He lit the lamp in the cold kitchen and started putting wood in the stove. He couldn't think very clearly. Father Malletti was here, and alive, and that was wonderful—but where was Wong? He was afraid for Wong.

He worked quickly, methodically, making some beef broth from cubes, sticking more wood in the fire, taking the cup up to Father Malletti when it was steaming in his hand. He couldn't wonder about Wong now. Later—later . . .

Father Malletti took the beef broth very slowly, fed by Dennis from a spoon. The room was getting warmer. The light glowed from the lovely lamp of the old-fashioned oil burner set on the bureau. Father Malletti opened his deep eyes again and saw Dennis bending over him, intent frown between his brows, lips apart a little in his intensity. Father Malletti's face was warming to life again—the waxen whiteness displaced by a slightly softer color and contour. The soft gold light was kind to his face. Dennis breathed heavily and unconsciously through his parted lips, and looked at Father Malletti with his intent little frown stabbing his forehead.

"Are you all right, sir?" said Dennis, forgetting with the arrogance of superbly supple youth that Father Malletti was an old man and had a lot longer to go back from danger than he or Peter would have had. Father Malletti moved his lips faintly. Dennis frankly grinned. He took that for a good sign. Then he leaned forward to listen to that faint murmur of breath coming from the thin lips.

"Another," said Father Malletti in a thin thread of a voice.

"Another?" said Dennis. "Is there?" He considered this to himself. "Here?" he demanded.

Father Malletti said something that Dennis took for a "Yes." Only a very hopeful person could have translated that faint sign so.

"We'll get him," he said confidently. "Drink this, sir."

They finished the cup of broth. Dennis took Father Malletti's thin cold hands in his vital warm brown ones and rubbed them gently. He took off Father Malletti's shoes and rubbed the cold feet evenly and gently till he felt the warmth creeping into them. He put a white woolen blanket over the thin blackness on the bed, and Father Malletti lay there drowned in whiteness like snow, only his dark eyes alive, watching Dennis.

Then Dennis turned to go. He wasn't sure that Father Malletti understood what he was saying, but he felt that he owed it to him to explain anyway.

"I'm going to hunt for the other," he told him. "I'll be back, soon, sir—before you can get cold again. I've got to go."

He turned back again, slipped the overcoat from his shoulders, laid it over the white blanket carefully, and, satisfied with his work, departed.

He'd searched the two bedrooms upstairs. He'd been in the kitchen. He went, kitchen lamp in hand, through the rest of the house. There wasn't anything there except the dim furniture. Was it Wong that Father Malletti had meant? He wasn't there. Or was it—another? The other— the killer. Dennis frankly didn't feel like meeting him yet. Things were too darned uncertain. Father Malletti was just on the edge yet, and he might slip backwards into the cold again. Wong was somewhere, and he might need help. And Dennis was only one person—not really a fighting outfit, just a rescue squad. He needed reinforcements.

He wondered a bit dizzily why he hadn't thought of that before. He'd just gone ahead. Something inside of him had driven him on, regardless. Had taken charge of him for a while, all down the road to Delroy. He hadn't, in fact, been quite—responsible. He'd been like those monomaniacs, people with just one idea in their heads at a time. His idea had driven him down here, alone, without leaving any definite word to anybody. Dennis wondered vaguely why he'd been impelled to do it so at the time.

He came out of the kitchen door and surveyed the landscape, holding the lamp up. The whitewashed tool shed and the outhouses were dim bulks against the dark. The black frost caught his breath in a terrible damp chill, as though he were breathing ice. He left the kitchen steps and went on across to the sheds and lean-tos, and there was no one there. So then he thought that Wong was dead, after all, and the terrible cold chill fell on him silently, freezing all feeling, all tears.

He came back to the kitchen, went up to Father Malletti again, stoked wood downstairs, all in a silence that wouldn't let him go. Then he went to the phone, called San Francisco, got Kennedy on the line again.

"It's Dennis," he said.

"Wait a second," said Kennedy at that. "I'll take it in a closed booth."

He waited till that crisp and indomitably cheerful voice came over the line again: "Well, Dennis? What's the good news this time? I suppose you know Sullivan's searching San Francisco for you, looking behind every cushion and shaking out the curtains?"

"Yes, well," said Dennis dully, "he can find me down here, Kennedy. In Delroy. I've found Father Malletti."

Kennedy was stricken dumb. For a definite space of time there was silence on the line. Then he asked, only, quietly:

"Alive?"

"Yes," Dennis said, "but—"

"That's all, Dennis," Kennedy said in a new and very quiet tone of authority that Dennis unconsciously responded to. "Don't say any more—over the phone. You've said plenty! Only—wait a second. Are you at —the same place you were last time?"

"Yes," said Dennis.

"All right—stick there. We'll be right down. Are you—okay?"

"Yes," said Dennis. He heard the phone click as Kennedy hung up the receiver at his end of the line. He stuck his on the hook again and went up to Father Malletti.

Upstairs again he looked at his watch. How long would Kennedy take? He saw with a faint shock of surprise that it wasn't midnight, after all. It was only ten o'clock. He'd thought that hours and hours had gone by, in that ride down to here. The night was the longest he'd ever known. Longer than hospital nights, when he'd broken a leg once. It was the longest and darkest night.

He sat down by Father Malletti and sometimes he felt his face and hands and feet to see if they were cold, and sometimes he stirred to give him water or a bit of broth. A long time later Father Malletti looked at him more clearly and spoke in the lingering remnants of a tone of lifelong authority.

"What are you doing here, then?"

It was like a ghost summoning one to judgment. Dennis answered it straightly:

"This is my house, sir. Someone brought you here, and I found you. Someone wanted to know what Bianca Farnese told you, last Saturday night when she saw you."

Father Malletti considered this, eyes closed. Then he spoke.

"She asked me," said Father Malletti, "whether a dead man can live again. What do you make of that, now? I thought myself"—the thin breath labored to bring out each word—"it was a riddle."

"Either a riddle or a miracle, maybe," said Dennis. But his eyes were bright in thought. "What did you tell her?"

The deep old eyes shone darkly alive as Dennis's own eyes, in that sunken mask of an indomitable old face.

"I told her," said Father Malletti, "the best way for a dead man to live again in this world was in his works, and for her to be on her knees and pray for him in the next world."

Father Malletti was throwing aside the handicap of his frail and ill-used old body as a man much used to conquering it. His mind was bright and clear now.

"Dead men do rise up," mused Dennis. "Look at you, Father Malletti. Look at me. I'm supposed to be dead, too. And we're both here."

He smiled at his companion. "Are you warm, sir? It's a cold night, and very dark. It's like—death, I think."

He gave a little shudder.

"Be putting something around you," commanded Father Malletti, rising in spirit to the occasion from his bed of frailness. "And surely don't be telling me you're afraid of death. A fine boy like you!"

"That's just it," said Dennis frankly. "When I go, I'm—nothing. A body that can run a hundred in ten, sometimes, that can kick and block and tackle as well as you'd choose, that can feel the sun and the wind on it—all this means nothing. I can't take it with me. And it's all I've got. I have a great joy in it, Father Malletti. Can you understand that?"

Dennis could talk to Father Malletti the way he'd never talked to anyone before.

"Now you're different," he said earnestly. "You've got practically nothing to do with your body any more — you're a guest in it, you don't do things with it like running and kicking for the sheer joy in doing them, sir. You're different—you don't have to worry about going to heaven, or if*there is any heaven, sir."

"Haven't you any faith?" said Father Malletti sternly.

"I don't know," said Dennis. "I prayed for you when I thought you were dead here, sir. I prayed that you'd gone to heaven. I think that's a pretty good act of faith, to pray for another person's entrance to a place you hardly believe in yourself."

Something almost like a laugh came into Father Malletti's piercing eyes.

"That'll hardly be counted against you," he assured his host a bit dryly. He fell silent again.

After a while:

"When I was a young man," said Father Malletti, as though to himself, "I was a great swimmer. I loved to swim in the ocean, when it was a fine day or a rough one. Many a time . . ."

He lay there smiling a bit. Then he roused himself again.

"You're not of our faith?" he said again.

"I've never thought much about it, sir."

"You will," said the old man surely. "You will."

He didn't speak again after that, but fell into sleep again. Dennis thought that saints were very single-minded people.

After a while he heard false dawn being heralded from just outside by a sleepy cock, and he roused himself to go down to the stove again and stoke. He unwrapped himself from his blanket, thrust it sleepily away from him, stumbling in its folds, and went nearly in total darkness, eyes closed sleepily, down the stairs he knew so well.

He came into the kitchen, bent over the oil lamp again, struck a match—heard a slight sound, and remained, head bent, hand poised, above the globe as he looked up.

The kitchen door was opening. Dennis waited. The man who Dennis knew would come was there, pale face looking at him for a second.

"You!" said Dennis softly.

He wasn't surprised.

The match flared and went out. He dropped its blackened stem from his fingers. The door had closed. He knew that by the cessation of cold draft along the floor, by the slight thud of its jamming.

He was alone in there with a killer. The pale face still looked at him, the eyes burned brightly, in a sort of inhuman, unswerving, even dispassionate hatred. It was no use arguing with that sort of look—no use pleading, or playing for time, or doing anything but fighting now. Those eyes didn't see—reason. They hated, and watched their chance ... in the dark.

Dennis in the dark poised himself on his toes, ready for attack, hands held up to his chest, ready to launch himself. This was the last great line smash, maybe, and he wanted to make it good. He wasn't afraid. Not any more. He was in the game now, and he wanted to play it. He wanted to fight, and play a good game. He was impatient for the signal.

He heard the sound he'd been waiting for, body poised like a back's ready to plunge forward, and he located it — scrape of foot against the floor, there—and plunged. He hit something solid that grunted in a startled way as though the breath were out of its body. Then he was met by attack as fierce as his own, after that first irresistible giving away as his body struck the other's.

Their arms around each other, they rolled to the floor, struck the table, wrestled up again. Dennis tore his right arm free from those powerful smothering ones and began hitting, with a monotonous regularity. He heard, above their hoarse breathing, the smacking thud of his fist going in each time. The other grunted in a distressed way and got an arm across Dennis's throat, pulling it back in a way that almost cut off breathing. Dennis knew he couldn't stand much of that. He couldn't see to hit, either. He put his fist straight forward, hit the other's face, and felt the arm strangling him slip from his neck. Encouraged, he hit again, missed, shook his dazed head and plunged in again, felt something solid in front of his blows again and stood there and socked like a boxer gone blood-wild, all science cast aside for the moment.

They used each other for punching bags for a minute, then Dennis felt his opponent soften, fade away from before his blows, slipping. He heard a heavy crash that shook the floor. He was down. There was only a curious rasping sort of snore from the ground. Dennis stood there a second, raised shaking hands and wiped the sweat from his wet face with the palms of both hands, gasping for breath. He was shaking, and his heart was hammering like a loud clanging bell in his body. He wanted air and plenty of it. He went to the door, opened it, stood there dizzily, heard someone say:

"Reach for heaven, guy!"

He sidestepped automatically, lunged forward, hand stretched out stiffly, in a last effort of command over his sagging body. His hand struck someone's hard chin and shoved it out of the way.

There was a bright light there now. He looked with nearly darkened weary sight down at the man he'd spilled, and, in the bright glare of the automobile headlights trained on them, saw too late that he'd stuck his fist again too hastily into the face of his friend Peter.

He felt himself falling forward helplessly. He felt a heavy hand on his shoulder, yanking him to his feet. It spun him around, and as his dark head fell forward on his chest he saw Sullivan, and slid down to his feet.

A little while later he was talking to Peter.

"He looked at me," said Dennis, "at the inquest, and afterwards in the hotel, and his eyes were red as a cornered rat's. He was a very pleasant man," said Dennis dizzily, "only his eyes were red like a rat's."

"Dennis, come to," said Peter, shaking him. Dennis opened a pair of dazed dark eyes and found himself in some sort of semidarkness that shifted and moved a little, with his head on Peter's broad shoulder.

"You're so beautifully sane, Peter," he said drowsily. "I do like blue eyes. There aren't any shadows or red lights in them. Except once in a while clouds, like the sky."

"Dennis," said Peter, "how did you know?"

Dennis obligingly opened weary eyes again in slight surprise.

"He did everything short of shoving the knife in my hand and giving me a push," he said. "I sort of wondered. It was so perfect."

That was that. He heard Sullivan's deep voice say something about "concussed" and slid without any further interruptions into that sunlit ocean of sleep.

XXIV. —AND SAW THE STARS AGAIN

It was afternoon in San Francisco.

"Dennis," said Kennedy, "doesn't it strike you as somewhat of a miracle that Father Malletti was kept alive, on a wild sea coast, from Saturday to Thursday—when he was placed in your house, in his condition?"

"Why—no," said Dennis wonderingly. "I didn't at the time."

"How is Father Malletti?" asked Blake of Sullivan softly.

That massive gentleman smiled on them affably.

"Getting along fine," he said. "He's got Father O'Bannon with him now. That was a smart trick of yours, Dennis, to get Father O'Bannon to identify that hotel-manager rat Fersen as their visitor that Saturday night, by listening to his voice in the next room."

"He didn't see Fersen's face that night," said Dennis, "but I knew a man with a voice like Father O'Bannon's had a good ear."

He smiled in great satisfaction at Sullivan. "As long as you give me credit for suggesting that, I'll take it," he said. "But to tell you the whole truth, I don't remember that part of it at all. When was that?"

Peter grinned. "That was in the police car coming back from Delroy," he said. "You sat and babbled to me, Dennis. You were talking at first about a man with rat's eyes looking at you. At first we thought you were punch-drunk. You and Fersen gave each other a swell cleaning up. He was very messy when we went in and found him. He's got a scalp wound where his head got laid open on the edge of the stove, too. It was lucky for you I'm a pretty slow shot, when you didn't stop, coming out of the house.

I nearly got you, then I saw in time who it was. But you weren't punch-drunk."

"No," said Sullivan heartily. "It was just a little concussion."

"Just a little concussion," said Kennedy softly. "Nothing at all. In fact, a lot of people think that's the normal state of brain of a wirehaired pup anyway."

Dennis grinned at him. " Do you want me to go on?"

"By all means," Kennedy told him. "You might explain the main point of this, anyway, Dennis. Fersen sits there—he sat there last night—while we tried to reason with him about spilling the story, and he sort of snarls at us, showing his teeth slightly, and reminds me as you say of a nice plump rat that knows he's caught."

"Yes," nodded Peter to Dennis's inquiring look, "you weren't there in spirit with us, Dennis. We dumped you down on the leather couch in Kennedy's editor's office when we came back last night from Delroy, and you slept there peacefully while the *Star* Building was barricaded, telephone switchboard guarded, the chief of police and a number of detectives and reporters and such gathered around Fersen, trying to get him to talk—it was the biggest night the *Star* has ever seen. They didn't even issue any early editions until the other morning papers had all come out, so there wouldn't be any leaks. A couple of huskies from another paper tried to break in by the alley, and there was a swell fight. No one could get in or out after we came home with the bacon. And you were sleeping away on the couch in the same room with all of this rumpus about Fersen!"

"He didn't talk?" asked Dennis.

"Not unless you call that snarl of his articulate," said Peter. "I don't care much for it myself."

"Well," said Dennis, "this is it. There were two brothers—must have been brothers, or else why the change in name of one? One was Victor Farnese, a wholesale produce dealer of San Francisco. The other was trained in Switzerland, near Italy, for a hotel career. He came out here after a while, probably in accordance with his brother's suggestion. He got a hotel. He was a pretty good man at his job. But there was a flaw in him, a big one. It found him out. He and his brother Victor agreed to cook the hotel's accounts; they fixed it up on Victor Farnese's bills. I'll bet Farnese was the moving spirit in this, for two reasons—he was first on the ground here, knew the lay of the land, and also he was the one who either suggested that his brother change his name or actually picked it out for him. In fact, I know he did. Fersen never picked out that name for himself. So," said Dennis, "they fiddled with a lot of accounts, and took big profits for a while. For a lad who can't add three and four without getting something he shouldn't, I'm doing well in this rarefied atmosphere of high finance," added Dennis modestly, pausing to admire himself.

"You have us all gasping for breath," agreed Peter. "Go on."

"The inevitable happened," said Dennis, going literary under the stimulus of an audience. "He and Farnese had a fight. They didn't trust each other. I don't blame 'em. I wouldn't have either. He—Fersen— killed his brother down at Del Monte last year. Blamed it onto me. He was safe for a year. Then his brother rose up and slew him— or is going to hang him, anyway. The first intimation he had of it was what Bianca said to him."

Blake and Kennedy made it a dead heat.

"What did Bianca say?" demanded Blake.

"How did Farnese kill her?" demanded Kennedy.

"Don't you know?" asked Dennis. Peter growled warningly. "Well," hastened Dennis, "Fersen was in love with Bianca. I guess that was partly why he killed his brother, too. Envied him. But Bianca didn't know he was Farnese's brother. After Farnese was dead, Fersen made love to his brother's widow. Then the hotel was going to be sold and an accounting demanded. Fersen had made a lot of money. Some he'd spent on Bianca, and some on the stock market, I'll bet a nickel. Anyway, it went. He didn't

have any to show the accountants, and he knew it. He
was planning for a getaway with what he had. He wasn't
cleaning up hotel affairs, he was cleaning up his own late
at night. Then for once he got reckless. He knew he was
going to be forced to leave soon anyway, and he wanted
desperately to take Bianca with him. He sent her a letter.
A passionate, signed letter. Probably begging her to come
with him and giving her some directions for tickets—
things like that—if she agreed to run away with him. And
in his emotional stress he signed his real name—
Farnese—to his reckless, desperate letter."

"Dennis," said Sullivan heavily, "have you been
holding out on me again?"

Dennis shook his head decidedly.

"Then it's just a guess?"

"Oh, spring it on Fersen!" Dennis said impatiently.
"He'll tell you it's true. It must be."

"Go on."

"And Bianca looked at the note and wondered. And
she called Fersen around to her and asked him a
question."

"What question?" Sullivan asked.

"She asked him why his name was Farnese," Dennis
said.

The others sighed sharply.

"He couldn't answer. He was dumfounded, confused.
He'd thought that was too well hidden from anyone.
Bianca got suspicious. He couldn't bluff it out then—too
late. She told him she was going to ask Father Malletti
for advice. She went to Father Malletti. That night
Father Malletti was—called away to a parishioner.
Bianca didn't connect the two events then. Fersen called
her and asked her to come see him privately at the hotel
and he'd explain everything. Bianca came—and he killed
her. He knew she would be merciless now that her
suspicions were roused. She was his brother's widow.
She'd already talked."

"But you said that all she had asked Father Malletti was if a dead man could live again?" Kennedy asked keenly.

Dennis nodded. "Yes. She meant Farnese. Why was Fersen taking the name of Farnese? She didn't know. She talked in riddles around the subject. She was puzzled. And Farnese did live again. He came out of his grave and slew his brother."

"Dennis!" said Blake in a soft little wail.

"D-darling," said Dennis to her alone, "you'll see it. Farnese had a sense of humor—rough, but serviceable. When he made up his brother's fake name, he made it up out of the letters of his own name. No one saw it then. Bianca's been playing anagrams since then with some of her gentlemen friends. She saw it all, when she saw that signature—A. Fersen. It was Farnese and had always been Farnese. I saw it when he put it on the hotel bill. That's why I gave the bill to Sullivan. I was scared to tell him anything, in that hotel. I left him the bill as a hint. Fersen wasn't a humorous or a playful man. He'd never played anagrams in his life. Many people do nowadays. It amused Farnese to have his brother labeled with his own name all the time."

"It'll help hang him," said Sullivan. "I hope that'll amuse Victor Farnese."

"Probably," agreed Dennis. "Now you tell tales for a while. Just how'd you find Wong?"

"That was Blake," said Peter proudly.

"I sent for Louie," said Blake clearly, "when I came up from Monterey yesterday afternoon—I'd had lots of time to think on the road up—and I just said, 'Louie, where's Wong?' And he was hiding out in Louie's place in Chinatown. They belong to the same tong, and are very brotherly about it."

"The old heathen!" said Dennis proudly. A sharp high cackle answered him. Wong had been listening to his Dennis talking, hearing the sound of the loved voice, though he couldn't understand just what Dennis was driving at. "Why'd you skip out, Wong? Tell the company so they can understand it."

"He say, 'Dennis, he one mudderer,'" he shrilled. Peter stirred protestingly and got red.

"That was when Blake and I were discussing things around the stove at your place, Dennis," he protested. "After the sheriff took you up for the Bowden affair. We were saying what other people would say about you now.

"I know," said Dennis soothingly. "Go on, Wong."

"Wong say, 'Oh-h-h no,'" the brown heathen image shrilled out defiantly. "He say, yes-s-s, he one time kill man, one time kill woman, plenty bad fo' Dennis. What fo' Bowden dies when Dennis comes back heah again? He say, suppose one time Wong does that fo' Dennis. Wong think suppose he one time disappeah, no mo' Wong, they think Wong do it. Wong he makes bed, take his clo', go with tluck dlivah all up load, Sanfacisco. Goo'bye, till Dennis no mudderer again. Tha's all."

"Well," said Dennis, looking at them with eyes darkly bright, suspiciously bright, "I was wrong, that's all. Men have died for love, from time to time, though worms have eaten them for it. You know," said Dennis humbly, "I think at times I've been a damned fool," said Dennis very humbly indeed. "It's so difficult not to be, isn't it, Inspector?"

Sullivan got red under his broad tan. Peter snorted joyfully.

"But," said Dennis gravely, "if you hadn't skipped out for me, Wong, it would have been just too bad for you. Because Wednesday night, after Bowden was killed, after Blake and Peter had left my house, Father Malletti was planted there, still alive but very weak, from some hiding place where he'd been lying since Saturday night, to die. And if Wong had been there when the killer came to do that—there wouldn't have been any Wong.

"Here is the series of events: Saturday night, Father Malletti taken. Monday night, Bianca killed at the hotel, Dennis held for questioning by police. Tuesday, investigation in San Francisco. Wednesday, we went down to Delroy, didn't find Father Malletti, saw Bowden. Bowden was killed that night, afterwards. Wong went away. Fersen brought Father Malletti from where he'd hidden him since Saturday night in some little cove along the coast, up to my house, to be discovered—dead—in due time. Thursday, yesterday, up at the hotel here, Fersen was getting worried. Things were crowding him. He went down to Delroy to kill Father Malletti—in my house—for good. He was getting a bit cracked about me. He didn't like it because the police had let me go after Bianca's killing. He rang me in there because I was just out of a mansalughter sentence for Farnese's killing, and he thought it would be a swell coincidence for the police. Sure, he knew me, all right. He'd seen me at the trial. He was doing so well, after the Bowden killing, that he began to think he could wipe out anyone he didn't want on this case. He tried it on Sullivan, there, thinking he was Peter with some mysterious clue that might lead to him. As he was, of course."

"But the money-order receipts were found to be for printed applications," Sullivan objected. "It's hard to tell a man's handwriting from his printed writing."

"You didn't really expect to get a nice sample of the killer's writing especially written out for you on those very incriminating applications, did you?" asked Dennis, with lifted eyebrow. "I could have told you he'd print 'em, and saved you the disappointment. Only if I'd told you in advance, you'd have thought I was the one who'd printed 'em. Anyway, they served their purpose. They had Fersen getting panicky. What did we know that he didn't? He was a coward—and a most cautious guy, for a killer. Only bold when he was top dog. He chose his own hotel for the murder because it was safest. No one would think of a hotel manager capable of raising all this fuss in his hotel."

Peter bent a mild but accusing blue eye on Dennis.

"You knew I was in that hotel last night," he said. "Don't deny it. Billy Morgan told me he met you and talked about me. Why didn't you let me in on this midnight trip to Delroy?"

Dennis grinned. "You were having dinner with a chorus girl. Who was I to interfere? I withdrew."

"Withdrew!" snorted Peter. "You should have known I was following a clue—the clue of the white Spanish shawl. She was the girl we told you about, the one on Morgan's yacht."

"How'd I know you were following a clue?" said Dennis unrepentantly. "You didn't look an awful lot like it. You looked to me like Pete Byrne having dinner with a beautiful girl. Did you ever get around to the question of the Spanish shawl?"

"We did. We were talking about it when the fire engines came along," Peter said, brooding. "She said you could buy swell ones in Chinatown for practically nothing at all. She mentioned the store she'd bought it at. Then the fire engines came. That was a swell idea of yours, Dennis. I only hope you won't want to break up any more tete-a-tetes. Next time you might use tear-gas bombs, or something. We all tore out to the lobby, milled around a bit, quieted down, and I saw Sullivan looking at a piece of paper in his hand. It was your bill. We began putting the pieces of evidence together, Dennis, and found a dim sort of logic among them. Sullivan, for instance, thought this might possibly be your way of summoning him in a hurry."

"It was," said Dennis. "Kennedy gave me the idea."

"I? Me?" said the debonair gentleman, sitting up straighter. "I didn't tell you to go around ringing false alarms any time you wanted to see a friend, Dennis."

"Don't be so modest," said Dennis. "It was a swell idea. I wanted Sullivan there in a hurry, and he came."

"We all did," said Kennedy.

"Well, you see," said Dennis irrefutably.

"Dennis," said Peter again, "how did you know it was Fersen?"

"How'd you begin to suspect Fersen?" Sullivan asked. "There wasn't anything—"

"Enough," said Dennis, "when you came to add it all up. Bits of this and that. What he did. What he said. What he—was."

"He looked all right to me," said Sullivan.

Dennis dropped his cigarette carefully into the tray, put his clenched hands up to his face in the gesture that was as familiar to Blake and Peter as though they'd known him all their lives.

"Bits," said Dennis. "I don't dignify them by the name of clues. I leave that to the detective bureau. They want clues. Clues?" said Dennis with a certain scorn. "Clues are swell. But suppose a man doesn't smoke, drink, swear, or use profanity. How are you going to trace him then? If it's cigarette stubs you want, or empty glasses for fingerprints on them for him to be traced by, it ought to have been me. No, the clues I mean are the ones he leaves of his living self. First clue—he had a passkey, and he used it. Came busting into my room, when he really didn't have to. He was too eager. He wanted to make sure I wouldn't skip out. He was going to make sure I was held for and by the police, as a victim. Having one victim, they naturally wouldn't look around for more. He had a passkey.

"He knew I wasn't really a killer. That careful, rather soft-living guy wouldn't have stayed there alone with a killer, or someone he thought was a killer. No, he wasn't afraid of me. That was curious.

"Then he was too eager again to get me, when he didn't open a window in my room. He left it all locked and closed, so the police would be sure to suspect me of the murder. Sullivan outsmarted him on that one, and I got off—temporarily.

"At the inquest he laid himself out to get me, giving me the worst of every break he could. Nothing dishonest, you know, but it was a dishonesty of the mind, all right. And I saw him get mad there, too, once, when he was too closely questioned. He had a red light in his eyes. And when Sullivan said that about the killer being crazy at times, I saw, just for a second, the red light of madness flickering in someone's otherwise pleasant eyes. I couldn't quite place it then. It wasn't until afterwards—I placed it. He was a bit cuckoo, you know. He kept Bianca's evening bag and shawl.

"Then Fersen's alibi for that night was smashed. You wouldn't remember it like I did, maybe," said Dennis frankly, "because I've got some artistic vanity, I guess. At the inquest Fersen said he'd never heard me singing over the radio. Well, I was singing that night over the radio— in the Hotel Ancaster—in the Etruscan Room and through the lobby—and announced by name between each song, too. And Morgan called him up and found him out of his office then, when I was singing. He evidently wasn't in the lobby, though he'd said at the inquest the only times he left his office that hour were to go to the lobby. He didn't hear me singing. Where was he? Up in my room, reached from the service stairs in his corridor. He was up there with Bianca. He'd made this date with her because he was desperate; he went to it with a knife in one nicely kept hand. It's easy," said Dennis reminiscently, "to get knives in the Hotel Ancaster. I saw one sent up from the kitchens when I was in Mrs. Appleby's suite. It was the same sort of common breadknife Bianca was stabbed with. It put the idea into my head that if that one was from the hotel kitchens, probably Bianca's knife was, too. Easy to get, you see, for a hotel manager on a kitchen tour of inspection, earlier. That's why 1 was scared about old Mrs. Appleby and Lucy. It was a little thing, really. The police of course didn't get it—they didn't have tea there, in her suite. But I knew we were dealing with a man who made almost a mania of caution—a careful guy—and he might think I'd picked up something handy in that visit. As I had. So I was scared for them. But you put the policeman at their door, didn't you, Sullivan?"

"Sure I did," said Sullivan. "And Fersen, after the excitement of the fire, came up and touched off some fireworks about that, too. You were sure getting under his skin, Dennis."

"Yes, I meant to," Dennis said. "He was worried. He'd taken a shot at Sullivan and got me. Then you remember Peter said that about my being like a ghost. That I'd scare the murderer if he saw me. He probably thought he'd gotten me. The police veiled my end in mystery, as you'd say, Kennedy. They didn't give out any information about this particular shooting. So when I came into Fersen's office, and he saw me, and at first didn't see the bandage around my head—I had your hat on, Kennedy— he went up in the air. He looked at me as if he'd seen a ghost. I remembered what Peter'd said. I was a ghost, and he saw me there. For a second. But all this," said Dennis carefully, "isn't much good without a motive, is it? Why should Fersen, that nice soft-living pleasant man, want to kill Victor Farnese a year ago, and then his widow Bianca, and then stop Bowden's too loose mouth? Farnese was a wholesale produce dealer. Fersen was the manager of a hotel which he ran to suit himself. He didn't have to show his accounts to prying eyes. Not till lately. The hotel's going to be bought by Morgan's father and some of his friends. That meant an accounting. Morgan told me that, quite innocently. Then I remembered Fersen had been working late, alone, in his office the night Bianca was killed. Why should he? I wondered. So what?

"Then," said Dennis cheerfully, "I proceeded to get under his skin, for a couple of reasons—I wanted to see what he was like under all his fine walnut veneer, and I wanted to get his handwriting plausibly. And he was cheap wood under his fine grain, and he gave me his signature on the hotel bill, and I gave it to Sullivan. Then I played hob with him a bit more—fire alarms, cops, and so forth—and he scurried like a rat down to Delroy to kill Father Malletti and plant that on me. And he found—"

"A wirehaired terrier pup at his rat hole," said Kennedy.

Dennis grinned. "Being a detective's rather fun," he said. "I'm pretty good at it, I think. I think maybe I'll keep on."

"I never thought I'd be begging you to stick to radio, Dennis," said Kennedy. "But I am. Your detectiving is too rough on us—it's wearing. We're not all as young as we were. Stick to radio, Dennis."

"Oh, but I am," said Dennis. "I'm singing again tonight."

Kennedy said appreciatively, "There'll be a big mob to hear you, boy!"

Dennis said, "I don't mind that—as long as there's—one person."

His dark glance flickered on Blake's fair young face.

"I'll sing a song for you, Blake."

"Which one?" asked Blake.

"Ah, you'll know," said Dennis. "If you're listening."

He whistled, very softly, the first bar of "Drink to me only" as they all strolled out to the grass-covered terrace on the highest level of the hill-built house.

"What country, love, is this?" said Dennis to himself, as though he were trying to remember something he'd forgotten. It ran through his head. *"This is Illyria, stranger.* Stranger? No, not any more."

Peter and Blake stayed in the doorway, watching him.

"Are you really in love with him, Blake?" Peter said.

"Well," said Blake, thrusting her hands deep in her pockets, regarding Dennis, "he'll have to have someone to save him from being too chivalrous again. And then think of yourself, Peter. Life would be very dull for you without Dennis. You ought to be grateful to me for keeping him in the family permanently."

"I've felt like a three-ring circus since I saw him," agreed Peter.

"Besides," said Blake deeply, "I simply can't bear the thought of his marrying anyone but me. It must be love."

"I'm always waiting to see what he'll do next, or what'll turn up next," observed Peter with anticipation. "We'd better find out his proper name, by the way, if he's going to be our relative."

"Does it matter?" asked Blake.

"No," said Peter, consulting himself with surprise. "I suppose it doesn't."

Dennis looked at them from the goldfish pond and smiled and began to come over the grass to them. "I wonder what he'll do next," said Peter.

They stared in fascination at his ingenuous face.

THE END

Murder at Bridge

When an afternoon bridge party attended by some of Hamilton's leading citizens ends with the hostess being murdered in her boudoir, Special Investigator Dundee of the District Attorney's office is called in. But one of the attendees is guilty? There are plenty of suspects: the victim's former lover, her current suitor, the retired judge who is being blackmailed, the victim's maid who had been horribly disfigured accidentally by the murdered woman, or any of the women who's husbands had flirted with the victim. Or was she murdered by an outsider whose motive had nothing to do with the town of Hamilton. Find the answer in... **Murder at Bridge**

One Drop of Blood

When Dr. Koenig, head of Mayfield Sanitarium is murdered, the District Attorney's Special Investigator, "Bonnie" Dundee must go undercover to find the killer. Were any of the inmates of the asylum insane enough to have committed the crime? Or, was it one of the staff, motivated by jealousy? And what was is the secret in the murdered man's past. Find the answer in... **One Drop of Blood**

AVAILABLE FROM RESURRECTED PRESS!

THE EDWARDIAN DETECTIVES
LITERARY SLEUTHS OF THE EDWARDIAN ERA

The exploits of the great Victorian Detectives, Poe's C. Auguste Dupin, Gaboriau's Lecoq, and most famously, Arthur Conan Doyle's Sherlock Holmes, are well known. But what of those fictional detectives that came after, those of the Edwardian Age? The period between the death of Queen Victoria and the First World War had been called the Golden Age of the detective short story, but how familiar is the modern reader with the sleuths of this era? And such an extraordinary group they were, including in their numbers an unassuming English priest, a blind man, a master of disguises, a lecturer in medical jurisprudence, a noble woman working for Scotland Yard, and a savant so brilliant he was known as "The Thinking Machine."

To introduce readers to these detectives, Resurrected Press has assembled a collection of stories featuring these and other remarkable sleuths in The Edwardian Detectives.

- The Case of Laker, Absconded by Arthur Morrison
- The Fenchurch Street Mystery by Baroness Orczy
- The Crime of the French Café by Nick Carter
- The Man with Nailed Shoes by R Austin Freeman
- The Blue Cross by G. K. Chesterton
- The Case of the Pocket Diary Found in the Snow by Augusta Groner
- The Ninescore Mystery by Baroness Orczy
- The Riddle of the Ninth Finger by Thomas W. Hanshew
- The Knight's Cross Signal Problem by Ernest Bramah

- The Problem of Cell 13 by Jacques Futrelle
- The Conundrum of the Golf Links by Percy James Brebner
- The Silkworms of Florence by Clifford Ashdown
- The Gateway of the Monster by William Hope Hodgson
- The Affair at the Semiramis Hotel by A. E. W. Mason
- The Affair of the Avalanche Bicycle & Tyre Co., LTD by Arthur Morrison

RESURRECTED PRESS CLASSIC MYSTERY CATALOGUE

Journeys into Mystery
Travel and Mystery in a More Elegant Time

The Edwardian Detectives
Literary Sleuths of the Edwardian Era

Gems of Mystery
Lost Jewels from a More Elegant Age

E. C. Bentley
Trent's Last Case: The Woman in Black

Ernest Bramah
Max Carrados Resurrected:
The Detective Stories of Max Carrados

Agatha Christie
The Secret Adversary
The Mysterious Affair at Styles

Octavus Roy Cohen
Midnight

Freeman Wills Croft
The Ponson Case
The Pit Prop Syndicate

J. S. Fletcher
The Herapath Property
The Rayner-Slade Amalgamation
The Chestermarke Instinct
The Paradise Mystery
Dead Men's Money

The Middle of Things
Ravensdene Court
Scarhaven Keep
The Orange-Yellow Diamond
The Middle Temple Murder
The Tallyrand Maxim
The Borough Treasurer
In the Mayor's Parlour
The Saftey Pin

R. Austin Freeman
*The Mystery of 31 New Inn from the Dr. Thorndyke
Series*
*John Thorndyke's Cases from the Dr. Thorndyke
Series*
The Red Thumb Mark from The Dr. Thorndyke Series
The Eye of Osiris from The Dr. Thorndyke Series
A Silent Witness from the Dr. John Thorndyke Series
The Cat's Eye from the Dr. John Thorndyke Series
*Helen Vardon's Confession: A Dr. John Thorndyke
Story*
As a Thief in the Night: A Dr. John Thorndyke Story
*Mr. Pottermack's Oversight: A Dr. John Thorndyke
Story*
*Dr. Thorndyke Intervenes: A Dr. John Thorndyke
Story*
The Singing Bone: The Adventures of Dr. Thorndyke
The Stoneware Monkey: A Dr. John Thorndyke Story
*The Great Portrait Mystery, and Other Stories: A
Collection of Dr. John Thorndyke and Other Stories*
The Penrose Mystery: A Dr. John Thorndyke Story
The Uttermost Farthing: A Savant's Vendetta

Arthur Griffiths
The Passenger From Calais
The Rome Express

Fergus Hume
The Mystery of a Hansom Cab
The Green Mummy
The Silent House
The Secret Passage

Edgar Jepson
The Loudwater Mystery

A. E. W. Mason
At the Villa Rose

A. A. Milne
The Red House Mystery
Baroness Emma Orczy
The Old Man in the Corner

Edgar Allan Poe
The Detective Stories of Edgar Allan Poe

Arthur J. Rees
The Hampstead Mystery
The Shrieking Pit
The Hand In The Dark
The Moon Rock
The Mystery of the Downs

Mary Roberts Rinehart
Sight Unseen and The Confession

Dorothy L. Sayers
Whose Body?

Sir William Magnay
The Hunt Ball Mystery

Mabel and Paul Thorne
The Sheridan Road Mystery

Louis Tracy
The Strange Case of Mortimer Fenley
The Albert Gate Mystery
The Bartlett Mystery
The Postmaster's Daughter
The House of Peril
The Sandling Case: What Would You Have Done?
Charles Edmonds Walk
The Paternoster Ruby

John R. Watson
The Mystery of the Downs
The Hampstead Mystery

Edgar Wallace
The Daffodil Mystery
The Crimson Circle

Carolyn Wells
Vicky Van
The Man Who Fell Through the Earth
In the Onyx Lobby
Raspberry Jam
The Clue
The Room with the Tassels
The Vanishing of Betty Varian
The Mystery Girl
The White Alley
The Curved Blades
Anybody but Anne
The Bride of a Moment
Faulkner's Folly
The Diamond Pin
The Gold Bag
The Mystery of the Sycamore
The Come Backy

Raoul Whitfield
Death in a Bowl

And much more!
Visit ResurrectedPress.com
for our complete catalogue

About Resurrected Press

A division of Intrepid Ink, LLC, Resurrected Press is dedicated to bringing high quality, vintage books back into publication. See our entire catalogue and find out more at www.ResurrectedPress.com.

About Intrepid Ink, LLC

Intrepid Ink, LLC provides full publishing services to authors of fiction and non-fiction books, eBooks and websites. From editing to formatting, from publishing to marketing, Intrepid Ink gets your creative works into the hands of the people who want to read them. Find out more at www.IntrepidInk.com.

www.ingramcontent.com/pod-product-compliance
Lightning Source LLC
Chambersburg PA
CBHW070700280626
47159CB00022B/1012